EMMA'S ANGEL

By

Mi Mi Roberts

Front Cover Illustration and Graphic Design by
Anna Roberts, artbyannaroberts

Cover Layout by Emma Grace, Inksplatter Design

Print layout and eBook editions by eBooks By Barb
for booknook.biz

TABLE OF CONTENTS

CHAPTER I: THE VISITORS

Her father had been gone almost two weeks, these disappearances of his occurring seldom and bringing relief as well as anxiety about what would happen when he returned. They came when he had been sober long enough to make a significant amount of money as a body man in a car repair garage, enough to last for a good long spree, usually with a drinking buddy who had a car, he having lost his license many times and wrecked numerous cars. On a cold, dry, brilliantly starlit Saturday night in mid-January, 1961, Emma; her younger sister, Martha; her mother, Helen; and her paternal Grandmother Ila had finished their supper and given the meager scraps to the cats who kept the mice from coming into the house.

Once the kitchen was clean, Emma, Martha, and Grandmother went into the sitting room to watch *Oh, Susannah* and then *Loretta Young*. Emma thought she would stay up late once the television was turned off and read her literature assignment. School was the only social outlet for Emma as an eighth-grader and Martha, a sixth-grader. This year Emma's teacher at the small country school was smarter and more demanding than any of her previous teachers.

Mother never sat down with them to watch TV. Because she had little time at home, working uptown as a floor manager in Ledford's department store, she always had something to do. Tonight it was sewing a woolen skirt for Emma, a gray and red tweed material that Emma had picked out herself, a rare oppor-tunity.

Just as Emma was about to take her glass of tea to the sitting room to settle down, she heard the back door open and voices, her father's and two other voices. A cold, sickening, and fright-ening surge started in her stomach. She stepped into the bedroom to avoid the intruders. She heard her father speaking to her grandmother among the lower voices of a man and a woman. "This is a good pal of mine, Talton, and this is his wife, Gerta. She's from Germany. They're on their way to Florida, and I told them they could stay here tonight. They need a bite to eat; that's all."

"We appreciate your hospitality, ma'am," the man said. "Jiley thinks a lot of his family, I can tell you that. He's been talking about all of you."

"Nice to meet you," the woman said in a low, mellow voice.

"This is my first time in North Carolina. I thought I would see cotton fields, but Jiley told us you grow tobacco and corn in this part of the state," Talton said. "I think Jiley said this is Winn County, and you are about a hundred miles from the coast?"

"Yes," said Grandmother, "we used to grow cotton when the price was good."

Mother, whose sewing machine was in the little bedroom Emma slept in near the back door, walked through the kitchen where the couple had taken a seat. The man and woman spoke to Mother, who ignored them, looking at the grandmother, who, sensing the tension rising, asked Mother if the couple could sleep in Emma's room. "If they take Emma's room, she can sleep with me and make out one night," Grandmother said to Mother.

"I don't care what you do," said Mother, with a clear go-to-hell-all-of-you tone. Everyone knew the pattern: Father would come home drunk; Mother would arch her back like an angry cat, spitting at anyone who humored him. But Grandmother tried to keep the peace.

Father had lain down on his bed, being the drunkest of the three, not caring what happened to his company now that he was home. Mother went to the bedroom where she and Martha often slept on twin beds. It was an odd bedroom, having a large freezer in it that took up most of one wall.

Emma was curious to see the woman from Germany. She conjured up a mysterious person who could have been Hitler's mistress. She could also feel the knots in her stomach tighten as her father cursed her mother when she walked through their bedroom to get her night clothes. Emma had seen her father sometimes, seemingly asleep, get up and start fighting with her mother when he heard some derogatory remark she made about him and his drinking buddies.

"Jiley says the woman is the man's wife," Grandmother said to Mother.

"I'm not so sure. I don't see any rings."

"Well, I will fix them a bite of something. They said they'd leave early in the morning. Let's try not to start a fuss."

"I'm going to bed; you can do whatever you want to."

Emma, curious to see this woman from Germany who had disgruntled her mother, followed her grandmother into the kitchen. Talton and Gerta sat in the two chairs on the wall side, the table in front of them. The window behind them would make them chilly. No one sat there usually, but they were out of the way, looking as discreet as any unwanted guests could.

"Hello," said Emma.

"You must be Emma," Talton said. "I recognize you from Jiley's description.

He says you are smart in school."

"I'm Gerta."

"So where are you from?"

"Germany. My parents were German, and I grew up there."

Grandmother poured two cups of coffee left over from supper.

"Would you like to have a tomato and bacon sandwich?" Emma asked.

It was all she could think of that she could make quickly herself.

"That sounds great!" Gerta said. The man nodded.

Emma inspected the couple as closely as she could as she moved about to get the bacon, tomato, and salad dressing out of the refrigerator. It was a combination Emma would never choose —coffee with a sandwich? But the man sounded like a Northerner, and Gerta was a German. The man called Talton looked to be in his thirties, lean, and rugged, dressed in brown corduroy trousers and a gray shirt. Nothing in his demeanor was frightening. He talked quietly to the woman as he lighted a Camel and searched for an ash tray. Emma found one and handed it to him. She took another look at the woman, who to her disappointment was a pretty redhead, about thirty, well-mannered or acting so in her present predicament. Her fiery curls accentuated her large, dark greenish eyes. Emma thought her complexion the creamiest she had ever seen. Gerta held her cup sipping the coffee with delicate fingers, her nails manicured and polished wine. Her hands looked younger than Emma's. This woman had never looped tobacco, dug potatoes, or even shelled butter beans. She resented this woman who had the audacity to travel with her father and come uninvited to the house.

Emma turned over the bacon twice and took it up to drain and cool while she put dressing on the bread and added tomato slices, salt, and pepper. She added two strips of bacon to each sandwich, placed each on a small plate, cut the sandwiches in half, and placed them in front of the man and woman.

They thanked Emma, and each picked up a half and took a bite. She washed the dishes and left the room. It was nine-thirty now. Mother was in bed reading, Martha asleep already in her twin bed. Grandmother was moving around slowly in the dark with only her gown on. Father snored, still fully dressed down to his shoes, as he lay across his bed.

Emma lingered in the shadows, not eager to sleep with her grandmother, and thinking about the man and woman sleeping in her tiny bedroom when they may not even be married. What kind of woman would travel with drunks anyway?

"Are you coming to bed, Emma?" Grandmother whispered from her room at the front of the house.

"Not yet, I'm going to sit here on the floor and read some homework."

"Well, see if you can slip your daddy's shoes off and cover him up so he will sleep on until morning."

Emma crouched in a corner by the kitchen stove where the light shone on the page of her literature text. She was halfway through *Great Expectations* and enthralled by every sentence. Poor Pip. She identified with him thoroughly. Talton and Gerta had turned off their light and perhaps were already asleep. Emma was reading about Miss Havisham and wondering how anyone could be so heartless when she heard the door of her bedroom open to a crack as if the couple were checking to see if anyone was still up. Emma slid as far back in her corner as she could putting her head down low. The door opened wider, Talton emerging still dressed except for his shoes. Emma could see him take a look around in all directions. All the bedroom doors were closed except her father's. She had not yet taken off his shoes and covered him. Talton stepped stealthily into the room where Jiley snored. Emma crept forward keeping low to see what the man was doing. She saw him, his back to her, picking up her father's wallet and taking several bills out of it. She slipped back to her hiding place, not seeing what else he did.

Was there anything valuable in that room? Emma remembered hearing her mother and grandmother talk about drinking buddies hauling her father around and stealing his money. When they had it all, they would bring him home. Well, this guy's luck had run out. She would wait until she felt both he and Gerta were asleep and then go into their room and steal the money back. If they woke up, she would say she needed her bottle of cough syrup, which was sitting on her dresser. Maybe the man's wallet would be on the dresser, but likely he put it in his trousers. The worst that could happen would be if he caught her. Then she would tell him she saw him take the money.

She waited, reading for an hour in the corner by the stove. Suddenly her bedroom door opened, and the woman came out and into the kitchen. Emma stood up.

"Oh, you're still up? You scared me! I just need a drink of water. That bacon has made me thirsty."

"I'll get some for you. I was just reading a novel I have to read by Monday. It's about a man who has a lot of money hidden around in different places," she suddenly made this up. "It reminds me a lot of Daddy."

"How's that?" asked Gerta, taking the glass of water Emma handed her.

"Well, Daddy is always hiding whiskey and money around. Sometimes I watch him, although I never tell Mother or Grandmother Ila because that would cause a family fight, and we have enough of those already."

"I would think there are a lot of places to hide money on a farm."

"Sure," said Emma, "but Daddy is pretty smart. He knows where people won't look."

"Does he have a large amount of money hidden? I would think, judging by how proud he is of you, that he would tell you his hiding places so that if anything happened, you would get it."

This woman was not as smart as she looked, Emma thought, and Emma, who relished a chance to make up a story, went on with her story, trying to think ahead of how it would play out. "Well, he has told me of his best hiding place. I even checked it just yesterday because he had been gone longer than usual, and I wondered if he took all his money. I found twelve hundred dollars in hundred dollar bills. Daddy makes good money when he's sober. People from all around have heard that he can fix wrecked cars to look like brand new. He's a good welder and painter. They call him a body man."

"I'm sure he is the best and has a smart daughter that he trusts to look out for him, someone who can keep his secrets."

Emma tried to act pleased to be complimented. "Yes, I know he is proud of me in his own way. I do try to keep the peace. I do check his best hiding place, but it is not something I like to do because it stinks, and I have to wash everything afterwards."

"What on earth?"

"Well, it is where the hogs and pigs live."

"I didn't know you had hogs. Jiley pointed out the chicken houses when we drove into yard. Where are the hogs?"

"Oh, the hog houses are almost a mile down that path that runs to the back of the farm."

"You must be brave to go down there by yourself to check the hiding place. Aren't you afraid?"

"No, I go down there almost every day with my Uncle Milton. He takes care of the hogs. The funny thing is he has no idea about the money hidden down there. I wait until my uncle is in a pen a good distance away from the pen where the money is hidden; then, I go check to make sure it is still there."

"How many hog houses are there?"

"Oh, it's just one long building with separate pens to house sows and their baby pigs, so I have plenty of time while I wait for my uncle to feed and water. Sometimes he has to give the hogs shots when they get sick and cough. Something is always broken it seems like, and Uncle Milton has to repair it. When he is finished, we go back to the house, and he washes up and takes me to the store for a Pepsi and an oatmeal cookie."

"Wow, you are one smart girl. You have everybody fooled, don't you? It must be a really good hiding place. It's a wonder the hogs don't eat the money. I hear they will eat anything."

"Yes, ma'am, they will, especially a sow that has pigs, even their own pigs if one dies and the mother gets hungry. They would eat the money if they could get to it. Well, I know I won't ever see you after tonight. I heard Mr. Talton say you are going to Florida to start a job next week."

"Yes, that's right. Unfortunately, I don't think we will ever see you again, but it has been a pleasure to find such a smart girl way out here in the country. You are no country bumpkin, as some might expect."

"Well, I'll tell you the hiding place, but please don't tell anyone. Do you promise?"

Emma acted eager to share her secret.

Gerta nodded. "Of course. I am curious about your clever secret, but I won't remember tomorrow any way. I've had too much to drink and can hardly hold a thought in my head."

"It is in the next to the last pen at the end of the building. Under the slat in the right corner of the pen is a plastic bag, which you can pull up through the opening between the slats. The money is wrapped in more plastic. Sometimes I have trouble stuffing the bag back because Daddy has it folded so carefully in a square, which I can never get tidy again. Don't you think it is a clever place no one would ever find? I am the one who told Daddy he needed to hide some money when he got paid for a big job and not carry it around in his wallet."

"This sounds all too complicated for me," Gerta said. She yawned and put the glass in the sink. "It's late, Emma. I need my beauty rest." She laughed.

"Yes, it is almost eleven o'clock. I'm tired too. Good night."

Emma could just imagine Gerta sneaking out in ten minutes to go find the money. Not only would she not find any money she would also come back smelling like hog manure! With no intention of going to bed, Emma turned off the stove light and sat down on the floor again beside the stove out of sight. She closed the book, resting her head on her knees. She had dozed off when she heard her bedroom door open slightly, then wider, Talton emerging staggering a little in the dark. He had a pint jar of Jiley's whiskey in his hand and had apparently drunk a good deal of it. She heard Gerta whisper something, and he went back into the room. Then they both emerged, she following him to the back door, opening it very slowly. Talton went outside but she stayed in, returning to the bedroom.

Emma held her breath until Gerta had closed the bedroom door. Maybe Talton was looking for the whiskey, which her father always hid in bushes beside the house, knowing Helen poured out all whiskey she found. But Emma wondered if by some wild chance Talton was going to walk a mile in the moonlight on this cold night to look for the hidden money in the hog house. He was already staggering. The cold air would sober him though, and the cold was a dry cold that did not feel icy. Emma fell asleep waiting. When she awoke, it was two o'clock. She heard her bedroom door open again. She crept forward to look, expecting to see Talton going back to bed after his fool-hardy adventure. Instead, she saw Gerta closing the bedroom door. Had she missed Talton entering the room ahead of Gerta?

A minute later Gerta turned on the light and came out. She knocked on Grandmother Ila's door.

"Miss Ila, Miss Ila." She opened the door and called in a low shriek.

"Miss Ila, I need your help."

"What is it? What time is it?"

"It's the middle of the night, but Talton's missing and I'm worried about him. He went out to find the toilet about two hours ago and hasn't come back. I walked outside about an hour ago and called him, but couldn't find him. Now, I am getting panicky."

Emma could imagine the fool still looking for the hidden money, thinking he was in the wrong pen. She wondered why Gerta had said he was missing when she had to know what he was doing. He was probably staggering back now empty handed and smelling like hog manure.

Grandmother was dumbfounded at first. Emma came out of the kitchen to see what the commotion was. "Emma, have you been to bed?"

"Yes, Grandmother. You were snoring when I lay down about eleven, but I got up when I heard a noise. I guess it was Gerta looking for Talton."

"Let's look in the yard to see if he fell down," Grandmother suggested. "He could've blacked out."

The three put on coats and went outside, searching all areas of the large yard, the night being bright with a full moon, but had no luck. Grandmother seemed concerned then. "It could be Jiley told Talton about the man down the road who sells whiskey any time day or night. He could be down there playing poker and drinking with Ray Moss," said Grandmother. Gerta didn't seem satisfied.

"As soon as it gets light, I'll get Milton next door to go down the road and find him," Grandmother added. "Now we might as well all lie back down. That crowd down the road plays poker all night every Saturday. He may be passed out down there."

Gerta said she would like to make some coffee and wait up in the kitchen if it was all right. Grandmother said it was okay but to be quiet and not wake up Jiley. Jiley might take a notion to go looking for Talton himself when he woke up. Emma lay down on the bed with her grandmother, keeping as close to the edge as she could without rolling off. She woke to the loud morning voice of her grandmother.

It was 6:30 a.m. Father was still sleeping, and Grandmother had called Uncle Milton to go look for Talton. Mother, who normally would be up, stayed in her bed, knowing Gerta was still in the house. Martha came out rubbing her eyes and asking Emma what was going on.

"That man who came home with Daddy last night has disappeared. Grandmother asked Uncle Milton to go look for him as soon as it got light, but he came back saying there was no sign of him. The poker players hadn't seen him, or at least those who could be woke up. I think he's dumped Gerta and left with Daddy's money. The only thing I can't figure out is why the car is still here. Maybe he wanted her to have a way to get to Florida. He could hitchhike."

"What do you mean he took Daddy's money?"

"I saw him during the night take some out of Daddy's wallet while he was snoring dead to the world."

"Have you told Mother and Grandmother?"

"No, not yet."

Worried about Jiley, who had awakened about six o'clock

with a fever and nausea, Mother and Grandmother were not much concerned about Gerta, who sat at the kitchen table waiting, getting up every five minutes to look out the window to see if Talton was coming up the dirt road from the poker house. Finally at noon, Uncle Milton knocked on the back door. Having worked in the hog houses, he would not come into the house. Grandmother went out to speak with him. Emma watched through the window beside the door, trying to catch the words, but her uncle mumbled at best and she could make out only a word or two. "Eat im," she thought he said. His face was ashen in the cold winter morning air. It must be about business that he had to report to Grandmother. Then her grandmother, turning around, said, "I'll call the sheriff." As she came back into the house, Emma thought she was shaking a little. "Where's your mother?"

"In there with Martha, changing the sheets."

Grandmother went through the kitchen, not speaking to Gerta, who looked anxiously at her, and opened the bedroom door where Mother and Martha were quietly making up the twin beds. Then Martha came out, and the door closed. In five minutes, Grandmother came out and went to the phone, which was in her room, and dialed the sheriff. Gerta would not be able to hear, but, Emma stood by the door to listen.

"I need to speak to Sheriff Greene," she said. "Jim, I need for you to come out here as soon as you can. We've got a situation. No, it's not Jiley this time—well, not directly. It's a pal of his who stayed here last night. All right, I'll be here in the house, so stop by and let me ride down with you."

Emma could tell by her grandmother's tone that something was wrong. Suddenly she was frightened. Something had happened to Talton, and it must have happened down at the hog house. That was what Uncle Milton had told Grandmother. Oh,

Lord, she would be blamed for making up such a lie about money hidden under the slats! But would Talton be dumb enough to explain what he was doing down there? Surely not! But Gerta might tell. No, that would only be admitting they were thieves. Talton must have been so drunk that he stumbled and broke his leg or something. He may have been lying all night in the path. Maybe he fell before he ever reached the hog house.

When Grandmother came out of her room, Emma heard her saying a prayer as she often did when she was troubled. "Lord, give me the strength to face whatever is my due." Emma walked with her grandmother to the kitchen, where Gerta looked up. "I've called the sheriff," said Miss Ila. "He's a friend of mine. I've known him since he was a baby. He'll solve this, and maybe you can be on your way this afternoon. Helen will fix something for us to eat. We got some good homemade soup."

Jiley lay in bed, too sick to notice that Talton was gone and that Gerta was up and down, smoking one Camel after another. Gerta ran out, and asked Emma if she could borrow a cigarette from her father. Emma, wanting to be as nice as possible now, was quick to get her one.

Sheriff Greene and a deputy pulled up in the driveway about two o'clock. Gerta saw the car first and called Grandmother from her room where she rocked and read the Bible.

"Come in, Jim."

"Ila, is this young lady the one who accompanied the missing person?"

"Yes, I'm the one. My name is Gerta Steinman." Emma took note that she did not say she was his wife.

"Well, ma'am, Miss Ila is going with me to look around, and Deputy Barnes will stay here and ask all of you some questions. We'll be back shortly."

Emma's heart beat irregularly, her chest tightening as she

imagined what the deputy would ask her. Could she be arrested for lying to strangers? It was Gerta, however, whom Deputy Barnes took outside to question. Emma watched through her bedroom window as Gerta shook her head. Something he said had upset her, and she wiped her eyes with a handkerchief he handed her.

Turning her gaze toward the path, Emma saw the sheriff's car winding and bouncing back to the house. Grandmother got out, and the deputy and Gerta got in. Sheriff Greene rolled down his window to speak briefly to Grandmother, then drove away quickly.

Emma prayed silently that God forgive her for whatever she had done. She watched her grandmother come in through the back screen door, stepping carefully and steadying herself on the handrail. Emma, seeing her pause as if to catch her breath, opened the wooden door to let her in. She was shivering and shaking.

"I need to lie down a while. Tell your mother I want to see her."

"Okay. She's in there where Daddy is. He hasn't been up all day. She says he's worse."

"I don't think I'll live through this night." Grandmother lay down, turning her head toward the wall as Emma closed her door and went to find her mother. Slowly she opened the bedroom door where her father lay talking out of his head. Simultaneously Mother and Martha looked up from their magazines. They both sat on the floor where a lamp provided a dim light. Emma wondered how they could possibly see to read. She motioned them to come out.

"Grandmother is lying down. She seemed upset and wants to see you, Mama."

"You girls stay with your daddy while I see what she wants. I think he'll have to go to the hospital. I can't get his fever down this morning."

Emma and Martha sat down in the dim light. Mother had marked her page in *Reader's Digest*. Martha was reading her *Weekly Reader*.

"What's wrong with Grandmother?" Martha asked.

"I don't know, but stay here, and I'll see if I can find out something." Emma went out of the room and went to her grandmother's door, which was slightly open. She peaked in and then put her ear to the crack and listened. The women were not whispering but not talking loud. Grandmother was speaking, still lying on the bed, her head propped on her big bolster. Mother sat in a chair by the bed.

"The thing Jim can't figure out is why Talton went down there in the first place. There wasn't much left except some bones, mostly the head and face that fell in the aisle. He talked like it was the worst sight he'd ever come across in twenty-seven years with the law."

Emma's mind could not comprehend the meaning of the words at first, trying to listen to both voices that sometimes spoke at once. "Those sows eat their own dead. They'll eat a man who doesn't get out of their way. I know that from what Jiley told me when he worked down there," Mother's voice was matter of fact.

"They're taking the remains to the morgue," Grandmother said. "I feel like I cannot live through this."

"We need to get Jiley to the hospital," Emma heard her mother say, reminding her to get back to her place with Martha.

At four-thirty in the afternoon, Deputy Barnes' car drove to the back door. Emma heard the knock on the door and saw him through the kitchen window. Her heart skipped a beat when she noticed Gerta sitting in the passenger's seat. Emma waited until the knocking became loud enough for someone else to hear. Mother went to the door to see what the deputy wanted.

"Hello, Helen, sorry to bother you all again, but I need to speak with Miss Ila briefly."

"Come in, John," Mother said, waving him to Grandmother's bedroom, where she was sitting in her rocking chair reading the Bible.

"Oh, and is Emma here?"

"Yes," said Mother. "What do you want with her?"

"Miss Gerta is in the car. She wanted to ride out with me so she could stop by the post office, and she said she had a present for Emma for being so kind to her fixing her dinner and all."

"Emma!" Mother called. "She's usually got her head stuck in a book somewhere."

Emma emerged, trying to appear as if she had been engaged in her studies.

"Hello, Emma. Miss Gerta is in the car and wanted to say good bye to you especially for being so kind to her if you would like to walk out. She's not up to coming in this house again."

"Sure, I'll walk out there."

Deputy Barnes walked to the front of the house to see Miss Ila.

"You would think that woman had had enough of us, wouldn't you?" Mother said. "Don't tell her anything about your daddy or anything else. She probably just wants to see what she can find out."

"Don't worry," said Emma, walking out the door.

The long winter day was closing. The dark, smoky clouds thickened the wet, icy wind. Gerta, smiling as she rolled down her window to greet Emma, wore her black coat, black fur hat, and black leather gloves. She extended to Emma a box of chocolate candy.

"Hello, Emma, thanks for coming out in the cold. This is just a little present for you."

Emma did not speak at first but took the box. She avoided looking into Gerta's eyes. "Thank you, but you shouldn't have gone to the trouble."

"Well, you have been such a kind and helpful young lady that I just had to say you will be—remembered." Gerta's tone changed to something ominous and, to Emma, threatening. Emma looked at her closely to read her meaning. Sunlight streaked through the clouds at this moment as if invoked to turn Gerta's green eyes into yellow green slits smoldering under the heat of her fiery hair, burning in the setting sun.

"Well, thanks again, and good luck." Emma was eager to get away.

"I guess you know what happened to my husband." Emma felt the iciness in her tone.

"You mean they found him?"

"They didn't tell you? I guess young ladies like you—so sweet and innocent—are to be sheltered. But I think they underestimate your—maturity. Your uncle found his remains in one of the hog pens this morning when he went to work his rounds. There wasn't much left except bones and part of his head and face. The sheriff has questioned me about why we were visiting and why Talton would have gone to the hog house during the night. Of course, no one can imagine why, can we?" Gerta looked hard at Emma. She no longer smiled. Instead, a steely smirk curled her small red mouth.

"No, no, I cannot imagine. How horrible! I'm so sorry and hope you will be all right."

"I have to move on as soon as the law will give me some peace, but we'll meet again. I will pop up when you least expect to see me. I want to make sure I never forget your kindness."

Emma backed up, speechless, and waved good bye. Her heart jumped and skipped beats. She opened the back door and looked back at Gerta as she stepped inside. Gerta glowed in the one streak of sunlight stealing through the heavy clouds. The image, ominous in her black attire and orange-red hair, was forever fixed in Emma's mind.

Grandmother and Mother did not discuss any details of the disappearance of Talton with the girls. Their attention was focused on getting Jiley to the hospital. By nightfall, his fever was up again, yet he was shaking from chills. At daybreak Grandmother walked next door and asked Uncle Milton to help her and Mother take Jiley to the hospital.

CHAPTER II: FATHER'S DEATH

Exhaust fumes trailed the rattling old school bus, Number 35, as it lurched down the dirt road on Friday afternoon in late January, 1961, and screeched to a stop at the farm house to let off Emma and Martha. The only other two houses on the mile-long stretch leading to the highway were too far away to be seen. The sun burned through the distant blazing woods bathing the frozen, grey fields, the corn stubbles and brown tobacco stalks, cut into the ground. The sleeping earth waited for spring.

Ten-year-old Martha hopped from the bottom step of the bus to the ground, throwing her book sack across the lawn, her curly light brown ringlets bouncing wildly, and raced to scoop up the stray puppy that ran out to meet her. Behind her, Emma followed, tall for her thirteen years and slender, her dark brown eyes squinting. The copper tones of her short dark brown hair, soaked up the sun and made her think of the freckles that always popped out on her cheeks in sunlight. Nonetheless, she walked slowly, balancing a big three-ringed notebook with a stack of five books on top of it and a shoulder bag bulging on her left side.

Three unfamiliar cars were parked in the yard out of the way of the dirt driveway. Emma's father had been in the hospital all week, and she imagined relatives and church folks were visiting Grandmother. Her mother would be at the hospital, where she had stayed since he was taken Tuesday. This was not the first time he had been hospitalized after a spree of drinking. Most of the time he got through the last stage by staying in bed several days, swallowing whole raw oysters and eggs until his stomach would let something stick. A bucket sat beside his bed for him to vomit in; often the vomit was bloody. Emma remembered times when a doctor came to the house and set up an IV for him, but this time Grandmother could not persuade the doctor to come out on a Sunday night.

Emma entered the screen door, dropped her books on the floor of the tiny bedroom at the back of the house, and walked through the kitchen to the family room at the front of the house. Aunt Ophelia, her father's sister who lived on the farm and whose husband, Uncle Milton, tended the farm, sat in a rocking chair facing the grandmother, who rocked slowly in an identical chair.

"Home early, ain't you?" her aunt said, as both women looked up at Emma.

"A little. Some people were not on the bus this afternoon, so we didn't have as many stops to make."

"Martha says she's hungry. I've got chicken and pastry done and on the table," Aunt Ophelia said. "Both of you go on over and eat all you want. There's some banana pudding too."

"I'm not really hungry."

"Well, go on over, honey, with Martha, and I bet you might change your mind. I left everything out on the table for you."

It was a short walk out the back, across the yard, and into her aunt's kitchen.

Everyone said Aunt Ophelia made the best chicken and pastry of anyone in the family. Emma had eaten at this table many times, but not many over the last few years. Such special meals were not uncommon on Sunday but never on Friday.

The large Formica-topped table stood in the middle of the kitchen. Emma had always liked dining tables not cramped in the corner of a room as theirs was. Martha waited for her older sister to fix her plate, having been reprimanded in the past for playing in the food. She was eager to eat and go play with her dog. The girls ate quietly, commenting only that the food was good.

Then they heard someone coming into the back porch, banging the screen door. It was their little second cousin, Robert, who was five. "Jiley's dead!" he announced to the girls, who stopped eating and looked at him. "Your mama just got here. She said Jiley's dead."

Emma felt a numbness filling her body. She looked at Martha, not knowing what to do or say. Robert ran out, speaking to someone as the door banged again.

Aunt Ophelia came in to check on the girls. "You all go ahead and finish eating before you go home. Your mama's all right. She knows you are over here eating."

Martha picked up her corn bread halfheartedly and took a bite. Emma looked at her plate of pastry. Her stomach wasn't full, but a sickening feeling was welling up in her. She slid out of her chair and walked out into the yard between the houses. Mother stood talking with Aunt Ophelia on the back porch of her grandmother's house, where they had lived for as long as Emma could remember.

"He died of cerebral hemorrhaging," Emma heard her mother tell her aunt. "That's what they put on the death certificate." It sounded foreign to Emma. What would she have imagined the cause? Well, after all, they wouldn't put drank himself to death. At the last, all his systems had broken down. He was thirty-four.

Not noticed, tiptoeing in silence, Emma followed her mother and aunt into the family sitting room, where Grandmother sat rocking. Someone had told her. Mother walked over to Grandmother and hugged her. Neither woman said anything; they grieved in silence, still in the denial stage. It was the first time Emma had seen her mother hug her grandmother.

Emma could remember many times when her grandmother had prayed for Jiley's life to be taken naturally as he slept. She herself had prayed the same prayer.

Now his death was not real and would not be for a long time.

*****

She had sat up with her father the last night he was home. There had been many times when he was trying to get back on his feet after a long spree when a doctor had to be called in or he had to be taken to the hospital. But this last night had been the first time Emma had ever been awakened during the night—a school night at that—to sit with him so that her mother could lie down for an hour.

"Emma." Her mother shook her shoulder. "I need you to take my place for a while so I can lie down. Just watch him and get him some water if he wakes up. He has a fever."

Mother left the room in the dark to lie down in the next room on the couch. It was one o'clock. Grandmother and Martha were sound asleep. The only light came from a stove light in the kitchen. Emma tried to focus as she sat on the foot of her father's bed. She had seen his thin, pale face and thick red beard many times as he lay helpless in bed. There was always a cycle to the spree from sober to irritable after the drinking started, to angry, to violent, to sick, to humble and pitifully near death. Grandmother would buy oysters for him to pour vinegar on and swallow whole. It took several tries and half a day to get one to stay down.

For half an hour, she sat listening to her father breathe shallowly, thinking about the math test she had the next day and wishing she could lie back down. When her father turned his head and opened his eyes, Emma got up and leaned down to ask him if he wanted some water.

"I want my medicine," he said. Emma knew his prescribed medication was out.

"How about some aspirins for your fever?"

"Give me some of that red medicine in the bottle." Emma got up and went to the kitchen cabinet. Suddenly she thought about the red food coloring her grandmother used for red velvet cakes. She mixed some aspirin, water, and food coloring to make some red medicine. Father drank it from the little vial without commenting.

Then Emma found a wash cloth, wet it, and wiped her father's mouth and forehead as she had seen her mother do. He was restless, his fever a little hotter. Lying down at the foot of the bed, Emma propped her head up with her elbow, her eyelids growing heavy. Her body and mind numbed until her elbow slipped and jolted her brain. She sat up, afraid her mother would catch her dozing. Father had fallen back asleep. He snored lightly, breathing seemingly from the top of his chest. Her red medicine had worked!

Mother entered the room and saw Father sleeping. "You go back to bed now. I just needed a little break." She felt of Father's forehead.

"He woke up and wanted his medicine, so I just gave him some aspirin. His fever was up then but is back down now." Emma did not tell her mother about the food coloring.

*****

About five o'clock on Friday, the phone started ringing and never stopped until bedtime. Grandmother told everyone Father died in the hospital and that his body would stay at Landau's Funeral Home in town. Some people brought the body of dead relatives to lie in the living room, and Emma was glad not to have to deal with a casket in the house. A cold sensation ran through her. Her father would be in a casket like she had seen other dead people in, but they were strangers, people who made her afraid of the dead.

While Grandmother was on the phone, Mother started to clean up.

"Emma," she said, "get down here and help me scrub this kitchen floor before folks start coming in."

Emma could hardly believe her mother could think of such a thing when her father lay dead. What in the world did it matter if the floor was waxed and shining or not? But they scrubbed every square of the cheap linoleum, scraping grime from the cracks with little knives put aside just for that purpose. They stooped and slid, scouring, then rinsing with clean rags, and finally putting a coat of wax, backing out of the kitchen to let the floor dry.

The rest of day and evening blurred into whispers among family members who sat in the bedrooms away from Grand-mother, while she talked loudly to the elite elders and preacher who sat in the living room. "I hope I'm saved," she said. "The Bible says you have to have faith and be saved through grace. I know I'm a sinner."

"I know I'm saved," said Elder Blackstone, as he spat tobacco juice in Grandmother's cuspidor. "Who's goin' to preach Jiley's funeral Sunday?"

Emma stood in the next room listening. There would be a funeral Sunday, and Saturday night a visitation at the house. The body would not come home again. Her mother's voice mention-ing her name caught her attention. "Emma has nothing to wear."

"Eula has a dark blue dress Emma could wear Sunday," said

her Aunt Carrie, who had driven out from town. "It might be too long but I could put a false hem in it. I'll bring it tomorrow and let her try it on so I can mark a hem."

"She has some black shoes," Mother said.

Did she not have a dress good enough for her father's funeral? Emma wondered. She had to wear her cousin's dress? Eula wore dresses from the small dress shops run by the Jews uptown. Emma's mother never bought those clothes because they were too expensive.

On Saturday a steady flow of folks stopped by to see Grandmother and Mother. Martha stayed close to her mother while Emma kept aloof, not wanting to have to hug all those old people who smelled like moth balls in their best woolen clothes. The kitchen table was full of covered dishes people had brought: collards, corn bread, ham, peas, corn, butter beans, even homemade apple jacks. Emma ate a pimento cheese sandwich in her bedroom. Then someone was calling her. Aunt Carrie was ready for her to try on Eula's blue woolen dress. It fit except for being too long, the fashion being that girls wore dresses mid-calf. That done, Emma went outside to watch the traffic coming into the yard. Cars were parked all over the front and back yards and in the driveways. As she observed, she grew weary and then angry. These people didn't care about her father or her or anyone else in the house. They were laughing and talking loud at every door and every corner, the men congregating in the yard where they could talk and smoke freely.

Emma needed to find a place to get rid of those people. Her Aunt Ophelia had a little cot in her house where she slept by a window looking out onto the front porch. She sidled up to her aunt and, whispering, asked if she might go over to her house to lie down.

It was almost dark on Saturday evening when Emma walked

over to her aunt's house. The screen door was unlatched, and no one was in the house, her aunt and uncle being among those offering condolences to her mother and grandmother. She passed through the kitchen into the family room. She paused in the dark room where the window pane emitted enough light to see the vinyl couch and chair, the wooden rocker, and the television sitting on a small table in the corner. Her uncle had bought a television a year or more before her grandmother did, and consequently she would go over to watch whenever her mother would let her on the weekends. She and Martha were small then. One Saturday night, Emma and Martha came over to watch the fights at ten o'clock because her father was watching with Uncle Milton. It was a rare memory of being with her father, sober, sitting there in the dark, watching men in shorts hit each other with gloves until one fell down and the referee counted to ten. Martha had sat in Emma's lap and fallen asleep before the fight was over. Her father carried her home in his arms. That was the only good memory Emma could conjure before walking to the small front bedroom that had been added on to Aunt Ophelia and Uncle Milton's house for their boys years ago, but which now was her aunt's own room, isolated yet providing a view of the road and her grandmother's front porch where all the guests were coming and going, laughing and hugging one another.

Aunt Ophelia had put a cot in the room several years ago when she started having insomnia and didn't want to bother Uncle Milton by getting up and down during the night. Emma lay down in the cold room, always shut off from the heater in the sitting room and kitchen. Most likely Mother would miss her and send someone with a message to return to the company, but an hour passed as darkness fell, making the house spooky except for the light shining in the window where Emma watched the crowd that grew by the minute.

Who were these strangers who descended like vultures at the news of a death? Emma raised the window beside the cot to catch the dialogues and reached for the blanket at the foot of the cot. The muffled voices of men standing in the front yard, visible only by the red tips of their cigarettes, reached her ears when the chilly breeze flowed through the window screen. Suddenly she heaved, disgusted by the stupid women laughing on the porch who would meander to the kitchen and eat cake and pie while her father lay alone and cold in the funeral home in town, and she cried harder than she had ever cried before in her life. There was no one who had even missed her, but if someone did come, she would not join the irreverent dunces who took the opportunity of her father's death to socialize.

It was true she had few good memories of her father, and she had dreamed of one day not having to be afraid of him and not having to be ashamed of him, but now all the emptiness of what could have been and what would never be rose in her throat like mashed potatoes she could not swallow. She forgave him for the illness he could not control and for the lack of treasured childhood memories he had not been able to give her.

Suddenly Emma heard the back screen door open and then the kitchen door. Not wanting anyone to see her, she slid off the cot and into the closet beside it.

It was pitch black in the closet. Then she heard Martha calling her. "Emma, Emma, Mother says you need to come home." The voice rang through the small house and back outside. Martha stopped to ask the men if they had seen Emma.

Meanwhile Emma looked around to find an escape. She would be seen leaving by the back or the front doors. The only side of the house not visible to the visitors was next to a field. She decided to go out the back, ask the men if someone had called her, walk toward her back door, but rather than go inside, circle behind the smokehouse and through the neighbor's field until she could get on the road. She just needed to walk a while and breathe deeply.

The trek through the field to the dirt road was treacherous in her cousin's dressy outfit her mother had insisted she wear for the visitation. She stepped carefully, avoiding the icy patches. A sharp wind chilled Emma's face and neck. She pulled the hood of the borrowed red coat over her head. Her Aunt Carrie had brought the coat along with the blue dress to complete her funeral attire. As Emma walked down the road, she thought she must look like little red riding hood under the brilliant stars and crescent moon.

As she walked, she studied the moon, hanging so yellow and so shaped like a banana. A poem started in her brain, and she composed it orally as she walked.

> The moon a ripe banana bright,
> hanging sturdy turned upright.
> One banana dangling free,
> On one great black banana tree.

No, this was not quite right.

Suddenly a loud crashing sound and the appearance of head-lights at the end of the dirt road a half mile away scared Emma. She must get off the road and out of sight. She ran, almost stumbling in the uncomfortable shoes, until she reached a path leading to a small pond, always known to her as the fish pond she had always been forbidden to play in, unlike her male cousins who swam and fished there. Water had never intrigued her as it did most children. In fact, Emma had a fear of water. Now though, the pond invited her, the tall pines and wild shrubs on either side of the winding path blocked the wind, and she pushed back the red hood. A short pier, where she had often sat with her cousins fishing, appeared rickety, some of the boards rotten, but Emma wanted to look at the water in the moonlight. She walked carefully on the precarious boards until she reached the end of the pier where she could see small ripples in the water. This forbidden place was a refuge this night.

One winter she walked down to the pond with her father, mother, and Martha looking for a Christmas tree. They never bought one but would look in the woods for a cedar that would do. Her father carried an axe and spotted one on the far side of the pond. He seemed pleased that he found the tree that year. That was the only time Emma could remember her father doing anything related to Christmas.

A frog jumped off the bank into water, reminding her she would be missed by now. As she turned to face the path, she thought she saw a figure moving in the shadow of the pines. She shrieked, terrified, and started to run. The heel of her shoe stuck between two boards causing her to lose her balance and fall into the water. Flailing her arms, she lounged forward fast, the dark, cold water slapping her face as her arms and legs struggled to stay afloat. But her heavy coat pulled her down as she tried to swim and she felt herself gulping air and water. She didn't hear anyone coming. Suddenly she felt arms around her waist and a pulling against the water. Her chest felt as if it would explode. Someone laid her on her side and pressed her back. She coughed and coughed, not raising her head. Her heart was racing.

"Are you all right, Miss?"

Emma turned her head and looked up. The face, in the moonlight, was that of a black man about her father's age or a little older. His brown eyes and copper tints in his hair reminded her of her father. The man was tall and strong. She had felt like a bird as he carried her out of the pond and set her down in the field.

"You scared me to death! And then you saved me!" Emma was breathing deeply and shivering in the cold.

"I'm so sorry. I was just walking to get rid of some built-up stress. My mother lives nearby. She is ill, and I am staying with her and was just walking for exercise. I never would have expected a little girl to be out here at night."

"You sound just like Sidney Poitier. Did anyone ever tell you that?"

"No, Miss, I can't say anyone has."

"Oh, Lord, my mother will kill me for ruining these clothes!" Eula's expensive dress and coat were ruined.

"Your mother will be delighted that you are safe! May I see you to your house? Where do you live? And why are you out here by yourself in the dark?"

"Well, it's a long story. My father is dead, and so many folks had come that I thought I would go crazy unless I got away until they left. I live right down this road a quarter of a mile. I need to get back, hide these clothes, and try to clean them before noon tomorrow! Thank you for not letting me drown! As my grandmother would say, 'The Lord must have sent you.'"

"I must see that you get back and speak with your mother. I can see all the lights down there now. Some cars are leaving."

"No, no, she would be too upset. She has enough to worry her tonight. Don't you see? I know what to do. I'll be all right." And Emma started running away from the man who stood staring at her. In five minutes she was back to her short cut across the field to the back yard. She turned and looked down the road. She could see the man still looking at her. She waved.

Luckily a number of visitors still lingered, giving Emma time to sneak back into Aunt Ophelia's house. She took off her wet clothes, shoes, and stockings and wrapped them all up in the red coat. Then she found her aunt's gown and robe in a drawer and put them on. The only thing she could do was try to sneak in to her house unnoticed. The last of the guests were in the front room, and judging by the raised voices, they were standing and about to leave.

Aunt Ophelia came through to the back of the house on her way to her house as the guests were exiting the front. "There you are! We were looking for you. Where have you been?"

"I have a little problem, and you are the only person that I think can help me."

Aunt Ophelia always wanted to be the heroine especially in helping Emma and Martha. She always said they were her girls since he had only two boys. "What is it?"

"Well, of all times, I don't want to worry Mother tonight, but I have messed up the clothes Aunt Carrie loaned me to wear tonight and tomorrow. They are all wet, and I wonder if there is any way you can dry them by in the morning?"

"What in the world happened? Did you slide down in that ditch of water out there where you girls play?"

"Yes, but please don't tell Mother."

"I can tell her that you want to stay with me tonight. That way she won't see your wet hair either."

"Please, tell her for me, and I'll go back to your house now."

On Sunday Emma, Martha, Mother, and Grandmother rode into town to the funeral home an hour before the funeral so that they could say good bye to Jiley privately. Few words were spoken on the way in, and those were exchanged between the funeral home director, who drove the long black hearse, and Grandmother. Mother and the girls sat in the backseat. Emma watched the raindrops sliding down the side window and the people walking, umbrella in hand, the day being unseasonably warm and balmy.

Once inside the funeral home, Mother encouraged Emma and Martha to touch their father's hand. "If you touch him, you won't be afraid," she said as she held her husband's hand and looked at his waxen face and examined his clothes. Martha reached to touch the right hand placed on her father's chest. Emma did not want to touch her father but felt she might later regret not doing so. She reached to place her fingers on his hand. It did not make her feel better. His hand was hard and cold, the wiry hairs reminding her of hog killings when she once helped scrape the bristles off scalded pig skin with a jar top.

During the ceremony Emma sat beside her mother near the front, the casket open in clear view. Just to get through the long hour, the preacher made up text because he never knew Jiley, only the Grandmother. It was surreal, something one endured until Emma noticed a damnable fly buzzing over her father's face and then lighting on his nose. How in the world could a fly get in at this most sacred time in the presence of all the mourners? The fly flew away. Emma breathed deeply. In four seconds, the fly alighted on her father's nose again. Damn fly. Should she get up and shoo it out of the room? No, she couldn't move. The fly buzzed and crawled. Suddenly she snickered loud enough that Helen put her hand out to silence her. That was all she remembered.

At the family grave yard, only a short way down the dirt road from the house, people mulled around after the last prayer, the family waiting for everyone else to leave. The funeral director again conversed with Grandmother.

"Miss Ila, you've been through a lot. How many children have you lost?"

"Seven. There's just two left."

"Well, I know you are hurt."

"Yes, but I'd rather it be one of them than me."

Emma, listening, was a bit surprised that her grandmother would say something like that, but maybe it was just the effects of old age or all she had been through. Or maybe she meant just what she said. The director walked away.

CHAPTER III: MEMORIES

It would take years before Emma stopped dreaming of her father. Fear, a tumor that had grown in her stomach her whole life, would not begin to recede until the shock and denial ended. Turning fourteen soon after her father died, she could not comprehend the change in her life. When she woke up every morning for the next year, she would feel the same old sickening fear in her stomach, and then her brain would say, He's gone. He's dead. You won't ever have to dread his coming home again or fear being awakened during the night by loud cursing and window panes being broken or your mother whispering, *He's got a knife, or He's got a gun; you and Martha go outside and wait for your grandmother to pick you up.*

The routine was that Emma and Martha would put on their clothes and shoes quickly and run quietly outside the house and down the road, where they waited to see the headlights of their grandmother's car, which she might not turn on until the car was headed down the dirt road towards them. Once in the car, they sped a mile to the secondary paved road and then usually to Grandmother's friend's house or to her brother's house for a visit. When they returned a couple of hours later, usually Mother was doing some work and Daddy was asleep, out for the night. However, if they returned to find that he was still out of his mind, Mother would either join them or tell them to stay away until morning. Daddy would eventually wear himself out and when he did he would be out for hours. The raving and violence was caused by the need for more whiskey or was a case of what was commonly called the monkeys. At this stage even Mother, who was gritty and brave and obnoxious to Daddy, had learned to stay out of his way until she could get the knife or the gun and hide it.

Often Grandmother would take the girls to see Thelma, her church sister. Here Emma and Martha would sit politely answering initial questions to the old woman, who had gummy yellow teeth and who grinned like a wrinkled Alice's cat. Thelma rocked hard as she talked to Grandmother about the preachers, church members, their children, and her one granddaughter, whose formal portrait hung on the wall behind the piano. That was Abigail, called Precious, by Thelma, the prettiest and smartest girl in her school, winning a full scholarship to the university. Emma thought Precious must be smug and shallow if the smirk on her face was any clue. Once the questions were answered, the girls were left at the farther end of the long living room to do their homework while the old women talked and rocked. Sometimes Miss Thelma would lean close to the grandmother and whisper, causing Emma to strain her ears to catch the secret such as the time Miss Thelma brought out a thick catalog and pointed to an item, turning red and giggling. "I ordered me one." Emma looked up but could not comprehend what the item was, but it must have been risque to make Miss Thelma snicker like a teenager.

"I don't blame, you," said Grandmother, changing the conversation to ask about Miss Thelma's housemate, an ancient, skinny woman named Mary, who stayed out of the way of company.

"Mary is in her room. She don't come out except to eat. She pays me fifteen dollars a month on the groceries." Apparently hearing her name, Mary appeared like a ghost from a back room, frail and hollow-eyed, her gray hair straight and matted.

"How are you, Mary?" asked Grandmother. Mary smiled faintly and walked slowly to the kitchen.

"She don't talk hardly ever. She just eats and goes back to bed," Thelma explained.

Emma thought Mary was the oldest, frailest person she had ever seen. She was scary, maybe crazy, and probably kept locked in the back room when Thelma went to bed. Trying to focus on her spelling lessons, the endless exercises she did every week, she accidentally dropped a notebook on the piano keys. This was a serious faux pas. But Miss Thelma, knowing she did not mean to, let it go without comment. Emma wished she could take piano lessons as did some of her friends who left class to go to piano for thirty minutes twice a week, but a piano was too much to wish for.

*****

Emma knew the story Mother had told her about the time when she was about eight months pregnant with Emma. Mother and Daddy had moved away from Grandmother Ila, he having taken a job in another town. They stayed in an upstairs apartment. One day when Mother was washing clothes in the laundry room, her arms deep in suds, she and Daddy argued, and he opened his knife and held it to her stomach. Even though Mother was not openly religious as was Grandmother, she would end such stories with "The Lord was looking after us."

The knife triggered another memory. Emma checked out of the A & P grocery store with her mother. She reached up to put two cartons of candy Camel cigarettes on the counter to be rung up by the cashier. "One is for me, and one is for my daddy," she told the clerk. It was Saturday, and the next day Emma, her mother, Grandmother, and Martha, a toddler, would drive to a distant town to visit her father. She did not know until years later that he was in prison. She just recalled the wire fence and people standing and talking on either side. When Emma was older and thought to ask her mother why her father was in prison, she said only that he had cut a man.

*****

The year Emma started first grade, Mother started a job in town, ten miles in from the farm, at Ledford's department store. She had worked downtown for years already at different jobs, such as taking tickets at the theater and working at the candy counter at Woolworth's. Emma would never forget the smell of the butter scotch candy, lying individually wrapped under the glass counter or the smell of corn candy. Emma was fascinated to explore the aisles, careful not to touch anything, something her mother strictly forbade. She did not want Emma and Martha to look suspicious of stealing, the worst sin, it seemed to Mother, perhaps because she saw a good deal of it going on in the store.

The Ledford job was more professional, one that would last twenty years until the store burned down when Emma was grown, out of college and working. In the early years of the job when Daddy was still alive, Mother was off every Tuesday, working every Saturday, stores not being open on Sunday. Mother could squeeze in a miraculous amount of work into that one day and past miraculous in the summer when vegetables were ripe. Emma and Martha looked forward to Tuesdays because, if nothing else, during school days, they could count on a scrumptious supper to be devoured early after a long day at school without anything good to eat. School lunches were sometimes not even edible, the worst being dry hamburgers and hard corn, hot dogs and sourkraut, fish sticks and cold slaw, and sickening soup and peanut butter sandwiches. Maybe it was just the overpowering steam and smell of food and body odors that hit Emma's nostrils every day when she opened the cafeteria door in line with her classmates, all prisoners of the system, at once liberating and brainwashing, beating them into future lower middle class workers.

One cold, sunny Tuesday, Emma's mother's day off, the girls got off the bus, knowing their mother was there working and cooking a special meal, entered the back screen door, and were greeted by the waft of a medley of delicious aromas. The kitchen table was set and full of bowls of food with several still sitting on the stove. There were fresh turnip greens, home pickled beets, boiled potatoes, lima beans from the home freezer, okra, corn, fried corn bread, sweet iced tea, still hot but cooling on the table. On the stove waited ham hock that had been boiled with the greens and an apple pie, bubbling, ready for the cold vanilla ice cream to cool it. This was the girls' favorite meal! Emma loved the apple pie and ice cream.

Emma's second glance was from the table to the floor, where her father lay on his side in the doorway of the kitchen in the narrow space between the wall and the refrigerator. He was drunk and almost passed out, mumbling some incoherent phrases when Helen made some hateful remark. Grandmother sat in her room, waiting to be called for supper. It had been a full day of work for Helen, the washing of several loads of clothes in the wringer washer and wash tubs, hanging clothes on the line in the backyard, taking the clothes in, folding, putting them away. Probably Father had come home early in the afternoon already drunk, perhaps fired from his job. This was the pattern. The girls had seen it over and over. It still chilled their hearts and rendered the table full of food a mirage. Father was almost out, however, and the meal could be eaten in peace. With luck, he would sleep through the night.

Mother told the girls to wash up and call their grandmother to eat. Emma went to the sink to wash her hands. All of a sudden Emma saw her father get up from the floor, where he had appeared to be in a drunken stupor, incapable of standing, and start cursing her mother. He picked up a broom, handy in a corner of the kitchen, and swept it across the kitchen table, scraping the bowls to the floor. He beat the table as if trying to break it down and knocked all the dishes off, food splattering on the walls and floor, glass breaking and mixing with the carefully prepared food.

When Mother tried to stop the destruction of the meal, Daddy took her down to the floor and started choking her. Grandmother came quickly to see what was happening. The girls stood frozen, horrified, at this, the worst scene they had yet to witness. Mother could not speak, her throat turning red as he choked her more. Grandmother pleaded with her son to let her go. He did not relent, getting strength from madness and desire to free himself from the demons that drove him insane.

Grandmother kept on begging, "Please, Jiley, let her up. I beg you, not to hurt her. What would the children do? If you want whiskey, I can get you some. Let her go, Jiley."

Finally after an eternity of several minutes, Emma's heart beating fast in her throat, Father grew tired and released his hold on Mother's neck, now blue and red. She did not move at first. Emma did not know if her mother was going to die or could breathe. The moment, pregnant with uncertainty, Grandmother motioned the girls out the door. They knew what she meant. They ran to an outside shop and hid around the corner, where they could watch the back door. Here they waited for the next signal. Five minutes passed before they saw their grandmother's car roll slowly out the driveway. They ran to open the back door of the car and jumped in.

Grandmother's new two-toned blue Impala Chevrolet, luxurious and grand, picked up speed as it kicked up dust on the dirt road. "I'm going to get him a pint of whiskey if I can find some," she said. "Maybe he will drink himself to death tonight. I pray the Lord will take him this very night before he kills somebody."

The girls did not speak. The destination would be one of three places they had been previously with their grandmother. This time they drove what seemed like a long way, seven or eight miles out farther into the country to an old farm house set back from the black-top road, down a winding, bumpy dirt driveway. Grandmother blew her horn and waited. In a few seconds, a man opened the front door and looked, then closed it. In another minute, he returned, his coat pocket bulging.

"How are you, Cousin Ila?"

"I'm aliving. That's all I can tell you. I came to get a pint of whiskey. Jiley is on a spree, and I'm trying to keep him from killing somebody and hoping this whiskey will kill him. I pray the Lord will take him this very night."

"I know you've been through some torment with them boys. It's still five dollars."

He took the bill. "I appreciate it, Jasper. You all doing all right?"

"As well as can be expected. You take care now."

The Impala rolled down the path to the road and back home.

"You younguns wait out by the shop until I see what is going on."

All the lights in the house seemed to be on. All was quiet.

Emma wondered where her mother was and if her father was blacked out by now or still crazy and violent.

In ten minutes, Grandmother stepped out to the shop, accompanied by Mother. She must have wanted the girls to see she was okay.

"I think as long as he has his whiskey when he wakes up, he will just drink more and go back to sleep," Mother said. "That's what all this acting is about." She always down played the violence that paralyzed the rest of them.

"Do you think we had better stay away tonight?" Grandmother asked Mother.

"I don't know. I think you and the children might better stay off until morning so you can get some sleep since tomorrow is a school day. I can stay out of the way until he is out for sure. Then I can sleep some before he wakes up. It's not going to be cold tonight. I can stay outside out of the way if I need to."

"Well, I hate to leave you here, but I can't make you come. I think I'll take the younguns and go to Frank's."

Uncle Frank was Grandmother's older brother. He was Emma and Martha's great uncle, the kind of man who felt duty bound to help his sister. He and his wife, Mabel, and house full of children lived just a few miles away on another dirt road more populated with farm families than Grandmother's. A tall, burly man, sixty-three years old, Uncle Frank, Grandmother's only male sibling, had inherited all the farms from their father. Grandmother and her three sisters inherited a few thousand dollars cash. Grandmother's husband died and left her with five children of their nine still alive and a farm to pay off or lose. She had hung on and paid off the debt. As a result, Frank could not tell her much. They loved each other for the blood kin. He had taken in his sister and granddaughters any time she came unannounced, fed them, and put them up for the night, sometimes two nights while Jiley, wielding a butcher's knife, ranted and raved, breaking out window panes, walking up and down the dirt road, trying to borrow money and find a ride to get more whiskey.

This night it was about five-thirty in the evening when the Impala pulled into Uncle Frank's drive. Grandmother and the girls got out and went to the door, which opened just as they reached the first step.

"You all come in," Aunt Mabel said matter of factly, knowing she had no choice. "How are you? Come on in and have a seat. Frank will be in here directly.

He is taking his muddy shoes off."

Patriarch of his family, Uncle Frank entered the dark pine panelled den, hanging his hat on a peg on the wall. "How are you, Ila?" he asked, sitting down heavily in his red leather recliner.

"I wanted to get away from the house. Jiley has gone on a wild spree. I thought he was going to choke Helen to death," she said, her voice quivering.

"Well, you and the younguns better eat supper with us and stay here tonight."

He looked at Aunt Mabel. "Go tell Sarah to cook enough for Ila and the girls."

She rose obediently and went into the kitchen. In a moment, Sarah, sixteen in her junior year of high school, the middle daughter of the three still living at home, came to the den door. "Hey, Aunt Ila, Emma, Martha. We're cooking supper in here if you want to come in and watch the chaos," she said, turning to Emma and Martha. That was their cue to leave the adults.

Once in the big kitchen, Carl and Damon, the two younger teenage sons still living at home, came in the back door, having been out feeding the hogs, chickens, and turkeys.

"Get those nasty shoes and clothes off, and get ready for supper," yelled fourteen-year-old Maude, turning around from the sink, her hands dripping suds. The boys laughed, mimicked her grumpy tone, and made faces behind her back. Yet they went straight to the bathroom down the long hall.

Sarah and the third daughter, Miriam, eighteen, bantered about an upcoming church bazaar. Emma, listened, smiling at them as they teased and fussed. Dim lights in the spacious kitchen emitted a thick, warm dusty aura befitting three high school sisters basking in security and dreams.

Carl and Damon emerged, clean but ragged, ready to play. Soon they coaxed Martha to the large living room, out of ear shot of the adults. There they would play cards, most likely setback until called to eat, Carl, acting like Moe of the three Stooges while Martha watched laughing, forgetting for the moment the scene she just left.

Emma listened to the sisters' chatter as they went about the task of fixing supper, now having to add more food for the unexpected, and, Emma sensed, inconvenient guests.

Maud was just learning to make biscuits. She kneaded the flour with butter milk and lard awkwardly in a large wooden bowl.

"Watch out, Maud," snapped Sarah, "you're sifting flour on the floor I just swept!"

"Well, the way you sweep, nobody would know the difference," Maud muttered, being used to her older sister's criticism.

Sarah broke eggs into a glass bowl deftly and after a dozen asked Miriam if that was enough. Glancing at Emma, Miriam told Sarah to add three more. That done, Sarah poured the eggs into a large frying pan already hot with a thin layer of lard ready to receive the mass of whites and yolks. Emma knew how to scramble eggs as her mother had taught her, but she watched Sarah, mesmerized by the slow careful stirring of the eggs. She had never seen scrambled eggs take more than a couple of minutes to cook, but here was Sarah, stirring slowly the loose mixture over low heat as if she were performing a religious ritual. As she stirred, her chatter stopped, and Miriam, the senior who would graduate in May, took over as if to allow Sarah to concentrate on stirring.

"Maud, we saw you today on the bus, making eyes at the preacher's son, stinky Binky, hoping he would move to sit with you," said Miriam. "I know you were heartbroken when he went by you and sat with the boys in the back."

"I did not!" Maud mumbled, becoming tongue-tied. "He's a … spoiled brat and puffed up football player."

"Sure, Maud," chimed in Sarah, still stirring the eggs. "That's why you gave his mother a valentine card to give to him after church last Sunday."

"That's a lie!" Maud screeched, almost losing her breath. "That card was for her, my Sunday School teacher! I'm gonna tell Mama that you're spreading lies. It'll be all over the church first thing you know. You know how just one girl on the bus can go home and tell her mother something and then she tells it at the next circle meeting, and then it's all over the community."

"Well, he is going off to that special college agriculture program in Raleigh that farmers send their sons to. Mama says the preacher's wife has over five hundred acres of land that Binky will tend and own one day," Sarah added. She and Miriam loved to get Maud going because she always got angry and tongue-tied.

"Girls, what on earth are you all doing in here?" Aunt Mabel said quietly and calmly as she poked her head in the kitchen. "Is supper about ready? Did you make extra coffee, Miriam?"

"Yes, ma'am, it's just Maud fussing and grumbling as usual."

"Well, let's get ready to eat," Aunt Mabel said in her no nonsense tone. "It's six o'clock, and we've got to make some pallets for our company. After you clean up the kitchen, go up in the attic and get some quilts and there're some pillows in my closet. Make one big one for Emma and Martha on the living room floor. Ila can sleep on your bed, Maud, and you can sleep in the den on the couch." Maud grimaced, but saw the reprimanding look on her mother's face and turned her head. Anyhow, you three should show Emma and Martha your Easter dresses after supper. I bet they might like a dress like yours if they don't already have one. They may want to go to church with us Easter. If Ila would buy the cloth, I know Ophelia would make the dresses. She can sew anything and she can borrow my patterns."

"Okay, we'll show them our dresses," said Sarah, catching her Mother's intention to shift the conversation to a pleasant topic.

"Mine is plain with no lace like Sarah's," said Miriam, "but I intend to get some satin shoes, a hat, and bag to dress it up."

"Maud's looks like an old lady's dress, like a suit," chirped Sarah.

"Well, I don't have to worry about my weight like some people. I can afford to show off my sophistication, unlike some people who don't know the meaning of the word," Maud had the last word before supper was served.

Aunt Mabel brought extra chairs from the bedrooms to the dining table. Still, there was not a place for one: Maud said she would eat later and go work on her homework for a while.

For Emma, the meal was like a grand breakfast: country ham and gravy, grits, eggs, homemade biscuits, and homemade butter and jam. She had never thought what a wonderful supper breakfast food could make. There was not much talk as the adults sipped coffee and avoided the topic of why Emma, Martha, and Ila were there uninvited. Carl and Damon had washed their faces and hands well enough to be admitted to the table, and Sarah and

Miriam ceased their chatter. The meal to them was something to endure, a time to be seen and not heard until the adults returned to the sitting room and left them to clean up.

"Eat up, Sarah," said Uncle Frank. "Aren't you hungry?"

"I'm on a diet."

"Always on a diet," said Grandmother. "You're not too fat; you're just a nice size. I don't think boys like skinny girls? Do they, Damon?"

Damon turned red, but realized he had to be polite. "Don't ask me. Carl would know."

"I think she *is* fat." Carl smiled and glanced at Sarah.

"Well, at least I'm not mangy."

"All right. That will do," Uncle Frank said. "You two must be finished eating. Go do your lessons."

"Everything was good, girls. Mabel, you've got some good cooks here," said Grandmother. "I guess you couldn't do without them now, but one day some handsome gentlemen will take them away from you." Grandmother knew how to compliment folks when she wanted to.

Sarah, Miriam, and Maud started cleaning the dishes from the table, and the adults went outside to stretch their legs and admire the shrubs.

Miriam asked Emma to take the scraps outside to the dog pan in the back yard. Emma and Martha did not have any pets unless a stray dog or cat came up after having been dumped out by someone who wanted to get rid of it. The dirt road they lived on was a favorite place to push a dog out of a vehicle without being seen. But Uncle Frank took care of his dozen bird dogs, vaccinating them himself.

There were also chickens, guineas, and turkeys walking around the yard pecking at apples that had fallen to the ground. Sometimes the turkeys scared Emma even now as old as she was.

This evening, thank God, the turkeys were not in sight. She did hear the hogs grunting from their pen in the nearby woods and smelled them faintly.

When Emma returned to the kitchen, the girls had finished cleaning up and had gone to the back to their rooms. She heard Grandmother talking with Uncle Frank. He was sending an older son, Tom, who had just come from work to ride by Grandmother's house and try to find out if Mother was okay or wanted to come over for the night.

In the back, Sarah and Miriam were in the living room dancing the cha-cha to "Tea for Two." "Come here, Damon," hollered Sarah. "I need a man to dance with, and you'll have to do." The boys always obeyed their older sisters in the presence of company.

"Emma, do you know how to cha-cha?" Miriam asked. Emma shook her head no. "Well, would you like to learn? It's easy."

"Sure, I'll try."

"I'll be the man and lead you. Just do what I say. Just face me and take one step back with your right foot; that's one. Lift your left foot up and back down; that's two. Then bring your right foot up and down, your left foot up and down, and the right again up and down quickly; that's one, two, three. Miriam pushed Emma back, then forward, then stamped one, two, three. Meanwhile, Damon and Martha were dancing. They all got the hang of the basic steps and were laughing when Emma noticed out the window Tom's black sports car drive up. Mother was not with him.

In a minute, Aunt Mabel came to the living room and told Emma and Martha privately that their mother was okay and wanted to stay home.

Once the cha-cha was mastered or destroyed, depending on

one's perspective, Sarah got out a stack of cards. She had taught Emma and Martha long ago how to play setback. Normally Emma did not like games, but her cousins were so entertaining, she forgot it was a game one was supposed to win, and consequently she never won.

It was nine o'clock when Aunt Mabel came in to break up the play. "All of you need to get a bath and go to bed. Did you all do your homework?"

No one responded as the group dispersed scattering in different directions.

"Sarah, find Emma and Martha something to sleep in while I make their pallet here in the living room."

"I can sleep in my clothes and bathe in the morning before school when I get home," said Emma, terrified by the thought of undressing and bathing here with no privacy and no clean clothes.

"Me too," said Martha. "I'm not very dirty anyway."

Aunt Mabel put a thick quilt down for a mattress, putting a sheet and blanket on top to make a bed. She brought two old, hard pillows in white cases.

"Do you think that's enough cover for you girls?"

"Yes, ma'am," Martha said.

"Thank you," Emma said.

Aunt Mabel turned off the light and closed the door behind her. Emma and Martha did not speak. They settled under the cover and turned away from each other. The acrid smell of the carpet and musty quilt was so strong Emma thought at first it would keep her awake. Here she was, an uninvited and most likely unwanted guest, sleeping on the floor in rank bedding. Her thoughts were interrupted by Martha's heavy breathing. She had fallen asleep already.

Suddenly Emma felt hot and pulled off the blanket. She turned on her side and wondered what her mother was doing.

She dreaded the early morning when Grandmother would arouse her from deep sleep at five o'clock, and say, "Get up. We'd better get home, so you can get ready for school. I'll fix your breakfast."

Emma could never eat breakfast; her stomach was always queasy in the morning. Then she thought of the wonderful supper her mother had fixed and saw once more her father get up from the floor, grab the broom, and knock bowls and dishes onto the floor, saw turnip greens spatter the wall, and then him choking her mother and Grandmother begging him to stop.

CHAPTER IV: THE TEENAGE YEARS

For the remainder of the school year after her father died, Emma was thankful he was gone, thankful that she would never be outside playing with her cousins and see him walking down the dirt road toward the house, someone having let him off at the highway; or see a yellow taxi drive into the yard, her father stumbling from it into the yard and into the house or falling down in the yard, the driver waiting until Grandmother came out and paid him.

A couple of weeks after the funeral, a distant cousin asked Emma and Martha if they wanted to go to a local children's theater performance. To the cousin's surprise, Emma declined and Martha followed suit. Emma felt the cousin was asking only out of sympathy, something that did not make her feel better. A week later, Dorothy, one of Emma's classmates who lived a few miles away in the country, asked her if she wanted to go shopping one Saturday. This classmate was the prettiest, most popular girl in the eighth grade, and Emma was surprised to be asked. Again Emma wondered if Dorothy's mother made her ask Emma out of sympathy. Emma accepted the invitation, however, but would have to find a way to get to Dorothy's house and uptown twelve miles away. Uncle Milton agreed to take the girls, and Dorothy's father would bring them home. It was embarrassing that Emma had no father to drive her, and her mother always worked on Saturdays. Besides, her mother had no car or license.

The day of the event was cold but sunny. Both Emma and Dorothy wore long black coats. Uncle Milton did not speak all the way while the girls whispered in the back seat, discussing what they would buy. Once let out of the car at two o'clock in the afternoon, the girls walked up and down Center and Rhine Streets, browsing in all the popular stores from Woolworth's and Kress's to Penny's and Belk-Tyler's to the small elite dress and shoe stores. The girls avoided Ledford's because Emma did not want to disturb her mother. Emma had twenty dollars and some change; she imagined Dorothy had more and would buy some expensive items. Yet two hours passed, and they had looked casually at skirts, sweaters, jewelry, scarves, and shoes. Tired of walking, they decided to go to the movie early, their ultimate goal for the outing being to see Elvis in *Blue Hawaii*. This was only the third Elvis movie Emma had seen.

On rare occasions Emma and Martha spent a Saturday with their cousin, Eula, who lived in town and who was seven years older. They would walk twenty-five minutes with her to get to the theater in town. Eula's father managed the theater and allowed the girls to sit in the balcony during the day and see movies free. The few blacks sitting there looked at them curiously. Emma did not relate her previous movie going to Dorothy, whose parents had surely taken her any time she wanted to go. The songs and scenery were breathtaking and so romantic that Emma longed to step into the story and be taken away. The girls sat quietly absorbing the dazzling color and sounds. Emma would learn the words to all the songs and sing them all the next summer while looping tobacco on Uncle Milton's harvester. "Take my hand; take my whole life too, for I can't help falling in love with you."

The movie over, it was still too early for Dorothy's father, who had been instructed by his daughter to pick the girls up at 9 p.m. in front of the theater. At six fifteen, the street lights on, the air twenty degrees colder than it had been two hours before, the girls walked down to the only other theater a couple of blocks away and decided to go in to see a John Wayne movie playing there. By now, having had no supper, the fourteen-year-olds bought popcorn and drinks. Not as many people were watching this movie. After an hour of Indians and arrows, cavalry and flags, Emma began to think they had made a mistake: it would have been better to see *Blue Hawaii* twice. Surprisingly Dorothy was amenable to leaving the endless chase on the screen. It was only seven thirty, but the girls were not about to give up on their night out. They stopped to admire expensive diamond rings and watches in the window of the most exclusive jewelry store in town. Emma could see herself and Dorothy reflected in a wall mirror inside the store. They stood, both slender in black, young, and longing for the future as unknown as the dark night beyond the street lights.

"Let's go back to see Elvis again," suggested Emma, knowing they could not walk another hour and a half on the street. Uncharacteristically, Dorothy went along with Emma this night, and the girls paid once again to enter the theatre. At nine fifteen, the movie ended the second time, and the girls moved slowly through the crowd into the bitter, still winter night, a shock to their bodies, having steeped themselves in a summer in Hawaii. But there was Dorothy's father, and the girls hopped in, their big night over.

*****

During the summer, Emma and Martha helped their Uncle Milton and Aunt Ophelia on the farm, primarily working in tobacco. One scorching day when her uncle was on the tractor in the back field next to the hog houses, Aunt Ophelia asked Emma if she would take Uncle Milton a quart jar of ice water. The mile-long path, bordered by wild flowers and weeds, was shaded in sections by oaks and pines where the woods had not been cut. Walking briskly in the dusty middle, thinking of the lovely seclusion and privacy of the path she had traveled as long as she could remember, Emma hugged the sweating jar, changing arms when it got too cold. The summer was just beginning, corn had shot up after the last rain but she could still see the thick growth of small trees on the pond side of the farm. The shady patches she passed through and a light breeze refreshed her hot face. She was almost to the back field. She could see her uncle on the tractor at the farther end of a long row, his back to her, as he plowed the tobacco, one row at the time. She stopped to decide whether to walk to meet him or wait until he turned around and started back towards her. Just then she noticed something moving along the woods bordering the corn field, waist high; it was only a glance, but she saw a woman dressed in black, her head covered with a black hat. Emma felt her heart jump. Could this woman be Gerta come back to get her? Maybe Gerta had been stalking her and waiting for such a chance to attack her. So frightened was Emma that she threw down the jar and ran back towards the house. Once she was a good distance away, she stopped, out of breath, and felt foolish for being scared. Nonetheless, she went all the way back to the house. Once in the yard, her mother asked her if she delivered the water.

"No, I got scared because I saw somebody down there."

"Who was it?"

"I don't know. It looked like a woman dressed in black."

"Well, if it was somebody, it was probably somebody looking for huckleberries. You go back down there and give Milton that water!"

Emma went, embarrassed to have been scared by something

she probably did not really see. It was strange. She had been down that path a hundred times growing up and had never been frightened before. This time she looked carefully all the way but did not see anyone. Her uncle was at the near end of a row and was so happy to get the cold water, drinking nearly the whole jar at once. He kept the jar, and she started back watching again for the woman in black, who never appeared.

*****

The fall after her father died Emma started high school in the same small rural first-through-twelfth-grade school she had always attended. She still had nightmares about her father as well as Gerta and Talton. In one dream, Talton came to her bedroom window, raised to let the summer night breeze blow through the screen. She could hear a low wailing like that of a wounded Indian in the movies. When she looked out the window, she saw the bloody half-eaten face of a man unrecognizable, yet she knew it was Talton. Just as he was about to cut the screen with a knife, she woke up, wet with perspiration, her heart pounding in her throat.

*****

The ninth grade was a blur of adjusting to classes. There were only two sections each of all the courses. Emma surprised herself by questioning the grammatical diagram of a complex sentence her English teacher put on the board. The teacher, a confident, smart lady, explained the sentence again in a sharp tone just for Emma and asked her if she understood. The class fell silent, all eyes on Emma to see if she dare disagree. No, she did not understand, but saw nothing to gain from prolonging the impenetrable wall. She said yes. This year the class was actually assigned an essay that was graded meticulously with comments. What a shock to open the paper on a Friday to find an eighty-eight! Emma had never seen such a low grade on her writing. The comments were valid; she actually learned something about writing. This teacher meant business. How wonderful and how rare.

Even more wonderful, Emma was chosen to participate in an innovative class comprised of three freshmen, two sophomores, two juniors, and two seniors. The format would be a seminar. The plan was for the course to last at least six weeks, a grading period, and be taught by her ninth-grade teacher and a twelfth-grade English teacher. The teachers were friends and drove to work together from another town. The word was that the work would be difficult but creative and advanced. Intimidated and excited, Emma was so eager she could hardly contain herself.

The course proved as stimulating and difficult as she had expected. The group sat around a long table set up in a small room constructed in a corner of the auditorium. Students spoke freely, not having to raise their hands. The instruction was led primarily by the senior teacher. She assigned pieces of literature normally taught on the senior level, such as Wordsworth and Coleridge's more difficult poems. The weeks flew by as the students studied literature, wrote, and presented critiques as well as creative pieces.

At the end of six weeks, the special class was told the course would not continue. The teachers were facilitating the extra course without any release time or extra compensation. It was too much for them, and so it was back to the regular classroom, which now was dull in comparison.

By tenth grade sophomores began getting their driver's license. Emma, being in the higher classes in all subjects, suddenly did not want to deal with the cult of popularity worshipped by the group she had grown up with. Her mother refused to let her join a group of models, who paid to be in a program sponsored by the leading department store, saying she could not afford it. The family did not go to the basketball games; Helen was always working. Emma just wanted to do her work and be left alone. The breaking point occurred in French class when the teacher announced she was giving a pizza party for the class and that everyone should donate seventy-five cents for food. Emma, although knowing she would not go, turned in her money. On Monday after the party on Saturday, the teacher walked over to Emma's desk during a class work assignment and loudly threw three quarters on the top of the desk. "Here's your money back," the teacher said in a disgusted tone as if to say there was no hope for Emma's social deprivation.

Having gained some confidence the previous year in the special honors class, Emma decided to ask the principal to change her schedule to put her in the lower class sections. That would separate her from her childhood friends with whom she no longer felt comfortable. She was weary of pressure. Mr. Sauls at first just laughed. No, he could not change her schedule and why would she want to do so anyway? She insisted, saying she wanted sincerely to switch if it was not a problem for him. Reluctantly he relented, never mentioning that he should check with her mother. She started her new sections on a Monday, the teachers having been notified by the principal. The teachers were the same. They seemed puzzled. A few of the students looked at Emma with curiosity that lasted only a day. They were not aggressive. Emma had no problem staying ahead of all of them. Even the brightest student in these lower classes was not especially academic but more domestic, planning for an early marriage.

*****

One Saturday morning about two years after Father died, Sheriff Greene dropped in to see Grandmother. Not wanting to be disturbed by company, Emma was not pleased with the unexpected guest, who ventured no farther into the house than the small room leading in from the back door, once a porch. Grandmother and the sheriff chatted like old friends, Emma listening from her bedroom. The two talked so loud and laughed so heartily that Emma could not avoid distraction. Curiosity got the best of her when she heard a paper bag crunch.

"I appreciate it, Jim," Grandmother said off handed, as Emma walked past the talkers to get her sweater hanging in the bathroom. She saw Jim take his wallet out of his pocket and put a ten dollar bill in it as Grandmother slipped a pint of whiskey into her apron pocket.

"Hello, Mr. Greene, how are you?"

"I'm just fine. I see you're getting taller. What grade are you in now?"

"Tenth."

"She says she going to college," the grandmother interjected.

Emma never knew whether her grandmother would praise her or criticize her to company. Today they were on pretty good terms; other times, she might describe her granddaughters as "sassy strumpets."

"Oh, seeing you reminds me of your long-lost friend, Emma. I received a bulletin just last week on that so-called German woman who came here with her so-called husband." Emma was startled with the news and was instantly tense.

"Really," she said. "What was it?"

"Well, first of all, Gerta was not from Germany. She was from New York City. She may be in Germany now or some other country. Seems she is wanted for stealing jewelry and in the suspicious death of her husband. You see, Talton was her brother and accomplice in the jewel thefts. They had this routine of going into stores where the most valuable jewels were sold. First she would go in dressed up in the finest clothes. She usually wore a hat and gloves. She would talk with an accent and act like money was no object. She would ask to see the most expensive jewels and strike up a conversation with the salesperson. Then Talton would come in and distract the salesperson while she dropped a ring or some piece of jewelry in her purse or pocket. But the law is on to her now all over the country. She'd better stay abroad, but I know she has connections right here in North Carolina."

Emma rubbed her arms, feeling something like mites crawling on them.

"Well, I actually thought there was something too nice about her, if you know what I mean," she said. "What happened to her husband?"

"The report I read said authorities think he was poisoned slowly."

"When did the husband die?" asked Grandmother.

"A couple of years ago. Soon after she was here with that man who died on your place. Talton was his name. Of course, as I said, Talton was her brother."

"I sure am glad I threw that candy away she gave me," Emma said, feeling short of breath.

"I don't think she was stupid enough to poison you with the law investigating Talton's death," added Grandmother.

"No, she was in an all-fired hurry to get away from here, and now we know why." The sheriff leaned over the arm of his rocking chair and picked up his hat off the floor. "I'd better be going back to the house. I'm off today and have to do my chores. It was good to see you all again."

Grandmother went out the back with the sheriff while Emma went to her room. Her face in the dresser mirror was pale. Maybe she should tell the sheriff what she had done. If Gerta, or whatever her real name was, ever sought revenge, she might try to poison her or something worse.

Grandmother came back in and went to her room. Emma, wanting to quiz her, followed, entering the bedroom to see her grandmother put the whiskey under her mattress.

"Well, that was quite a story about Gerta, wasn't it?" Emma spoke as casually as she could.

"I suspect her game is up now without Talton to help her sell the stolen goods. I doubt she will come back to this country. She's a smart hussy." Grandmother's words were reassuring to Emma. She put the matter out of her mind and started on her biology drawings, a task that would take several hours.

*****

The high school years were a time of Emma's stabilizing in her cocoon. There was never enough time to study, but it was such a blessing now not to have to be afraid of her father, not to have to leave and spend the night away. There was a new worry of tension between her mother and grandmother, or maybe it had always been there and she had been too young to notice it or too preoccupied with her father. Her house remained a place where she hesitated to invite friends.

Sometimes her mother and grandmother did not speak. Emma learned the cycle: first, some cross words would pass between them; her grandmother stopped coming to the table when Mother cooked supper or dinner on Sunday; then Grandmother separated the groceries in the pantry as well as items in the refrigerator. Martha was too young to understand

and continued to use any food in the house. After about two weeks, Mother would break the cycle by preparing Grandmother's favorite supper and asking Emma to go call her to eat. Usually she would come on the first invitation, but if she felt she needed to pout more, she would wait until the next invitation.

Mother was promoted at Ledford's to sales manager for two floors, a change that meant she had to take trips to Charlotte to buy for her departments several times a year. From Sunday about one o'clock until Thursday afternoon was an eternity for Emma and Martha to be alone with Grandmother. Emma followed her mother's instructions to look after Martha's school clothes and see she took a bath at night. Grandmother was overprotective, checking on the girls several times a night when she thought she heard a strange noise. She also woke Emma up when she stumbled through her room to get to the bathroom during the night. Emma, having reached the age where she valued privacy above all else at home, wanted the doors to her bedroom closed at night. The old house had no hall, so the bedrooms opened to other rooms. Grandmother wanted the door between her room and Emma's to stay open during the night because she said if she had to go to the bathroom, she could not find the door knob and indeed she would wake Emma by scratching and clawing to find it. Sometimes Emma, infuriated to have been awakened in the middle of the night, would get up and open the door for her grandmother, who would either be thankful for her sweet granddaughter's help or irate for Emma's having closed the door when she was told not to. Normally Emma would keep the door open until she could hear Grandmother snoring, after having drunk her toddy of bourbon, taken, she claimed, for her health and recommended by the doctor. She kept her liquor and special candy and fruit hidden in her room under the quilts on the shelf in the closet. When she was feeling generous, she would bring out the candy and fruit to share.

One night when Grandmother was fumbling in the dark and could not find either the light or the door knob, Emma awoke so angry that she jumped up and opened the door, feeling she could strike her grandmother. Grandmother this night responded like a grateful child. She was so thankful and pleased that Emma had helped her find her way. The next day Grandmother was in a different mood, indignant with Emma for giving her a "sassy" answer to something, telling everybody she called on the phone. So wrought up was Emma in repressing her anger that she went to her grandmother's closet and tore the pockets on two of her best dresses, not caring what the consequence might be. For the moment she had her revenge. It was days later before Grandmother remarked that she did not know how her pockets got ripped, but she never linked the deed to Emma.

*****

Although she could not have explained why, Emma wanted to be the best student, to have the highest grades. Her studies defined who she was. It was easy to end up her high school years in the small clique of students who were known as the college bound. When the senior English teacher announced that *War and Peace* would be shown on a Wednesday afternoon uptown and that any students interested would be excused to go, of course, Emma and the three other academic girls went to sit through four hours of the classic, one of the novels on the college reading list she had not tackled.

The academic years blurred into nights of memorizing French, agonizing over chemistry and trigonometry, and reveling in literature. Only a few turn of events caught Emma off guard.

One occurred when a popular girl, who never had anything to do with Emma, came to her, saying Emma had to run for home-coming queen for the senior class. Emma was angry that this joke was not funny. However, several more popular students came to her, begging her to run yet they were vague on why the fervor. The decisive plea came from the English teacher, whom Emma trusted to tell her the right decision. And so she entered the race so anxious was she to please everyone. Then unbelievably she won! Something here was strange. Now she had to have a picture made with her crown, get an escort and a pretty car for him to drive! Thank heaven one of the girls who begged her to run had promised up front to take care of the logistics and did. A nice young junior, someone Emma hardly knew, was to drive his baby blue Mustang convertible and she would ride siting on the top of the back seat.

It was surreal. But she did it, waiting saying practically nothing the night of the game, until halftime when the ceremony took place. She was driven out, escorted onto the field, crowned and given roses, and had a picture taken. Then once safely back in the car and out of the field, she knew she was supposed to stay for the rest of the game, which she managed awkwardly to get through. That was the only high school football game she ever attended. On Monday after the event, one of the popular girls told Emma that the only reason the in-group had wanted her to be homecoming queen was to defeat the other senior who was running. Apparently there was a feud between the two most popular girls, and those against the candidate decided to beat the society queen by backing Emma. So it had nothing to do with supporting Emma or wanting her to win. It was totally Machiavellian.

One beautiful Thursday in April of the senior year a couple of the girls from the popular group cornered Emma to tell her that the teachers and principal had okayed an afternoon off for those who had at least a B average. They had a plan to leave school at lunch break and drive to one of the girls' house, her parents being at work. There they would gossip, play records, dance, and have a jolly time. By this time, Emma had gotten over the homecoming scam and wanted to be part of this group. She was flattered to be asked. In fact, they insisted the party would not be complete without her. The suitors were different yet part of the group that never included her. At last she relented and got into Michelle's small car, packed full of thin girls. They chattered and laughed, not to Emma but with each other. Once at the house, the ambience did not set quite right with Emma. She should have checked with the teachers. The thing that really worried her was that the friends of her small academic clique were not there as she had been told they would. The afternoon wore on with growing anxiety for Emma. These girls did not care about grades or anything but silly gossip and what the top ten songs were and baking chocolate chip cookies and wearing pretty clothes. About three o'clock when it was time for school to be out, Michelle said it was time to take everyone home. On the way to Emma's house, one of the girls sitting in the back seat beside Emma said, "Michelle really didn't have permission, but she thought if you were in on it, the teachers wouldn't punish them." This news put a sick feeling in Emma's stomach. Her first concern was that she had skipped school. Secondary was the fury of finding out she had been duped … again.

The next day Emma asked her teachers whose classes she had missed if indeed the group had been granted permission for the afternoon off. No, they were not. However, the group was right about the outcome: no one was punished. The topic was never brought up by any teacher or the principal.

A third bitter pill to swallow occurred when Emma was asked

to write a graduation speech, being valedictorian. She spent weeks perfecting it. The week before graduation, Jane, one of the popular gang, who wrote a weekly column about school events for the town newspaper, asked if she could read the speech. Emma, being flattered yet protective of her work, reluctantly let Jane borrow the speech. The next day Jane returned it, thanking Emma, but not commenting on the speech. That was Thursday. Graduation was scheduled for Friday of the next week. On Sunday, one of the academic clique called Emma to say her speech was in the paper—it was Jane's column. Evidently Jane, busy at the end of school with social events, did not have an article to turn in to the paper, and knowing how naive Emma was, borrowed the speech and simply submitted it for her column. Emma's family did not subscribe to the paper, but her friend brought the article to her on Monday. Emma was so hurt and so angry that she could not speak about it. At lunch, the principal found Emma. They looked at each other. He asked her if she still wanted to give the speech. No, she did not. How was she at ad libing? Not good. I'll just say a prayer, she finally said. Thus it was settled, but she did not tell a soul. Her grown cousins and family went to the ceremony. She went to the podium microphone and said, "Please bow your heads." There was a rumble of whispers in the front row of seniors who knew what she was supposed to say. At the end of the ceremony, marching out past Jane, Emma overheard her say, "I thought she was going to give a speech."

Chapter V: College

In the fall of 1966, Emma left her mother, grandmother, and sister to go to East State College, a four-hour drive from home. No one from her class was going to this college, where Emma had received a full scholarship with the stipulation that she teach four years. She had no idea who her roommate would be until the day she moved into her dormitory.

Mother had learned to drive with Eula's help after Father died, and Emma was grateful to have her mother and Martha help her move into her dorm. Mother's Chevy II, loaded with all Emma could pack into it, rolled out of the dirt driveway at the farm as Emma waved good-bye to Grandmother, standing in the shade on the already hot September morning.

The long trip evoked little conversation, Emma already homesick, never having been away from home for more than overnight with her cousin, Eula. The distance in itself isolated her from home, too far to travel home for weekends. Of course, the family would send her money to come home on a bus for holidays. But this was what she wanted, what she had studied so hard for. She couldn't fail. The alternative, Helen was always quick to point out, was standing on her feet all day as a salesclerk. "It's not how hard you work," her mother said, "but what you know."

Moving in on Sunday made a long first week. Freshmen had a

schedule already made for them to pick up in the hot gym, where they stood in long lines inching up to finally face wilted faculty rifling through schedules in alphabetical order in cardboard boxes. When Emma was handed her form, she found the nearest bench outside the hot building and sat down to decipher her schedule. She didn't know some of the abbreviations and had to go back to her room to get a catalog. One course was wrong: she was supposed to have social dance but had swimming instead. A swimming class was required or else passing a swimming test. However, she had planned to put off the course until she had time to adjust and find out about the course and the swimming pool. Now she panicked! She could not try to change the course until the next day when students were allowed to change their schedules.

The next morning she walked briskly back across campus, once again standing in a line not moving, this time for physical education courses. No social dance slot was open, no ballroom dancing—she gave up and kept the swimming. She would get it over with and be done with it one way or another. She would drown, fail, or pass. She called her mother collect from the hall phone that night to ask her to send a swim suit as soon as possible. Luckily the first swimming class would not be until Thursday of the next week.

Wednesday, the first day of classes, was Emma's longest day, having a biology class and three-hour lab that ran until six o'clock. Freshmen were supposed to be in their rooms every week night from seven until ten studying. Then from ten until eleven, they took showers. Lights were supposed to be out by eleven. These were the rules for the first semester. Anyone going out of the dorm after seven had to sign out even if only going to the library. The dorm doors were locked at ten, and anyone coming in after that received three demerits. Twelve demerits would send a girl home.

Her roommate, having already gone to the cafeteria for supper with two other girls who lived down the hall, Emma bought a cheese sandwich and coke from the vending machine on the first floor and took her dinner to the ironing room in the basement, the one place in the dorm where she could study without hearing any noise. The big ironing board stood in the center of the narrow room, bolted to the floor. In one corner sat a reclining chair, and although there was only a dim overhead light in the room, the high window in the room let in enough light to read by until the sun went down.

Once her eyes adjusted, Emma needed little light to read comfortably here. She wanted to read the first three chapters of her history text for the class that met the next morning at eight. Although the class had not met, she had picked up the syllabus from a folder hanging on the professor's door. She could not remember from one paragraph to the next what the text said. World civilization, part one, was to be digested in one semester. It seemed impossible. She was too tired to retain the information. She would have to do something to get through the course.

The light had waned. She closed the book and got up. No one ever came to iron, so Emma was surprised to hear footsteps coming down the dark stairwell. A woman she had not seen before stepped quietly and carefully, her long, full skirt rustling. She carried a large box, as she descended, and Emma stood to one side. When the woman, whose vision was blocked by the box, sensed the presence of someone, she gasped and almost dropped the box. "What are you doing down here! You should be in your room. It's almost eight o'clock."

"I'm sorry to have frightened you," said Emma. Sensing a strangely familiar threatening authority in the woman's tone, she hurried up the stairs to the first floor, walked quickly across the parlor to the large winding staircase that went up to the rooms. Emma and her roommate had the smallest room on the third floor, a few feet of the width having been sacrificed to the maid's storage room, where mops, brooms, and cleaning supplies were kept.

So far Emma had not gotten to know Elizabeth, her roommate, well. Elizabeth, who wanted to teach first grade, was a giggly lanky blonde, whose first priority was to watch the soap operas from two until four thirty. Loquacious and amiable, she socialized with girls on the hall who enjoyed playing cards and eating popcorn after classes. Sometimes they invited Emma to walk with them downtown to eat dinner to get away from the cafeteria. They always ordered fried chicken and French fries. Elizabeth always said, "Excuse me for eating with my fingers. My mama taught me better but she's not here." Emma, being the only member not majoring in elementary grades, listened to the discussion of arts and crafts projects and learning to play children's songs on the piano.

On Thursday night of the second week an important meeting was called for all dorm residents. The word was that the old dorm mother who had lived on the first floor for thirty-four years had died of a heart attack on Tuesday and that an assistant dorm mother from another dorm was coming that night to introduce herself as the new head dorm mother.

Although the meeting was at ten o'clock, girls started drifting down to the parlor at twenty till to claim a seat on one of the large couches or on a comfortable chair. By quarter of, when Emma and Elizabeth sauntered down the staircase in their pajamas and robes, the parlor was lighted as if for a party and decorated with eighteen-year-old girls, the few lucky ones claiming the sofas and chairs, legs drawn under them and not budging from their comfortable seats, others lounging on the floor and staircase, most donning pinks, yellows, and blues, bobbing like balloons as they discovered their friends, stepping over others to make their way to the perfect spot.

Strategically standing were the girls who preened, waiting to be seen by all who filed by. Emma had never seen so many girls in one place. Obviously the importance of the meeting did not produce enough anxiety to interrupt the most critical of tasks: the rolling of clean hair, as Thursday night marked the beginning of the weekend. Emma thought she was the only one whose hair was not already on pink curlers, ranging in size from four- to one-inch in diameter, as the crew waited for the arrival of the awesome new dorm mother, until she saw two black girls, hair uncurled, wearing T-shirts that read: "Brighten up your life; add color," and a second group, the Look-at-me-I-am-beautiful girls comprised of three white girls—a bleached blonde, a brunette, and a strawberry blonde threesome, whose modeling stance impressed only each other.

Beckoned by a group in a far corner, Elizabeth left Emma, who stopped on the stairs, where she could watch the commotion. The initial buzz turned into a roar rivaling the cafeteria lunch crowd. A sharp shriek from the bleached blonde caught the attention of half the room. "Susan, what is it?" the brunette yelled out as the bleached blonde scratched her head, her hair flying wildly.

"You've got some beige squiggly worms in your hair!" said the brunette.

"Oh, gross! They're a million of 'em!" One girl announced to the whole room. Now everyone looked at the aspiring models.

The brunette spoke up anxiously, "My head's been itching too. Somebody look at mine."

Eager to assist, the strawberry blonde inspected the brunette's scalp. "Sure as you're a sinner. You got 'em. Where have you two been? You must have thumbed your way here from the mountains, catching the goat trucks. My God! Somebody better look at mine!"

By now inspectors had acquired combs and went to work on the three heads.

"Get me some alcohol," a take-charge stout girl demanded of a demure girl close to the closet where the first-aid supplies were kept.

Meanwhile the assistant dorm mother, Miss Pollock, had arrived, having locked the outside doors. Her job was to pass around a roll sheet and get the crowd ready for the new dorm mother. Instead, Miss Pollock bent over the lice-infected threesome, who a moment before strutted like peacocks, now sparked a series of shrieks and giggles as word spread of their predicament.

"The best thing I have on hand at this late hour, girls," said Miss Pollock in a firm tone, "is the cure my mother would have used: snuff. There is some in the maid's closet."

"Snuff!" The girls could not believe they heard correctly. "That nasty stuff my grandma dips and spits!" said the bleached blonde.

"Yes, I have some, a big tin. What we'll do is wet your heads and rub in the snuff, then tie up your heads in plastic bags. The lice will smother and be dead when you wake up. Wait just a minute!" Moving more deftly than anyone thought possible, Miss Pollock scurried across the room to the little platform and podium set up for the occasion. "Girls," she yelled in her loudest dorm-mother voice, "I must have your attention quickly." She waved her long-sleeved covered arms, a white handkerchief waving from her short fingers. It took three tries before the girls group by group stopped talking and looked up at her.

"Girls, your new dorm mother, Miss Pierce, will be a few minutes late. She has to check out formally and bring her clothes for the night from Sampson Dorm. In the meantime, as some of you have seen, three of our girls need some immediate personal attention. Please stay put, and we will be back in fifteen minutes. By then, Miss Pierce should be here."

In fifteen seconds, the room was buzzing again. From her perch, Emma watched the kaleidoscopic beach-like scene as the girls grew restless and louder. In the left corner of her eye, she saw the front door open and someone hurry down the hall opposite the parlor, the hall where Miss Pollock had taken the patients to her private quarters for treatment. So fast was the unknown person's entrance that Emma saw only a swift flash of black attire.

In five more minutes, Miss Pollock reappeared, behind her three crest-fallen, slouching lice-infected princess elites, their locks matted with snuff and bound in plastic bags. They stopped this time at the nearest space and sat on the floor behind a tall girl. At first Emma did not see the woman in black standing behind Miss Pollock. She looked younger than Emma had expected.

The two women moved to the podium. Emma could see the new dorm mother well from her vantage point. An imposing figure, Miss Pierce stood straight, her head up, shoulders back, stiff as a general in her black suit and high-necked white blouse. Fortyish, she was attractive, yet stern looking. After Miss Pollock's brief introduction, which no one seemed to listen to, as all were sizing up the new lady, Miss Pierce walked briskly to the podium as if she were receiving an academy award, smiled artificially and paused fifteen seconds, observing what must have looked like a pajama fashion show. "Girls, thank you for waiting patiently for me. The residents in my now previous dorm gave me a surprise party. I enjoyed my job as assistant dorm mother for two years, and although I regret more than I can say the passing of Miss Taylor, I am honored to have been asked to move in here with you and Miss Pollock. She has already told me what a superior group you are."

"Sure, sure," someone behind Emma said loud enough for everyone to hear.

There was something uncannily familiar about Miss Pierce. Highlights shone from her short blonde hair as she turned her head from side to side. Her speech was sharp, her words carefully chosen. Emma's brain tried desperately to make a link. Miss Pierce raised her hand in an open gesture of embracing the group; she looked up to the girls sitting on the stairs. Emma caught the emerald eyes. Suddenly she knew what her mind strained to conjure! Those were the eyes of Gerta! And the voice was the same as she remembered it! She had dyed her hair blonde!" Emma did not hear any more of the speech as she slid back up one stair to get out of the speaker's view. How in the world could Gerta show up here! Emma felt warm and dizzy. The room was too stuffy. She saw black spots and knew she was blacking out. The girl beside Emma on the stair shook her shoulder. "Hey, are you all right? You look greenish. Too hot?"

The jolt brought Emma back. She scooted back out of view. "Yes, too hot. And I skipped supper. Thanks. I think I was almost gone."

The little commotion distracted the girls sitting on the stairs and consequently both house mothers. "What's wrong up there?" Miss Pollock called out.

"Need some air in here. Could you open the door?" the girl who rescued Emma yelled back. Miss Pollock scurried to the front door and opened it wide.

Miss Pierce resumed her talk, now explaining the rules that

must be strictly followed. "You are to keep your rooms clean, beds made, and clothes put away. Miss Pollock and I will make inspections when you least expect them, so do not skip a day. There is to be no cooking in the rooms as such is a fire hazard. In past years, I understand there were several fires started by cooking in the rooms. That means no hot plates, no toasters, no coffee pots." Among the groups several exchanged knowing glances. Only divine intervention could stop cooking in the rooms. "Furthermore, it is critical to keep food wrapped properly to prevent roaches and ants from infesting not only your room but everyone else's." Emma had already seen roaches bigger than she had imagined existed. On morning when she had an eight o'clock class and Elizabeth did not, she got ready for class without turning on the lights. When she reached for the towel on its rack by the sink to dry her hands, something dark had fallen to the floor. She screamed, looking down to see a roach as big as a fifty cent, squirming to upright itself.

Miss Pierce continued, "Another rule that I am adamant about is signing out when you leave the dorm for anything other than class. This includes day or night. Not signing out, if you are caught, carries two demerits. And finally, you are to be in the dorm every week night by ten, Saturday night by midnight, and Sunday night by eleven. Violation of these curfews carries three demerits each count. Your parents will be called after the first violation. Tomorrow at four we will have a social here in the parlor. I invite you to come so that we can meet informally. If you have any concern, please come to my office or to Miss Pollock's. One of us will be here at all times."

Emma realized this was the woman she had passed on the basement stairs. That night she could not sleep, reliving every detail of her encounter five years before with Gerta and Talton. Gerta would know her and was sure to discover her soon. She had to change dorms. It was three before Emma fell asleep. At seven when Emma's alarm rang loudly, Elizabeth groaned and turned over toward the wall. Although she did not feel up to French class, Emma got up quietly, reached behind the curtain that covered the closet and pulled out her electric coffee pot. Filling it with two cups of water from the sink, she plugged it in to boil while she went down the hall to the bathroom. Every morning she drank a cup of instant Maxwell House coffee and ate a fig Newton bar, dressing in the dark so Elizabeth could sleep. The coffee pot was well hidden in the bottom of the shallow closet the girls shared. Sometimes if the weather was bad, they ate a can of Campbell's soup, warmed in the same coffee pot, although eating such a dinner made a long, depressing evening in the cramped room.

It was a short walk to Cranton Hall, where the French literature course met at eight three times a week. The professor, a native of France, was a boisterous, insensitive middle-age woman with short, unruly black hair. Madame Cecille wore no makeup and no hose on her unshaven legs. To shake up the lethargic, taciturn group, she called on individuals, sometimes insulting them as well as demanding a response to the lesson. The females wore skirts and blouses, except one, a pretty, neat, sophisticated coed, of nineteen, who wore pantsuits, complete with blouse collar turned down on her jacket collar. She wore well a demeanor of nonchalance, a "this-too-will-pass" halo, which seemed to infuriate Madame. "You are not to wear pants to class," she declared, singling out the culprit.

"There is no rule against it. A lot of girls are wearing pantsuits," the student said in a matter of fact tone. "This is 1966. World War II changed things."

"I have a rule! No pants for girls in my class." Then to show she was not biased, she added, "And you," she pointed to a sleepy football player; "Comb your hair before class!" Madame snarled these comments before returning to the lesson while Emma studied her closely. This woman was as unkempt as any she had encountered, but she knew French.

Class over, unscathed, Emma sprinted back to the dorm to see Miss Pollock privately if possible. During the five-minute walk, she revisited the ideas that had kept her awake most of the night. She had to find a way to change dorms. So far the only thought she had was to say there was a girl in the dorm who hated her and had made her life miserable, but she would have to give facts, details which could be checked. If she told the truth, she would not be believed, plus she would certainly hasten Gerta's vengeance. If only she had someone to help her.

Once in the dorm, Emma walked slowly and quietly to the dorm mothers' offices and rooms on the south wing of the first floor. As she approached the office doors, one on either side of the hall, she saw that Miss Pierce's door was ajar; Miss Pollock's was closed, but had a notice on orange paper taped on it. Nervously, Emma moved toward the door to read the message, hardly breathing, lest Miss Pierce would hear her and come out. Miss Pollock was gone and would not be back for a week. Emma turned and stepped back to the parlor and up the stairs to the third floor to her room. It was ten o'clock, the prime hour for classes, and everyone was either in class or sleeping late. Emma sat on her bed in a daze about what to do. She was afraid to tell her mother about Gerta because then she would have to explain the elaborate lie she had told that led to Talton's horrible death. Helen had always taught her daughters that stealing and lying were the worst sins.

A gnawing in Emma's stomach reminded her that it was time for her snack before her next class at eleven o'clock. She decided to heat a cup of milk and cocoa in her coffee pot and have hot chocolate. That would hold her until an early dinner. Her history text lay on her bed, where she did most of her reading, sitting with her back against the bed rest. She must make herself study until time to walk to class. She read the same paragraph twice and still had not concentrated; midway through the third time she smelled scorched milk. Jumping up, she snatched the cord from the wall socket and detached the cord from the pot. She put the pot under the sink faucet, washing it the best she could with a rag.

Suddenly there was a shout on the hall near Emma's door. "Room check! Open your door if you are in! Room check!" Emma couldn't catch her breath. That was not Miss Pollock. It had to be Miss Pierce, even though she did not recognize the shouting voice. Grabbing her towel from the rack next to the sink, Emma wrapped the coffee pot, ran to the closet and stuffed it in a corner under a stack of Elizabeth's dirty clothes. She looked around. Elizabeth had left her side of the room a mess as always. She cleaned up only if there was an announced room check even though the girls had been warned of unannounced checks. Previously Emma had thought she would not rush to make Elizabeth's bed to prevent her from getting demerits, but rather than have Miss Pierce linger, she had rather clean up. However, it was too late. A fist pounded three times on the door. Almost visibly shaking, Emma stood and crossed the room reaching the knob just as the door swung back. Miss Pierce had unlocked it. She seemed to look past Emma's pale face to search the room, looking from her clip board check list to one side of the room and then the other. "Who's side is this?" she asked pointing to the unmade bed, strewn clothes, and uwrapped crackers on the sheets as well as the half bottle of coke and cigarette butts in the ash tray on Elizabeth's desk.

"My roommate's, Elizabeth Culbert," Emma answered in a

voice more husky than natural, hoping Miss Pierce would not remember her, moving to stand in front of the closet and out of the sunlight, and praying she would not smell the milk. Emma avoided eye contact as if doing so would prevent Miss Pierce from looking directly at her.

"Tell Miss Culbert to come to my office when she comes in."

"Yes, ma'am." Emma tried to maintain her huskiness, her thin body tense and straight. Then, giving no sign that she recognized Emma or smelled burned milk, Miss Pierce walked abruptly out into the hall to the next door, knocking loudly three times.

Elizabeth was irate when Emma told her the news. "Didn't she smell that stinking coffee pot of yours? I can't believe this!" She whisked out the door to tell the girls next door, making sure she could be heard up and down the hall. "Instead of making my bed and straightening my stuff, she just let me get two demerits! I'm out working in the cafeteria, and Emma's here with her damned nose in a book day and night! She won't even check our mailbox!"

An hour later Elizabeth came back to the room, looking sheepish and smiling coyly. "Emma, Page and I have a big psychology test in the morning at nine and need to stay up all night studying. I was wondering if you would mind staying with Page's roommate so we won't disturb you. Her roommate is nice. You know Barbara, don't you? On the first floor opposite end of the dorm?"

Not expecting the request, Emma nodded yes, glad at least Elizabeth had not fussed her out directly over the demerits. Emma stifled her emotions whereas Elizabeth blew up and put the event to rest. To solidify the deal, the four girls walked downtown at five and ate at the Old Towne Inn, all ordering the special country style steak, potatoes, and beans for $2.35. The consuming topic was what could be the reason for an unscheduled dorm meeting at seven o'clock. Emma's only thoughts centered on how she could avoid Miss Pierce.

Girls from the three floors were already assembling when the foursome returned at six forty. Instead of going up to their rooms, they decided to hear the gossip circulating. Someone said there had been a murder on campus, and the killer was still at large. Scanning the room carefully to pick a good place not to be seen from the podium, Emma sat on the floor beside the piano and did not move when two taller girls sat in front of her.

At two minutes past seven, the newly elected dorm president stepped onto the small platform to convene the meeting. After announcing that Miss Pollock was gone to see her sister for a week, she turned the meeting over to Miss Pierce, who again stood like a general, wearing a dark brown suit, ready to take charge.

"Good evening, ladies! It's time to start, ladies! Let me have your attention! I know you are anxious to find out what is going on. This won't take long, but I thought it critical to make some announcements. First, as some of you may have heard, there is a rapist on the loose. Last night a girl walking alone from a department store downtown back to Stanton Dorm was grabbed from behind, dragged to some shrubs, blindfolded, and raped. This happened before six o'clock, before dark." A hush fell over the parlor, as Miss Pierce raised her sharp voice even more. "Then at about ten thirty another girl, this one, from our dorm, was attacked as she walked back from the College Union snack bar. Again, she was grabbed from behind, dragged to some thick trees, blindfolded, and raped." Everyone turned around and looked all around the room, trying to determine who was missing.

Emma heard several names whispered. "The names of the girls are not being released. However, campus police, senior administrators, as well as dormitory directors are especially concerned that we do everything we possibly can to make sure you are aware of the danger and to give you some strict directives to follow until the attacker or attackers have been abducted. First of all, we are locking the front door an hour before sundown. You will have to ring the doorbell after six o'clock. Walk with others even to class. If you have to go out after dark, go in pairs, avoid dark areas. Don't establish any patterns in your daily walking after dark, and don't loiter talking to friends outside after dark. And whatever you do, don't forget to sign out. There will be security guards posted near the girls' dorms and around the snack bar and library after dark. Now what questions do you have?"

"Can you tell us what floor the girl who was raped in our dorm lives on?" asked a short, buxom freshman.

"No, we are trying to give her some privacy."

Emma didn't hear the other questions and answers. The buzz around her was too loud. "I know one of those wanna-be-models is missing—the tall redhead," said the stout girl beside her. The meeting over, the buzz quickly grew into a roar as the talkers stalled at the foot of the parlor staircase. No one seemed in a hurry to go upstairs.

It was seven thirty, time for Emma to read the short story to be discussed the next day. Once in the room, Elizabeth reminded Emma that Page would be up soon to spend the night. "You're so sweet to do this switch for us."

"No problem." Emma quickly gathered her books and night clothes. "I will need to come back about quarter past seven in the morning to get ready for class."

"Sure, we'll be dead to the world by then. We plan to stay up until two or three or as long as we can comprehend anything." Elizabeth waved pretentiously as Emma left with her arms full. On the stairs, she passed Page, her arms full also and already looking tired.

"Have fun," said Emma.

"I just want to pass that course with a C. All the tests are these stupid multiple choice that don't make any sense."

Page and Barbara's room on the first floor was larger than Emma and Elizabeth's. Emma found Barbara watching television, the volume louder than Emma could tolerate while trying to study. "It was nice of you to accommodate our roommates," Barbara said when Emma entered, looking around for a clear space to drop her armful. Seeing the problem, Barbara simply pushed Page's clothes, books, and makeup kit on the floor and then slid the stack to a corner. Emma dropped her belongings on the bed and sat down beside them, glancing at the sitcom on the screen.

"I hope you don't mind the TV. I just can't study without it on. I block it out but need the noise to concentrate."

"Oh, no—anyway, I have to go to the library to research some criticism on a story for my composition course, and I need to get on over there."

"Who is going with you? You can't go alone! You know what Miss Pierce said! Aren't you scared to go tonight!"

"Oh, a girl on the first floor is in my class," said Emma as if she had a companion. Barbara nodded, no longer concerned, as she turned to the television. There really was a girl on the first floor in her class; Emma thought she would stop by and ask the girl to go with her if she could find her. She picked up her literature book and notebook. "I will be back by ten. Will you be up?"

"Yeah, just knock and call me."

Emma left Barbara watching the sitcom and wondered if she would get around to studying at all. On the first floor, she turned down the hall to search out the girl in her class. She had forgotten her name and was not sure which room she had. Approaching an opened door, she looked in and asked the studious-looking, bespectacled girl if she knew the girl who took composition on Monday, Wednesday, Friday at three o'clock. "Hell, I'm smart, but I don't have everybody's schedule memorized!"

Emma laughed and moved on, deciding to speak to the proctor who was monitoring the front door. She was an overweight, introverted girl named Missy, who would gladly help Emma if she would just give her some attention. "Hey, Missy, I see they've put the most reliable proctor on for tonight." Missy brightened up and gave Emma a smile. "I really need your help tonight. You are someone I can trust, and I'm really in a bind. I need to go to the library but don't have anyone to go with, so I don't want to sign out. Also, I need to sneak back in about ten. I know you understand, being a serious student yourself. Is there any way you can help me out? I can't study with a TV program blaring. Can you?" Missy made a frown and shook her head no.

"Well, everyone has already gone to the library that I know," Missy said. "I don't think there is any danger if you stay within the courtyard. Okay, go on, but get my attention before you try to get back in so no one will see you come in alone. Maybe you can catch up with some girls and walk back with them. Yeah, you probably can do that."

"Sure, thanks a million, Missy. I owe you one!" Missy beamed and her double chin trembled. Looking around the parlor and down the hall where the dorm mothers lived, Emma saw no one watching and quietly opened the front door and escaped, walking fast toward the library. Evening was not quite night as Emma scurried along, catching up with a group of two females and one male student. Lights from the library lighted the surrounding grounds, and many students sat outside on benches, socializing and smoking.

Once inside, Emma took the elevator to the fourth floor to

her familiar row in the stacks. For two weeks, she had been studying Hawthorne, first "Young Goodman Brown" and this week "My Kinsman, Major Molineux," both packed with symbolism her professor expected students to be able to discuss. After locating a book with criticism on "Molineux," Emma found her usual carrel between the stacks and sat down to read and take notes. It was now five past eight. By nine forty-five, she should be ready to walk back to the dorm. The library, open until eleven o'clock, would still provide plenty of light and traffic walking back through the courtyard.

Emma was deeply engrossed in a critical essay comparing the main character's struggle for independence to the colonies' struggle against England, jotting down the main points when without any warning the lights went out. Thinking the power would come on again in a few seconds, Emma sat still, looking around in the dark while her eyes tried to adjust. She wasn't even sure there was anyone else on this floor. Then she heard the shuffling of feet on the stairs and muffled voices passing as students made their way slowly down the stairs. Better get out, she thought, feeling to gather her notebook and text, leaving the library book on the carrel. Moving carefully through the familiar stacks to the door leading to the stairs, she could see the end of the stack and the wall, but between the stacks was too dark to distinguish anything. She walked cautiously, remembering that often there were step stools left in the stacks that she might trip over.

Finally she reached the end of the long row of stacks, and turning left, as her eyes focused on the door where emergency lights lit the stairs, she bumped into someone, who groaned, as Emma screamed, though not loud enough to be heard, as the unseen man calmly said, "Excuse me." Both dropped books on impact and both stooped to gather them, almost knocking heads.

First to reach the door, Emma opened it and turned back to look at the man. For the first time, the thought of the rapist flashed across her mind. Somehow she never considered a rapist would be patient enough to hide in stacks where few people would choose to study. Furthermore, this man did not have the demeanor of a rapist. Fortyish, with graying hair and sad brown eyes, the tall, slim black man did not frighten Emma. "I believe you picked up one of my books and perhaps one of my papers," he said.

"Well, let's get to the first floor and sit down to check." The man nodded in agreement as they made their way down four floors. To her surprise there was no one at the circulation desk. A few people were still wandering around, hoping the lights would come on, but most had gone outside, huddling under dim emergency lights.

"It's getting stuffy in here. I think we can sort our materials better outside on a bench under the light," the man said pointing to the front door. The crowd had begun to scatter, tired of waiting. A few people, mainly library staff, sat down on benches lining the front walkway. The man was right: Emma did have two sheets of an article that did not belong to her. As she handed the papers to the man she realized he must be a professor or some-one from the community. There were not many students around as old or as well dressed as he.

"Are you studying or working here?" Emma asked.

"I'm Charles Di Yanni, professor of music, and I was both studying and working. And you?"

"Emma Applewhite. I'm a freshman, English major."

"I assume there is someone you came over with who is waiting for you? I heard about the rule about female students not walking alone." Suddenly the man's voice stirred a memory, and Emma tried hard to remember what it was.

"No, I broke the rule," Emma said, remembering that she needed to be back before ten. "What time is it?"

The man looked at his watch. "It's nine forty-three."

"I've got to go. The girl on door patrol promised to sneak me in." Emma stood up and extended her hand.

"Well, let me walk with you to your dorm. I wouldn't feel right letting you go back alone."

"I need to hurry."

The two walked at a brisk gait, not talking for a few minutes. Then Emma thought there was something so familiar about the man. "I am thinking I have met you somewhere—maybe orientation?"

"No, I didn't work during orientation. But now that you mention it, there is something familiar about you too. Where are you from?"

"My home is near Pikesboro in Wynn County, but is actually in the rural area—a farm."

"Yes, I know the area very well. I am actually from that neck of the woods myself."

"Oh, my, that's just a …" Emma looked strangely at Professor Di Yanni and put her hand over her mouth. "Are you the man who pulled me out of the pond on the dirt road a long time ago?"

"Oh, my, I remember that little, skinny girl! You?"

Emma was embarrassed. "Yes, I was only thirteen then. Just started the eighth grade."

"Well, it's a small world. I hope you didn't get into trouble that night. I always felt bad that you would not let me speak with your mother."

"I seem to always be in trouble. Right now, I have to get in the front door before ten, or I will be in big trouble! Thank you for walking with me. Bye!"

Emma turned and walked up the dorm steps to the front porch. Professor Di Yanni stopped in front of the dorm to watch her get safely inside. Emma looked back but did not speak as she closed the front door quickly and quietly.

Missy motioned Emma to a corner in the parlor. "I was worried sick! We got word a few minutes ago there was another rape tonight. A student from Hardy dorm went to the library by herself. When the lights went out, she left by herself and was attacked even though they say she put up a hell of a fight. Mighty brave bastard to do this a third time right on campus. Anyhow, I'm glad it wasn't you. I'd be kicked out of school, I bet!"

"I'm sorry, Missy! I won't ask you to do it again. It was a dumb thing to do. Anyway, I owe you one. Good night."

Missy went back to her desk. It was ten o'clock, and a group rang the doorbell as Emma walked quickly up the stairs to Barbara's room. She could hear the TV before she reached the door and knocked. "It's me, Emma!" She knocked again before Barbara opened the door, book in hand, her hair wrapped in a towel.

"Hey, we're all locked in! Did you hear the news?"

"About another rape tonight?"

"Yeah, I'm glad you're back. Let's push the desk against the door." Emma dropped her books and helped push Barbara's desk in front of the door.

"I doubt the son of a bitch would be dumb enough to try to come into a dorm, but you never know. They have security guards watching the dorms day and night." Barbara sounded almost hysterical.

"Let's go to bed. I have an eight o'clock class. It's going to take us a while to get to sleep, I think."

By ten forty-five Emma turned out the lights. Barbara talked to Emma in the dark until she calmed down and rolled over to face the wall. In fifteen minutes, Emma could hear her breathing heavily. Now she thought of her own problem: what to do about Miss Pierce, whom she was certain to encounter and who would surely remember her. Miss Pollock would return tomorrow. Emma would have to try to get help from her without the so-called Miss Pierce finding out.

Emma tossed and turned in the unfamiliar bed, the cover smelling of cigarettes and Barbara's breathing having turned into a light snoring. She thought she would be awake when her alarm clock went off at seven o'clock. At half past midnight, she got up and took four aspirins and heard muffled sounds of girls' voices passing the door.

She dreamed … drifting through the library stacks, taking her same study carrel, retrieving the biography of Hawthorne, and reading about his Puritan ancestry. Behind her, someone laughed absurdly, a laugh that made Emma look back to see who was sitting in the carrel. At first she saw no one, but getting up, she walked to the stack behind her, and there she was! Gerta, looking just the way she did the last time she confronted Emma, her eyes sparkling green slits in the light of the carrel where she sat. "Well, it's a small world, isn't it, Emma?" Gerta said, smiling and looking up.

Emma felt the blood drain from her brain. She couldn't think. Then the lights in the library went out. In the pitch dark, Gerta laughed again the same wicked chuckle. Emma ran to the door leading to the stairs, but it wouldn't open. She pulled as hard as she could but couldn't open it. Then she felt Gerta's cold hands on the back of her shoulders, shaking her hard.

"Wake up! Wake up, Emma!" Barbara hollered. "Something's happened. Everybody's getting up!"

"What time is it?" Emma asked, grateful to be rescued from Gerta. Whatever it was couldn't be as horrible as what she was dreaming.

"Close to four. Hey, I'm going out to see what happened."

Emma, left in the dark room, trying to gather her senses,

turned on a lamp and started getting dressed. Looking out the window, she saw lights on all the floors. Then she saw a ladder leaning against the wall on the north wing and firemen starting to climb it.

Then Barbara banged on the door. "Let me in! There's a fire on the third floor! "Let's go see what's going on!" Then the fire alarm sounded, sending all the girls on the floor scrambling downstairs to the parlor and out the front door. Once outside, Emma saw the occupants of the north wing of the third floor descending on the fire escape and looking up saw billows of black smoke piling out of the roof. She looked hard for Elizabeth and Page. The smoke was coming from a section close to their room. They must have gotten out early.

"The fire came from the maid's storage room, where supplies are kept at the end of the hall," someone in the crowd explained. "That's what I heard a fireman say."

"Hey, Emma, did you know Elizabeth and Page were taken out on stretchers?" It was Missy's voice, coming through the crowd. Emma strained to see where she was. Then Missy's bulky body shoved folks out of her way and there she was, her hair standing straight up as if frightened. "Emma, I think they were seriously hurt. I mean, they weren't saying anything, just lying still on the stretchers. They took them out right past me. I bet that son of a bitch rapist started it. Good thing he likes fires, 'cause he's headin' for one big time, and I hope I run into him soon to speed up his trip. I'm carrying clorox perfume in my pocket and a razor blade." Emma couldn't react. What was Missy saying?

"Were any other girls taken out?" Emma asked.

"Yes, the girls in the room beside Elizabeth's and your room. Just think, Emma, if you hadn't been down on the first, it would've been you instead of Page!" Missy's voice was high pitched and sounded strangely accusing, Emma thought.

All dorm residents were excused from classes, although only occupants of the third floor were moved out to another dorm. Emma could not go to her room to get any of her belongings. Counselors came to talk with the girls and then one of the deans. That night a meeting was held at seven o'clock in the dorm parlor. Instead of the dorm mothers, an administrator facilitated, saying the dorm mothers, sitting at his side, were distraught and concerned for the safety of the girls. A fireman spoke also, explaining that although the cause of the fire was being investigated, he suspected the fire started either in the maid's closet or the dorm room closet next to it. He had heard that two of the victims of the fire had been studying until early morning and had apparently been making hot chocolate in a coffee pot found in the ruins. The fire might have started from the overheated coffee pot. The second theory was that a cleaning product in a spray can had been placed on the floor next to the gas hot water heater in the maid's closet instead of placed on the shelf and had exploded.

"Making hot chocolate in a coffee pot"—the words froze in Emma mind. She saw herself scurrying around the room when she heard Miss Pierce call for room check the day before. Yes, she had snatched the cord from the wall socket and stuffed the pot under some clothes in the closet. The other side of the closet wall was the maid's closet. The fire must have started there. The woman Emma had passed on the stairs, the woman she now thought was Gerta, had been carrying a box of cleaning materials. She apparently monitored the inventory of the maid's closets on each floor. What if Gerta had not revealed to Emma that she recognized her and had purposely set the fire to get rid of her! Why did the fire just happen to start on her floor? There was a maid's closet on every floor. She must see Miss Pollock right away. Although Miss Pollock was not due to return until the end of the week, she had come back early after hearing about the fire.

The next speaker, the dean in charge of the dorms, announced that some rooms on the first and second floors would take in a third occupant but that the rest of the residents of the third floor would be housed in an apartment building downtown, arrangements to be worked out by the dorm mother. That was Emma's salvation if she could just see Miss Pollock alone after the meeting without Miss Pierce being present. How could she manage that? Maybe a note. She looked around for paper and pen, spying Missy, always doing her homework during meetings, and worked her way quietly, sliding on the carpet to Missy, who gladly shared her writing materials. Now Emma scooted back to her place behind the dorm mothers, who were seated on either side of the podium. Because she might be seen by Miss Pierce if she gave the note directly to Miss Pollock herself, Emma folded the note and put "To Miss Pollock" on the outside, then asked the girl beside her to send it down the line of girls closest to Miss Pollock. The dean speaking frowned and seemed about to pause when he glanced at the note passing but refrained, as if he reconsidered the tension in the room. Hence, the note was safely delivered to Miss Pollock, who, when the dean was not looking, opened the note and read "Miss Pollock, I desperately need to see you privately after this meeting! Sincerely, Emma Applewhite," then slipped the note in her pocket. She looked around to see where the Emma was seated but could not see her.

The meeting over, the girls who would have to move rushed to speak with Miss Pierce while Emma found Miss Pollock. With earnest but polite guidance, Emma led Miss Pollock out of the parlor whispering that she desperately needed to be one of those allowed to move into the apartment building. She explained that her nerves were a wreck, that she had worried herself sick over Elizabeth and Page, who reportedly were still in grave condition, having inhaled a great deal of smoke, something Emma could not understand unless they had been drinking or had taken something to put them out for a few hours until time to go take their tests. She had heard that Page's boyfriend supplied her with liquor on the weekends.

"It has fallen to my responsibility to reassign the displaced occupants," said Miss Pollock in her most sympathetic tone. "Miss Pierce is so new that she is overwhelmed right now with the financial side. Anyhow, I think you are correct in thinking you would be better off to move. You see, Emma, there is something I need to tell you before you hear it from someone else." Miss Pollock paused and took a deep breath. "Let's step into my office." This was precisely where Emma had led her, wanting to get out of Miss Pierce's way.

"Sit down, Emma." Suddenly Emma felt afraid. She knows, she thought. Miss Pierce really is Gerta and has told her all about me and what I did in the past. Would she be sent home or to the police?

"Emma, I received a call about two hours ago from the Dean of Student Life, Dr. Forest." She looked directly into Emma's eyes. "Elizabeth and Page died shortly after they arrived at the hospital early this morning. They never regained consciousness. All the girls will find out tomorrow, but I wanted you and Barbara to know first. I have already told her—just before the meeting, and she has gone home."

Emma's brain tried hard to process the meaning of the words, but she could only see Elizabeth and Page as they sat together at dinner with Barbara and her, hear their giggling at their children's lit professor.

"One more thing." Miss Pollock took a deep breath. "There is some question about how the fire started. A girl who was going to the bathroom about two thirty in the morning saw the door to the maid's closet ajar when she passed, or so I heard. So we don't know what to think yet. But, yes, let's move you out to the other housing. I plan to keep the names of those moved private."

"Thank you so very much!" Emma whispered, not registering all she had just heard. "I understand there are some boxes of things saved from our room?"

"Yes, you may look in the cloak room next to the parlor. The boxes have room numbers on them. Get your things out. Also, make a list of what you lost, and we will try to get you funds for those as soon as we possibly can. Any books lost, you can get for free at the bookstore. Here I have already made verification slips."

"When do I go?"

"Well, as you heard at the meeting. You should go tomorrow before six at night and go with someone. And, as you heard just now at the meeting, the displaced girls can sleep on pallets or cots in the parlor tonight unless invited to stay in another room, in which case, you must report where you are."

"I wish I could stay right here with you tonight, Miss Pollock. Somehow I feel scared in the parlor."

"Well, I think that you might be even safer in the parlor with numerous other girls as opposed to in here by yourself. You see, there is a rule."

"Oh, yes, of course."

"The maid is putting out cots and cover for pallets now. Go grab one, and see me early in the morning for your apartment assignment. Would you like to be assigned with Barbara? She wants to move also."

"Yes, ma'am. Thanks. Good night." Emma opened the door, looked each way down the hall, and seeing no one, headed for the crowded parlor, where with much commotion, bed covers were being tossed and placed on the floor. Wanting to keep out of sight of Miss Pierce, Emma grabbed a blanket, sheet, and pillow, and headed for the corner behind the piano, where she could not be seen by anyone passing through the room. The girls took a long time to settle down, whispering among themselves about the rapist, the fire, the girls they thought were still in the hospital but were by now in the morgue. Finally about eleven o'clock a nurse from the infirmary came in to check on them, going from cot to cot and pallet to pallet asking how everyone was. Some told her they were nervous and couldn't sleep. She gave them a tiny white pill and a cup of water. Emma raised up and asked for one. Then one by one the girls stopped whispering and went to sleep as the nurse sat close by at the desk usually occupied by Missy.

During the night Emma dreamed of Gerta prowling around the parlor looking in every cot and pallet, searching for her, as Emma sunk deeper under her blanket until finally the frightful face bent over her, peering to see if she was awake. Suddenly Emma found her voice and screamed out.

"Hey, it's all right. You're here safe in the parlor. It's all right," a soothing voice spoke to Emma. "You are having a bad dream." It was the nurse, still looking fresh in her white uniform and cap.

Emma sat up, hot from being under too much cover, and looked around at two girls who had been awakened by her scream. "Let's get some juice from the refrigerator," the nurse said, taking charge. She put her hand on Emma's forehead. "You're too warm. Let me take your temperature." The nurse left and came back with two aspirins and a cup of pineapple juice.

"Thank you. I'm sorry to have bothered everyone," Emma said.

"Try to go back to sleep. It's only 4:30. I'll be right here in this recliner beside you. You're not the only person who is having trouble sleeping. You just didn't hear them." The nurse was true to her word, still sitting in the recliner, reading, when Emma woke up at seven o'clock. Her first thought was to get dressed and head to Miss Pollock's office to get her assignment for the apartment. Most of the parlor sleepers were up now, headed for the bathrooms to shower and dress, but to beat them to the sign up, Emma dressed in the parlor and hurried to Miss Pollock's door.

There was one girl ahead of her, already sitting in the office waiting for Miss Pollock to return from some errand. Not wanting to risk Miss Pierce passing by and seeing her, Emma stepped inside the office, pulling the door almost shut. "She's expecting me early," she said to the girl waiting. Shortly, Miss Pollock appeared, coffee cup in hand, smiling, and eager to get the work done. In five minutes Emma was out, having secured her papers to move into the apartment building rented by the college to accommodate the students displaced by the fire. She hurried to collect her belongings, and with those stuffed in bags, started walking toward the town side of campus. Several times she had to stop and reposition the weight of the bags and to rest before walking on.

It took her fifteen minutes to reach the building, which looked even older than she had recalled from having passed it numerous times on her way downtown to make a purchase. Nonetheless, its old red bricks, cement porch, and unlatched screen front door reminded her of home. No one greeted her as she walked around and searched the outside doors for number 17. Finding it on the end, she put the key in and opened the door. What a big place compared to her tiny dorm room. But there was only one double bed. Another bed, perhaps a cot, would have to be brought in for her or Barbara, whoever was unlucky. Looking around, she did not see any sign of anyone having started to move in. She quickly walked through the sitting room, bedroom, bathroom, and tiny kitchen. This seemed like a mansion. But for now she must hurry to the bookstore and get the texts destroyed and go to classes.

The rest of the day Emma sat through history, English, and math, trying to concentrate but all the while imagining the dead bodies of Elizabeth and Page and wondering if Miss Pierce really was Gerta and if she had set the fire thinking Emma would be the victim. At four thirty the math professor dismissed the class, leaving abruptly himself ten minutes early. Emma sat staring at the homework on the board. She still needed to copy the last problem. Everyone else left. Closing her notebook and packing up, she gazed out the window toward the gym and thought about her swimming class. Instead of going to her room over a mile away, she needed to eat and go to the pool to practice so that she would have a chance of passing the course.

CHAPTER VI: DISPLACEMENT

Her mother had mailed Emma's two two-piece swim suits in time for the first class of swimming. Now after a month of classes and practice at least once a week, the size five bottoms were sliding down below the waist, and she had noticed the absence of her monthly period. The problem was she had always had a fear of water over waist deep, and even though the class was for beginners, there was only one other person in the class who could not already swim, a large young man who looked more distraught than Emma, and she felt sorry for him when she had a fleeting thought beyond her own misery. He had curly black hair, one curl hanging always in his eyes, and white skin that appeared never to have seen the sun, and when the instructor said, "Go," he would pretend to swim with his arms out, his feet touching the bottom, and then stand up when the water got deep. The instructor never smiled. His expression seemed to say, "What did I ever do to deserve having such dunces in my class?"

Emma had learned that the exam for the course was to swim ten laps up and down the pool. That seemed impossible unless she could swim nine on her back as the instructor had suggested was an option some might want to consider, certainly having Emma and the fat boy in mind. On Monday Emma went to practice. There were a few students diving off the high board, doing fancy turns in the air, and then there was Emma, diving off the side, hoping she was not attracting anyone's attention.

Thankfully the instructor was not around. At first swimming on her back seemed the worst position she could think of, but realizing she would never have the breath to swim more than a couple of laps with her face in the water, she knew she had to learn to turn over and swim on her back or she would not get a college degree, a fear worse than drowning. The instructor had said the students must dive off the side, swim at least one lap up and down on the front, and then they could swim the other laps on their backs. So the goal was clear. She had to start and build up her strength.

She dived off and started, swimming fast until she reached the deep end of the pool, using the wall to kick around and start back. Once back, she stopped, out of breath. The instructor had said she was not turning her head to breathe. As she stood in the water, resting, she watched a girl swimming on her back slowly as if she might go to sleep any second. Observing carefully how the girl kicked her feet and used her arms and hands like oars, Emma built up her courage, and when the girl left the pool, she decided to just start off on her back. No, that was too scary. She would start on her front and flip over as the instructor said she would have to do on the test.

Now she had a plan to dive off the side, swim half way to the deep end and flip over. If she sank, she would not be in very deep water and hopefully would not cause a scene. It was almost nine o'clock, and most people having left the pool, Emma dived for the last try, swimming face down, struggling to breathe until she got tired; then, she flipped over as she had seen the girl do, and flailing about to balance herself she remembered to put her head down, kick her feet, and use her arms to move forward. Miraculously it was working! She could breathe all she wanted to. The only problem now was she was going sideways. She wasn't using her left arm as much as her right. Once she corrected this problem, she moved forward to the end of the pool, kicked back and swam to the deep end on her back. One more time: she would try the exam test. She dived off the side, swimming and trying to turn her head to breathe. At the deep end, she hit the side of the pool with her foot and started back, determined to make it back. Halfway she thought her lungs would burst, so she flipped over and swam on her back. How wonderful to breathe all she wanted to, yet she found that she could not relax enough to float and must move to stay up. At the shallow end, she pushed off from the wall and swam face down to the deep end and back once again on her back. This was enough of a victory for one night. She had three more months. She could do it.

Outside the gym the campus lights were hazy, a heavy fog blurring the bookstore window as Emma passed, hurrying to her dorm. As she neared it, she realized as if she had awakened from a dream that she had moved and must walk another mile. She walked on, her wet hair covered with a fuzzy pink cap, to keep from catching cold in the cool night air. She passed a few students walking back from downtown or from the library. A man, older than most students, stepped out of an old building she usually never noticed. Someone had said graduate students had offices in it. He looked at her she thought in a strange way, and suddenly remembering the rapist, she turned around making a broad sweep in passing the man and walked fast back into the light of the library.

Outside the door, she sat down on a bench close to a group of smokers standing in a circle. She would wait until someone started walking her way. Meanwhile she could read from her history text by the night light near the bench. She had read a page on the chapter on Mesopotamia and looked up as she turned the page to see Professor Di Yanni coming out the door. Not in a mood to talk to him, Emma looked down at her page, hoping he would not see her or not stop to speak. But he did.

"Emma, how can you see to read out here? You will ruin your eyes!" He laughed, but she could tell he was serious.

"Well, I was just waiting a minute before walking to my room."

"You know they caught the rapist? Or a suspect, I should say."

"No, I hadn't heard. That's a great relief!"

"Yes, I think only about an hour ago when he tried to attack an undercover female cop. But, the police are still asking females to take caution until they investigate. Still, there is usually only one in cases like this. Do you have someone to walk with? Are you waiting for someone?"

"No, truthfully, I saw a suspicious man and got scared and stopped here."

"Well, let me walk you to your dorm. I have been wanting to talk with someone in the dorm about the fire. I heard at first there was minor damage, and then later heard two girls are in intensive care from smoke inhalation. Is that true?"

Emma stood up. "I live in Hedgewood Apartments now at the edge of campus. Really it's city property. I was one of the ones who had to move because of the fire.

And yes, the damage was bad." Emma felt tears coming to her eyes and looked away.

"I'm so sorry. I didn't mean to upset you. Here, let's walk. Now you are on my way. I live close by, just a couple of blocks from the apartment building."

Professor Di Yanni changed the subject. "I see you're taking World Civilization. Is that the first or second part?"

"First," Emma said, still crying quietly.

"It's a pity those survey courses are so broad as to read like outlines." He looked away from her, giving her time to calm herself, but when he looked her way again, her small face was streaked with wet lines that shown like zigzag streaks of rain.

"Did you know the girls well who were injured?"

"One was my roommate." Emma's voice was quivering.

"Oh, I had no idea. But I don't understand. Were you in the room too?"

"No." Emma started crying again.

"Look, I need a hot chocolate before I turn in. Helps me sleep. We're here at the coffee shop, where I normally get a cup. Would you care to join me? I would really like to know more about the fire. You see, I am on a committee that deals with student health issues." He extended his hand toward the door of the shop, and Emma turned at his directive.

Inside, students sat, drinking coffee and studying or talking quietly. The bedraggled young man behind the counter was cleaning up. One of the students spoke to Professor Di Yanni.

Professor Di Yanni handed Emma a five dollar bill. "Would you mind ordering?" he asked. "I need to speak with that student before he gets away."

Emma ordered the chocolates and turned from the counter to see the professor already seated in a booth.

"Sometime when you are up to it, I want you to tell me about the fire," he said. "Not now, I see you are tired. It's getting late too."

"Well, it's just that Elizabeth and Page are no longer in intensive care." Her voice quivered again and the tears sprang up again. "They died. They've been taken home. It should have been me, not them."

"I understand you were quite close to those girls, especially Elizabeth, but you shouldn't blame yourself. You had nothing to do with it. And you were saved—for a purpose, I'm sure."

Professor Di Yanni looked at Emma, who looked up at him surprised.

"You sound like my grandmother. Everything with her is for a purpose—the good and the bad. I never thought of professors as religious."

"Well, I have great faith. My mother is a strong, spiritual woman. She believes angels came into her life twice to help her through critical times when she was raising us kids by herself. How did you happen to be out of your room the night of the fire?"

"Elizabeth and Page wanted to stay up all night to study together and asked me to stay downstairs with Barbara, Page's roommate. I think there was a purpose in the fire all right but not a divine one."

"I said a purpose for your being saved, not a purpose for the fire. What do you mean a purpose in the fire?"

"Well, how can you pick and choose what was a divine purpose and what was not? God lets a lot of bad things happen."

"Let's not try to figure out the ways of God at this hour. I am just concerned about your health as a result of the trauma you've gone through and are still experiencing. Have you taken advantage of talking with the counselors made available at the dorm?"

"No, I've been busy moving and practicing swimming or trying to swim, I should say."

"Maybe a weekend at home would be good for you. Does your mother know what happened?"

"No, she is not doing well, and I don't want to worry her. Besides, I really don't have money for bus tickets. I should get a part-time job, I guess."

"I'm sorry to hear your mother is not well." Professor Di Yanni pushed his empty cup to the middle of the table. "Let's go. You can take yours. I can carry your books." Emma followed the professor out the door, taking her cup of chocolate with her. "Emma, you appear to be ill. We have an infirmary open all hours, you know. Would you like for me to walk with you over there?"

"No, it's just that I would like your advice on something."

"Perhaps we can talk tomorrow. I am happy to help if I can, but I am not trained to counsel. It's late now, ten thirty. What time do you get out of classes? I am free after four."

"Well, I will need to practice my swimming again after classes, so it will be seven thirty. Maybe I will be ready then."

"That's a good time. I usually eat between seven and eight. May I take you to dinner, a modest one albeit, just sandwiches at the coffee shop, where few people will be eating dinner?"

"All right. I think I'll be ready by then."

"Well, if you're not—ready, we can wait until you are. I just think you should let your family know what happened. Well, here we are. Which apartment is yours? Oh, by the way, who is your new roommate?"

"I don't have one yet and it's the one on the end."

"You should get in the habit of having your key out and go in quickly. It's rather dark on the end here with the shrubs shading the light. You need a whistle around your neck to blow if someone frightens you. I think I have one, come to think of it. I'll bring it to you tomorrow."

"Thank you. See you tomorrow evening about seven thirty."

The next day Emma felt she had been foolish to think she could tell Professor Di Yanni or anyone about her fear of Miss Pierce and why. After her swimming practice, she stopped by the coffee shop and asked one of the students working to give a note to the professor, which said: "Sorry I can't make it. Something has come up. Thanks anyway. Emma."

She decided to stay in the tiny apartment to study instead of going to the library to avoid seeing him there. Her assignment was Henry James's *Turn of the Screw*, and she found herself having to stop and reread the same page several times. Yet she identified with the country governess who took the job of teaching two orphans, who lived in an old mansion in the English countryside. When the governess walked at dusk, Emma imagined she were there, having taken such walks a thousand times on the farm. As she sat on the bed with her bed rest at her back concentrating on the scene, she was distracted by the shuffling of feet that sounded as if someone had stopped at her door. She looked up expecting a knock, but no one knocked. Quietly she got up, walked to the window and peered through the blinds. Walking slowly away from the apartment building toward the library was a man who did not look like a student.

At swimming practice the following evening, Emma had trouble breathing, and her swim suit clung to her hip bones reminding her she was losing weight. On her way to her apartment, she passed the infirmary and seeing the lights on, she stopped and considered going in. Maybe she could get something to help her breathe better. It was an old building, not much used. She turned in, walked up the steps, and opened the door, which led to a hall with rooms on either side. Peering into a sparsely furnished room, stark with a few wooden chairs, a desk, and linoleum rug on the floor, Emma called out, "Is anyone here?"

A nurse in uniform came out of a back room. "Yes, how can I help you?"

"I am not feeling well," Emma told her. "I feel as if I can't breathe deeply."

"Sit here. I will get the doctor to check you in a few minutes." Emma waited impatiently for about ten minutes. There was nothing to read, not even posters. She opened her book bag and pulled out her history text. She had just found the assigned chapters when a tall young man in a white coat came into the room followed by the nurse. "Hello, what seems to be the problem with you today?" He was pleasant enough although not very concerned.

"I just feel bad, mainly in my stomach, and I can't breathe too well." Emma tried to take a deep breath.

"Get up here on the table." The doctor did not mention taking any clothes off, so Emma lay on her back on the table, fully clothed, including her shoes. The doctor looked in her eyes, her ears, and her mouth. Then he felt of her stomach with his fingers pressing flat. "Are you getting enough sleep?" he asked.

Emma nodded yes. "Most nights I get about seven or eight hours."

"Do you ever get up in the morning and vomit?" he asked as nonchalantly as if that would be normal.

The question irritated Emma. She knew what he meant, and she did not appreciate it. No, she was not pregnant. "No, in fact, I can't remember the last time I vomited."

"Well, that's good." The doctor stepped back. "You can get up. I'm going to give you a few pills to relax you a little. If you don't feel better soon, you might check with your family doctor. Miss Turner will get the pills for you. Take one before you eat a meal," he said as he turned and whisked out of the room.

"Thank you." Emma said to his back as she slid off the table to the floor. The nurse returned shortly with a small white envelope, which Emma took and left the building, eager to take one of the tiny white pills, although she didn't think so small a pill could do much. As soon as she was away from the building, she took one of the three tiny pills in her mouth and swallowed it. Now she needed to eat something. It was seven o'clock and getting dark. She might as well stop at the coffee shop, where she could get in and out faster than in the cafeteria or going downtown.

As soon as she opened the door, she regretted her choice. There in the back booth was Professor Di Yanni. Seeing her come in, he smiled and waved her over. She was embarrassed over her bad manners toward him when he just wanted to help her seemingly. "Please forgive me, sir, for the bad manners I have shown lately. I have just not felt well."

"Oh, no apology necessary. I remember my first year of college. Even in the dark ages, it was stressful, but at least I did not get burned out of my dorm room! If you are alone, please get your food and join me. I have had only coffee and need to eat something before I go. Perhaps a chat would be good for both of us." His manner was so down-to-earth that Emma let down her guard and sat down. "May I order for you while I place mine?" he asked.

"No, let me go look at the specials posted." She rose and went to the counter and ordered a grilled cheese sandwich and Coke. Emma returned to her seat in the booth and thought how odd it was not to be eating with friends like everyone else. At least in the dorm, there had been Elizabeth, Page, and Barbara to eat with. Barbara had decided to stay in the dorm in a different room and would not be moving in with Emma. Emma had not been able to bear the thoughts of attending the funerals even though Barbara had offered her a ride.

Professor Di Yanni broke the ice. "How have you been doing?"

"Actually, I can't tell one day from another. Now that I am alone in the apartment. Well, I am supposed to get a roommate. Maybe I should request one, but it is so nice to have no TV on while I am studying!"

"I understand, but don't you know some of the students in

the other apartments in the building? I bet they would like to have your company at dinner."

"No, I doubt it."

"See here, young lady, the other students who were on your hall have attended meetings with a counselor and psychologist to help them through the trauma of the fire and losing their friends. You seem to think you are immune from the effects of the tragedy."

Emma looked down at her sandwich. "I have other effects I am more affected by."

"Can you be more specific? That is an enigmatic statement if I have ever heard one."

"Well, it's nothing your committee can help with."

"So how do you know? Why not let me decide that?"

"Well, it's somewhat incriminating, just something I have to live with."

"It must be an awful burden because you seem afraid all the time. Did you know that?"

Emma faked a laugh, surprised at the professor's insight. "The only thing I am afraid of is failing swimming or drowning trying to pass."

"Oh, yes, how is swimming coming along?"

"I am getting pretty good at swimming on my back. That will be the only way I will make ten laps up and down."

"The semester is almost half over. Have you been home?"

"No, my mother is so short of funds that I have not wanted to add traveling expenses."

"Are you sure there is not some other reason?"

"Well, actually my sister has been writing to me about rising conflict between my mother and grandmother, mainly over my mother seeing a man. My sister says he is nice but a lot older than she is. Anyway, my grandmother is talking bad about her even though our father died over four years ago. I'd just as soon not even get into that."

"I understand. To change the subject, before I forget it, I wanted to tell you there will be a dramatic reading of the play *Macbeth* tomorrow evening at seven in Winston 308. I thought you might enjoy it, and the walk is so close for you. It might be a good place to meet some other English majors."

"You don't need to take it upon yourself to counsel me. I'm really fine. Do you have a family?"

"I did have. In fact, I had a daughter who would be about your age. Perhaps that's why I was concerned about you after the fire."

"What happened to her?"

Professor Di Yanni looked at Emma but did not speak for a few seconds. "I lost her and her mother."

"How?" Emma asked quietly.

"We had stayed with my mother, who was seriously ill, until bedtime one night when my sister came to take our place. We had just started out for home, not even a mile from Mother's house, when a truck transporting a load of hogs crossed the center line .... My daughter was only thirteen. It's not something I want to talk about. You know how that is. Anyhow, you remind me of my daughter in some ways."

"I am so sorry."

"I rather meant it as a compliment. Of course, I'm not objective, but I thought my daughter extraordinarily talented."

"Oh, in what way?"

"She wanted to be a writer."

"Really?" Emma's eyes brightened. "That would be my dream too. But since most writers come close to starving, I thought I would prepare for a regular job. Actually, I also dreamed of being an actress when I was younger."

Emma was in no mood to linger over the meager dinner, having a history test to study for, and excused herself. The professor rose as she hurried out the door. She knew if she stayed he would walk with her to her apartment and ask more questions, which she did not feel like answering. She just wanted to be alone and study. A wind had blown up, whirling oak leaves on the shortcut path Emma took behind the library, a trail that took her through a low area where the shrubbery had grown thick and wild. She reached the short wooden bridge over a small brook, where a sea of grasshoppers jumped as she put her foot on the first plank. And then an unexpected shuttering startled her. She lurched forward almost stumbling as a long-legged blue heron with great wings flapped past over her head so close she felt the moving air. Ah, it must have a nest under the bridge, she thought. A few drops of rain began to fall, big drops that seem to say, "I may be one but I mean to splatter you hard." She started to run and once close enough to see her apartment window, saw that the blinds were aglow. Did she leave a light on? No, she did not think so. Turning into the walk, she stopped, hearing a dog barking behind the building. Then, she dropped her books and ran to the back. A small black mixed breed dog barked fiercely, staked out at the edge of a border of Weyland cypresses. Emma went forward warily, finding a break between two trees that appeared to be a common passage. On the other side was another apartment building, not used by the college. Not seeing anyone moving, she went back, afraid to venture further.

Inside the apartment she found the bathroom light on. Perhaps she had left it on. Nothing seemed violated or disturbed. Her desk was messy. She wouldn't miss much if anything were taken from it. She had no valuables anyway. She must calm herself and study history. After a hot bath, she leaned back on her bed rest, braced on the wall, and began to read and take notes. By eleven o'clock she had fallen asleep with the book on her lap.

The next morning her first class was at eight. She scrambled to throw everything in her book bag for the day. She looked for the weekly announcements of events that she had stuck in a library book she needed to return. She wanted to consider going to the reading Professor Di Yanni had mentioned. In fact, she had circled it on the flyer. She found the book but not the flyer. It was time to go, so she stuffed the book in the bag.

As soon as Emma walked out, making long strides to get to class, a middle-aged man accosted her, coming from the back of her building. "Hello, Miss," he called and ran a bit to catch her. She felt no danger, the area filled with students walking to class. "I'm sorry to bother you, but I am trying to find out if anyone in your building has seen any stranger around. Someone has fed my dog something, I think, that almost killed her."

He had caught up with Emma, who kept walking. "I have an eight o'clock test. I saw a black dog last night when I got home. It was barking at the back of the building. I had never heard or seen a dog around before, but I could not see anyone." Then she thought of the light. "I will keep a lookout, sir."

"Good! If you see anything, I'm in apartment 10B in the building behind you. Name's Harry Furlow." He turned around.

Emma got out of her last class, English, at four o'clock. Janice Littleton walked out with her, asking if she could borrow Emma's notes until the next day. "By the way," Emma said, "are you going to the reading of *Macbeth* tonight at seven?"

"Oh, I'm going out with my boyfriend. In fact, I can drop off your notes tonight because we will be going by your building. Will you be back by ten?"

"Sure. It can't last that long."

Emma ate in her room, soup and crackers and a coke. As she

ate, she looked through the opened blinds toward the border of cypress trees where the passage was and where the dog had barked the night before. Everything was peaceful, most students having gone to eat dinner between five and six either in the cafeteria or downtown. At twenty till seven, Emma decided she would go to the reading; the exposure would help her when she took the Shakespeare course. She passed only a few students on her way to Winston and no one on the stairs to the third floor. Maybe she had the time wrong. But, no, there was a group outside the door, whom she walked by to enter the room. Desks had been arranged in a semi-circle and a platform with chairs brought in for the readers. They had not come in yet. Someone said the characters were next door in costume waiting for the introduction of the reading, sponsored by the English Club. Emma looked around at the audience already seated. She recognized some students' faces but no one by name. There was Professor Di Yanni on the other side of the room. He nodded and looked down at his program. There was an empty seat near him, but Emma preferred to sit near the door.

The lights went off and the witches appeared, the hazy spotlight making the ugly faces lurid and red. The readers scarcely glanced at their texts, rendering an effective first scene. "Fair is foul, and foul is fair." Recognizing the readers entering as Macbeth, Banquo, and King Duncan as classmates, Emma became more engrossed in the reading. And then Lady Macbeth entered alone holding a candle and reading a letter: "They met me in the day of success," she read turning to face the audience. Her green eyes seem to fix on Emma even in the dark room. It was Miss Pierce, Gerta—whoever she was! Emma, stifling a choking gasp, moved her head to the right so that the person in front of her blocked her view. Emma was sure Miss Pierce's eyes lighted up when she looked at the audience and saw her. What in the world was Miss Pierce doing in the reading, she wondered.

She must get out of the room. Perhaps Miss Pierce had not seen her after all. There was no light on the audience. Yet something had made Miss Pierce flinch as she read "I fear thy nature./ It is too full o' th' milk of human kindness/ To catch the nearest way." What an appropriate part for her, Emma thought. When Lady Macbeth turned her attention to the messenger, Emma slipped out the door without making any audible sound. Her mouth was dry and her chest tight. The water fountain in the hall gave her only a dribble. Outside the building students who had been released early after a test loitered on the steps comparing answers. Emma passed them, not even looking back when someone spoke her name, but hurrying to the sidewalk. She felt that someone was behind her, following from a distance, yet when she finally turned to look back, she saw no one.

Taking the short cut through the back lots and crossing the little wooden bridge, she slowed to walk quietly, hoping to spy the blue heron. Somehow it seemed a good luck omen, something that related to the farm back home, where one summer a blue heron nested in a ditch bank along the path she walked every evening after supper. The bird would stand in the path waiting until Emma was close before whooping slowly and flying off over the field into the woods. And even though she was expecting the great wings to slap the wind as she approached, she jumped back when the secret bird once again startled her, this time rising from the opposite side of the bridge.

Behind her someone else was startled. She heard a loud "Whoa!" And turning to see who it was, recognized one of the students who had been on the steps, but she also saw Professor Di Yanni, who seemed to be walking a few yards behind the tall, slender girl, who had been startled. "What in the world was that big bird!" the girl yelled to Emma. "It scared me to death. I thought it was a huge bat at first."

"No, just a timid heron, nesting under the bridge," Emma said turning around again.

"I've seen that heron here before," Professor Di Yanni sang out, walking past the tall girl. "Hey, Emma, I wonder what you thought of the reading. I had forgotten that I have to write a report tonight that is due first thing in the morning, so I had to leave." He caught up with Emma.

"So did you, like me, go to the reading only to remember you needed to do something else or were you just bored?" Professor Di Yanni turned to look at Emma's face, and, she, hearing his tone of concern, turned away from him, unable to hold back the tears that melted mascara, making black streaks on her cheeks.

"Well, I've always heard 'bored to tears,' but this is the first time I've actually seen it." He chuckled but Emma only cried harder. She couldn't speak. It seemed that all the stress and homesickness and uncertainty built up in her came rolling out.

"Here, let's sit outside the library for a minute," he said, pulling a handkerchief out of his pocket and handing it to her. There was an empty bench a few yards away.

Taking the handkerchief, Emma muttered a thank you and walked to the bench.

They sat in silence while she cried and cried. Professor Di Yanni simply said, "You'll feel much better after a good cry. Everyone does. Even men who try not to let people see them."

A few people passing them, stared, but no one they knew passed by. Finally Emma stopped crying. "I'm sorry," she said, "I'm so silly, acting like a teenager."

"Which you are, by the way. Correct?"

Emma giggled a little. "Well, actually, yes, nineteen."

"Ah, just the age of my daughter. When is your birthday?"

"September."

"I don't believe it. So is hers. Don't tell me the seventeenth!"

Emma stared. "You're kidding me now. How did you know?"

"Know what?"

"The seventeenth is my birthday! This is getting to be weird. You said earlier that you lost your family."

"They will always be with me. I have many precious memories. They are in heaven now, and I hope to be with them some day."

"Maybe they are also with my father. Who knows what heaven is like?"

"Now, Emma, something I have been wanting to discuss with you. I want you to make an appointment with a counselor and tell him or her about the stress you are under. You must do this tomorrow. I can see that you are worried and soon your studying and progress otherwise will suffer."

"I'm not crazy!"

"Of course, not. You just need someone to talk with."

"How about you? Maybe I could tell you."

"I don't have the training."

"Well, I feel comfortable with you. I don't think I could tell a stranger."

"I supposed we could meet in the conference room where my Student Life Committee meets. I will have to make notes for my file. I could use the information anonymously in our research on students' adjustment to college. Shall we say tomorrow at three thirty?"

"I couldn't be there until four."

"All right, four o'clock, in Lowry, 204A.

Emma did not rest well, falling asleep with a book on her lap in bed as usual, waking to sounds of shuffling feet or doors opening. Once she thought someone stopped at her door and slowly turned the knob, and then she heard the barking of a dog in the distance, but in the morning light she thought she had only dreamed the noises.

During the day sitting in her classes she thought of the meeting scheduled with Professor Di Yanni. At ten till four when she finished her last class, she walked reluctantly to Lowry and climbed the steps to the second floor. Room 204A was a seminar room for round table discussions. The light was off, but when Emma turned the door knob, she found the room unlocked. Suddenly she felt she could not keep the appointment and turned to go back down the stairs. However, turning around, she was face to face with Professor Di Yanni.

"Sorry, I'm a few minutes late, but I unlocked the door in case you got here early. We're working on a Christmas concert, and I was late getting away from practice."

"Oh, how nice. When is it?"

"December 6. It's free to students, you know. So if you can make it, do attend in Wainscott auditorium.

"Do come in and let's talk. You look pale. Did you sleep well?"

Dr. Di Yanni took a chair facing the door, which he left open and gestured with open hand for Emma to sit across from him, her back to the door opening into the hallway.

"So what is it that is troubling you? Are you homesick?"

"Yes, very homesick. When I was in the dorm, I used to get up late at night and go sit on the steps of the parlor staircase and look at the big clock."

"Oh, that reminds me of some good news: the burned part of your dorm has been rebuilt and furnished. The plan is to move all of you back who had to go to the apartments for the second semester."

"I don't want to go back to that room. I don't think the fire was an accident, and I think someone wanted to burn certain rooms—and certain people."

"Well, you can request a different room or even a different floor for the second semester. I can intervene for that request through a counselor. So, let's begin. I know freshmen who are not used to traveling or being away from home are more prone to have serious homesickness but your stress seems something more. You seem to me to be thinner every time I see you."

"Well, I used to eat with the other girls, but now I just haven't tried to find anyone, and with that swimming class—yes, I have lost weight. And I keep thinking I hear someone at my door during the night."

"That will all change and get back to normal when the new semester starts in January. And you will have a nice visit home for the break—a month off with no studies!"

"What's wrong? You *are* looking forward to going home?"

"Yes, of course, it's just that my sister wrote to me that Mother is having financial trouble and my grandmother has been put in a nursing home. You see, Mother worked downtown at Ledford's, but the store burned in September, and she has had to take another job that pays less. So I have not traveled home to save her money. I should take a job, but I feel I need all my time to study."

"Perhaps next year a part-time job would be a good idea or even in the spring if you settle down. Maybe a job in the library would suit you, and you would meet some people."

"Yes, I'm sure a lot of people would enjoy getting to know me," Emma said sarcastically.

"You seem to have a low opinion of yourself, and there is no reason you should."

The remark started Emma crying again. She turned her head away. It was about a minute before either spoke. "Take me back to the night I pulled you out of the pond, the night of your father's wake. What happened to him?"

"He drank himself to death," Emma said. Professor Di Yanni made a note on a white legal pad. "You did say any report would not use my name or any identification, didn't you?"

"Yes, anything I report would be part of freshman research. We do try to improve the freshman program every year. Your father's death was a number of years ago, as I recall. How old were you?"

"Thirteen."

"So how was your life after his death? How was school?"

"Oh, better. I was able to study without interruption and was able to get out more. You know, not afraid someone would bring me home or that I would bring someone home and see him lying drunk in the yard. Also, I was not afraid of violence any more, although I dreamed about it for a long time."

"You did want to come to college, didn't you?"

"Oh, yes, it's been my goal to teach for as long as I can remember."

"So your worries here have been the usual homesickness, adjusting to a new environment, harder courses than high school, and, of course, the terrible fire and loss of your two friends."

Emma nodded yes.

"But you seem frightened, not just grieving."

"Was the cause of the dorm fire ever determined?"

"The report given to our committee by the dean said the police determined it started by some explosive chemicals in the maid's closet."

"Yes, I imagine there were some, plus perhaps something to set them afire, I bet, that they didn't find."

"Why do you say that? You said something before about being suspicious about the fire."

"It goes back to something that happened just before my father died that I can't really talk about."

"That long? I'm intrigued to know how you think your father, dead for six years, had anything to do with the fire."

"It was not my father, but some so-called friends of his he brought home one night. They spent the night with us, a man and woman, married supposedly, and they stole some money from my father while he was asleep drunk." Emma stopped, as if she had said more than she intended.

Professor Di Yanni leaned forward, putting his long-sleeved clad arms on the table and pushing the legal pad aside. He twiddled his thumbs slowly.

"You know all the old gestures and words that remind me of my grandmother," Emma said, smiling.

He laughed. "Well, grandmothers, I find, for the most part, are sagacious and solicitous."

"It's just the way you are twiddling your thumbs. She did that a lot while thinking and sitting in her rocking chair."

"Please go on. How was money stolen from your father?"

"Well, I happened to be up late that night. You see, I had heard Mother and Grandmother talking before about how buddies would drive my father around as long as he had money to buy their gas and liquor, and steal his money; then dump him home drunk and broke. Since these two were spending the night, it looked funny, or so my mother thought. Actually I was tense any time he came home drunk, and I was up trying to study or read some long assignment."

"So your father was passed out drunk?"

"Yes, and sick. Everyone else was asleep as I sat in the kitchen in a corner reading by the stove light. Then the man came out of the bedroom and when he saw my father lying snoring on his bed and his door open and his wallet right there on the corner of the dresser, he stepped into his room as light footed as a cat even though he had been drinking. Then I leaned around the kitchen corner to look and saw him take bills from his wallet and go back to the bedroom."

Professor Di Yanni stared across the table at Emma with calm, kind brown eyes, his body leaning forward as if he were hard of hearing. "Did you tell your mother and grandmother and confront the man?"

"No, I'm just getting started on a gruesome tale. I kept sitting in the kitchen thinking of how I would wait until they fell asleep and then steal the money back. But before that happened, the woman came out to get some water, and I made up a big lie about Father having a large amount of money hidden in a hog house about a mile from the house. She laughed and went back to bed, but not long afterwards the two of them came out, and the man staggered out the door and was gone all night. I thought she had told him to go find the money. I think I had told her over a thousand dollars. The man never came back all night. The woman was all upset, and I tried to stay out of the way. The next morning my uncle went down to check the hogs and do his daily work and found the remains of the man in one of the hog houses. He had been almost eaten up. My grandmother called the sheriff, and after questioning everyone, he and his deputy took the man's remains as well as Gerta away.

"She did not tell on me, but in a subtle way threatened me. I was scared to death I would be arrested for murder."

Professor Di Yanni's face was tense now but he spoke calmly. "Did you ever tell anyone?"

"No, the police finally let the woman leave town because we all knew she was in the house all night. They never figured out why the man went down there during the night, and she didn't tell."

"So was that the end of it? Is it just a nightmare you have lived with ever since?"

"Well, before she left, Gerta gave me a box of chocolates and said something threatening like 'I will not forget you.' Of course, I threw the candy away."

"Have you ever heard from her? She never knew you lied, did she? I mean she had no way of knowing there was no money there?"

"I guess not, but the point was if it hadn't been for me the man would have not been killed."

"Did she ever contact you?"

"No, the sheriff found out later that she and the man were brother and sister and that they were wanted for robberies. He told my grandmother that the woman would be caught soon and put in prison, so I had almost forgotten about her until I came here."

"Let me get this straight. You think that woman is connected to the fire?"

"I know she is. The first night we had a house meeting in the dorm for the new house mother, I knew she was the same woman, only here her name now is Miss Pierce.

"She is all made up and dressed up, but I know it is the same woman, and I think she remembered me, although I tried to hide from her, she certainly had my name and could look up where I was from."

"And you're sure Miss Pierce had something to do with the fire next to your room!" Emma nodded. "I'm sure of it. What would you think?"

"Well, let's think this through. I tell you what. Here take these coins and go down to get us a soda from the first floor while I make some notes and think. Please get me a Coke or Pepsi. Do you mind?"

Emma stood up and took the quarters and dimes. She walked out and down the stairs, feeling relieved but foolish for telling all this to someone who might tell on her. Maybe when she returned she would tell Professor Di Yanni she had made up the whole thing to see if he would believe it. But when she returned with the drinks, Professor Di Yanni stood up and with an open gesture of his hand, motioned for Emma to step to the window. "I was just admiring the white Christmas lights the students put up around the fountain."

"Oh, yes, they are beautiful. White lights are the most elegant."

"The most intriguing lights and most symbolic. They make me think of imagination, purity, mystery, magic." The professor turned to Emma. "Emma in your literature classes, did you study the term *poetic justice?*"

"Yes, it means you get what you deserve."

"But without anyone doing anything to inflict the punishments, an irony of nature or fate or whatever one chooses to call it. What happened to the man who tried to steal money from your father, to me, is a good example of poetic justice. I don't see that you caused his death. The farthest thing from your mind was killing someone, wasn't it?"

"I just wanted to send them on a wild goose chase to teach them a lesson. My family has been around animals all of our lives, and I really had no thoughts of anyone not knowing how to handle hogs. My uncle does it every day of his life, and he has never been hurt. I used to dream of the remains that my uncle found even though I never saw them but heard my grandmother talk about the sight. She went down with the sheriff and, of course, Gerta, or whatever her name is, saw them. They actually used the teeth to do an official identification. And since I have seen her here the dream comes back, and I wake up and think someone has been turning my door knob. There was evidence he hit his head, and being drunk, passed out in the pen with the sows."

Professor Di Yanni made a note and breathed deeply, not saying anything for a few seconds. "I hope you feel better just sharing your story with someone, and I can tell you that even if you had told the sheriff nothing would have happened to you. You did nothing criminal. They were the criminals." Emma looked at him with a blank expression. "Now I think I will do a little investigation about Miss Pierce to make sure she is not the same woman. I just can't imagine she is. After all, it has been six years since you saw her, and she probably just has some common features."

"What about the voice? She sounds like the same woman."

"Yes, well, I can do some discreet checking with our campus police. Every employee should be checked for a criminal record, especially house mothers."

"Emma, have you ever read the short story "Haircut" by Ring Lardner?"

"I don't think so."

"Well, you should. It is such a good example of poetic justice and reminds me of your case. In fact, I suggest you stop by the library and check out Lardner's stories. I know exams are coming up, but you could read it during the semester break. When will you go home?"

"December 18 on the bus. My uncle will pick me up. I have saved enough money, so I don't have to ask Mother for any."

"Well, when you return, let's discuss the story, and maybe by then I will have some report on Miss Pierce to give you. You have to put this burden to rest. You have carried it around too long already."

Chapter VII: Weaning

Emma savored every day at home during the month-long break before spring semester. Purposely avoiding long walks on the farm that might give rise to haunting thoughts, she stayed inside most of the time. Yet the ambience was different. Mother and Aunt Ophelia sat in the kitchen on Saturday morning after Emma arrived by bus Friday night. They spoke softly about funeral arrangements for Grandmother.

Emma reflected on the previous evening. Uncle Milton had picked up Emma at the bus station, the rest of the family having gone to the nursing home because Grandmother had taken a turn for the worse with a fever of 105. They drove to the nursing home before going to the farm. Uncle Milton stayed outside to smoke.

Exhausted and frightened, Emma walked into the plain brick building and immediately smelled urine and Lysol intermingled. "Watch out for the wet floor!" a housekeeping lady yelled, as Emma left the carpeted area of the parlor and turned down the first hallway. She thought of the young girl in "A Visit of Charity" who had to visit some old lady in a nursing home to earn points for the Girl Scouts.

But Emma was not visiting some old lady. Grandmother Ila had held an iron hand over the family as long as Emma could remember, and even though she had both loved and hated her, she could not imagine that her grandmother would ever die. She passed a lady in a wheel chair, her head and arm twisted to one side, who kept repeating "Lord, have mercy. Lord, have mercy." An attendant pushed a cart with racks of meals, all covered with little name tags sticking up, and suddenly Emma was sickened with the overwhelming stench of too old fish. Patients from their rooms looked at her; some smiled; one asked if she would turn the TV on, it being too high up for the woman to reach. She did, and the lady thanked her. On the second hall, a man in a wheel chair asked her to tell the head doctor he wanted to see him. Yes, she told him she would tell the doctor of his request. Finally she was on the 600 hall where her grandmother was boarded. A nurse was dispensing medication in little paper cups. Room 601 was apparently at the very end of the hall next to the emergency door. "Would you give me a pain pill?" a patient asked the nurse. Raising her voice to a shriek, the nurse replied that she had just given her one.

Passing the nurse, Emma found Grandmother's room. No one was there except her grandmother, lying on her back on a narrow bed. Emma was glad to be alone at this moment as she focused on the withered, old woman, much smaller than she remembered. Beads of perspiration popped and streamed the leathery forehead. Emma remembered that her mother had often remarked that Grandmother did not have any wrinkles in her face, but the frail body twitched in a feverish slumber. She did not respond when Emma leaned down to speak.

"She's been unconscious for almost twenty-four hours now," said a voice from the doorway, a nurse coming in to check vital signs. Emma nodded, wiped her eyes and walked out. At the end of the hall she saw her mother and sister turn the corner. Without speaking, they walked faster and hugged Emma, one on either side. Martha looked so pretty, her hair cut in a pixie, and her mother, thinner, was dressed up as Emma had rarely seen her.

They all left together to go to the farm, riding with Uncle Milton, who had waited outside. From the back seat, Martha chattered, asking Emma questions about college. Then, abruptly changing the subject, she interjected a surprise. "Did Mother tell you she is getting married to Mr. Willis right after Christmas? She wanted you to be home for the ceremony."

Emma, sitting in front with Uncle Milton, who laughed out loud, a gesture not often witnessed, turned around to face her mother.

"We were going to tell you together tonight," Mother said. "John is coming tonight for supper with us and may be already there."

Trying to keep her composure, Emma smiled. "Oh, that is a big surprise. Well, I think that is grand. What date?"

"The day after Christmas," said Helen. "It will be just the family at the church. I just hope we don't have a funeral to deal with. Miss Ila is mighty low."

At seven sharp John Willis drove into the dirt drive on an expensive black sedan. He was a reserved, sensitive, well-dressed man, who looked about twenty years older than Helen. Having heard Emma would be home, Mr. Willis brought her a present. After greeting her at the front door, he handed her a canister of assorted nuts. Someone had told him she loved nuts, no doubt. Mr. Willis was extremely polite, rising when Helen came into the living room. Emma liked him fine until he was there side by side with her mother. He seemed more like the old men who used to court her grandmother, bringing her nylon stockings for Christmas. The four ate the meal of chicken pastry Mother had prepared before going to the nursing home. They were interrupted during the dessert of pecan pie when the doctor called from the nursing home. Grandmother had died, never waking up again after going into a coma the day before.

Getting up from the table while Helen was still on the phone, Emma excused herself from Mr. Willis and Martha and went into the front bedroom, her grandmother's room. Her thick, old worn Bible lay on the dresser. Emma opened it where the black ribbon marker was inserted. It was the page where all the children's birthdates were recorded. There had been nine children. Only one was left: Emma's Aunt Ophelia. Emma's father had barely been conceived when his father died. Emma had always pictured her dead grandfather as a gentle man, unlike her grandmother.

Helen went next door to work out funeral plans with Aunt Ophelia. There would be another grave in the family cemetery on the farm, where Emma's father was buried. There would be another crowd of old people rejoicing to see each other, laughter, and food brought to feed any stranger who might come by. Mr. Willis and Martha sat in the living room talking in low voices as Emma sat rocking in her grandmother's chair in the dark bedroom, looking out the double windows where her grandmother had enjoyed observing farmers working in the fields year after year.

For the moment Emma could not remember anything cruel her grandmother had done. She saw herself as a little girl with her grandmother riding to the country store in her new Chevrolet Impala, the store owner, always a slow-talking old man, coming out to ask how she was doing and what he could get for her. If it were a mid-afternoon trip, as it usually was, Grandmother would say, "We both want coca colas, and do you have any good bananas, not too ripe?" If they were lucky, the store man said yes, he just got some in, and if they were parked close to the door, Emma could see a bunch of bananas hanging upright from the ceiling in the unlighted store. "Let me have two pounds," Grandmother would say, "and put a napkin around the bottles, Kenny." He was going to do that anyway, he would always say.

And how is the little granddaughter today, he would ask, peering inside the car. Emma smiled but did not speak.

"We fell out this morning," Grandmother said. "Coming back from town, Emma spotted some wild daisies and nothing would do but to stop to pick some. I told both the younguns to stay in the car while I parked on the shoulder and waded in the tall grass by the railroad tracks to pick some confounded daisies. And about the time I had picked three, I saw the biggest snake coiled up, ready to strike you ever saw in your life! Oh, I almost forgot what I came for. Do you have a box of Navy snuff?" Sure do, he would say, turning toward the store. In five minutes, he returned with the small Coca Cola bottles with thin white paper napkins wrapped around them, handing them one at a time to Grandmother, who handed one to Emma. Then the man handed Grandmother a medium-sized brown paper bag containing the bananas and small tin of snuff. She inspected the purchases, paid, and thanked Kenny before asking him about his family and neighbors, drinking a swallow, and not leaving until another customer drove up.

When they were little, Martha and Emma fought like cats especially if they had to wait for someone while sitting together in the back seat of Grandmother's car. Because Mother did not drive, Grandmother took her to the grocery store and waited in the car.

Mother was paid every two weeks and bought two weeks' worth of groceries every other Friday. Shopping for five people, she took her time checking prices and expiration dates in the crowed downtown A & P, coming out after forty-five minutes with the bag boy pushing two heaping carts of large brown paper bags overflowing with staples and goodies.

One day while the three waited, Grandmother was not in the mood for the pinches and knocks from the back seat. "If you girls don't stop fightin', I'm going to call that policeman over there, and he might lock you up. You can get locked up whether you know it or not for fightin' in town." Emma considered this declaration and knew it was not true that policemen locked up little girls. In a few seconds, the girls were at it again. Grandmother rolled down her window and whistled. Emma didn't even know she could. The policeman, middle-aged, looked around and saw Grandmother's waving hand. He walked up to the car window and asked if he could assist with anything. Perhaps Grandmother winked but her voice was stern. "Officer, these girls here are fightin' and won't stop. I told them that you would lock them up in the jail if you caught them."

"Well, ma'am, I might have to intervene at that." He stooped to look at the girls, who sat up straight, not believing Grandmother had really called the policeman. "I'm sure you pretty girls won't be fighting any more. You could cause your grandmother to have an accident while she's driving. Ma'am, you just call me if you have any more problems." That ended the fighting for that trip.

Emma remembered ninth-grade Home Economics when she had to come up with a significant project around the house to complete for the six-weeks. Finally she thought she might wash and wax her grandmother's car. Confidently she went in her grandmother's bedroom where she sat rocking and sat opposite her for a while asking if she had bought any material lately for a dress. Not being sure how to get her grandmother to buy into the project, not to mention needing her to buy the car wax, Emma started by asking if she would like to have her car washed and waxed. "I know you can't stoop down or get up to reach the top," having laughed at her washing the top of the car with a rag wrapped around a broom. "It's looking a little dull." So pleased was Grandmother that Emma immediately felt guilty and decided to explain later that her offer was not entirely magnanimous.

During the weeks leading up to the Saturday when Emma would wash and wax the car, a 1962 two-toned blue Impala, she was the model granddaughter or as close to it as she could make herself endure. Finally time was running out, the wax was purchased, and Emma put down her books and pulled out a pail, detergent, and rags to wash the car. Knowing Ms. Brinson, the Home Economics teacher, would come to inspect her work and talk with her grandmother, or so she threatened, Emma washed the car meticulously, spraying the suds off every few minutes. The tire rims and hub caps were the worst to clean, but after an hour of scrubbing, Emma declared the car ready to wipe dry with towels. That done, she started the waxing, smearing a thick coat of the cream wax with a clean cloth, waited fifteen minutes until it turned white, and then with more clean rags started rubbing it off. Her arms already tired, she huffed and puffed, hating the course her mother made her take because everyone needed to know how to sew on buttons and hem dresses. Most of the girls in the course sat around admiring themselves in the mirrors they would sneak from their pocket books during class while Ms. Brinson droned on about the color wheel and how one could wear three colors as long as one was a neutral. These were the girls whose mothers took turns holding circle meetings for their church, of which Ms. Brinson was a member.

Twice Emma took a break from polishing the car to go inside for water. It was April but already eight-five degrees. After two hours of hard work, the task was done. Emma wrote up her report and had her grandmother to sign it. Grandmother gave Emma a ten dollar bill for the job. Emma told her Ms. Brinson might come by but she was hoping not. If she did, Grandmother was to tell her how Emma did and if the job was a good one or not. Emma was betting Ms. Brinson would not really show up, so she took the ten dollars and never told her grandmother she was not supposed to get paid. Sure enough two Saturdays later about three in the afternoon, Ms. Brinson's little grey car pulled in the driveway. Emma saw her and ran to warn Grandmother. Emma opened the door, forcing a smile, and invited in the guest, showing her to her grandmother's room.

"I'm Ella Brinson, the Home Economics teacher." She extended her hand.

"I'm Emma's grandmother."

"Well, I'm glad to meet you, Grandmother. I came to check on Emma's project of washing and waxing your car. Is that it out there?"

"Yes, she done a good job. It's got dusty now, but it still looks better."

"So you were pleased with the quality of the work?"

"Yes, I thought she done a real good job."

Emma held her breath, crossing her fingers behind her back, hoping her grandmother would not tell about paying her. She didn't tell. Ms. Brinson went out to inspect the car and soon was on her way to the next house. Emma never mentioned the fact that she should not have been paid. Maybe her grandmother did not know any better, but now as Emma rocked in her dead grandmother's chair, she knew she had known.

*****

The funeral was held two days later on Sunday, the visitation and ceremony a blur to Emma, who remained aloof while Mother and Aunt Ophelia talked earnestly with friends and relatives. Mother put off her wedding and told Emma it would be after she returned to college but that it would be so small and informal that she need not attend if she didn't want to miss any of her classes. Emma accepted the plan and left on the bus on January 12 to return to her old dorm. At least she had passed swimming. Everything else had to be as easy as swimming on one's back.

Emma's dorm had been repaired, and she was assigned to a different room. The move back into the dorm went smoothly because Emma did not have much to move. Miss Pollock had assigned a Big Sister who had car to help all the displaced girls move back in before classes started. When Emma checked her mailbox, she had a sealed note from Professor Di Yanni. He had news for her as soon as she was back and settled. Having arrived a day before classes started, Emma had the first night free from studying, and thinking she might run into the professor in the library or at the coffee shop, she headed out after her Big Sister had left.

She walked fast in the sharp, cold air, as the sky relinquished day to night, a full orange moon rising fast through the black trees. Entering the coffee shop, Emma looked around, and not seeing the professor, went out and turned toward the library. She heard a musical voice rising above the murmur of several students standing by a bench outside the library. Approaching slowly, she heard someone say "Not everyone can be a Mozart, you know, but whatever talent one has, it still must be harnessed. You have to study and practice!" It was unmistakably the professor's voice.

Emma walked past the group glancing quickly but not making eye contact. Then she heard her name. "Emma, hello!" Professor Di Yanni called out from a bench behind the students.

Stopping and turning toward the familiar voice, Emma was accosted by another voice. "Hello, Emma, I'm Jarret Bridgewater. I recognize you from our World Civilization class. You're the one the professor calls on because he knows you will either know the answer or make up something."

Emma laughed. "Well, hello. Yes, I remember you. You sat behind me. Aren't you glad we're finished with that nightmare?"

"Yes, and I am so proud of my C. From what I hear, that professor is the worst in the undergraduate program."

"Well, it's good to see you, Jarret. I need to speak with someone. Have a good spring semester."

"Hey, wait! I hereby extend to you an invitation to our rehearsal party for our first spring concert in three weeks. I have a friend who is also an English major who will be attending. Here write it down," he said, handing Emma a pen. "February 5, a Thursday, at seven o'clock in Wainscott, 305. Professor Di Yanni told me to be sure to invite you."

"I will if I can. What do you play?"

"The violin, and I'm a rising star, someone to watch."

Emma laughed. "It's nice to see such confidence!"

"By the way, won't you join us for a walk downtown for dinner? These two guys are harmless musicians. This is Justin Chadwick and Daryl Medlin. Guys, meet Miss Emma Apple-white."

Emma couldn't believe he knew her full name. Well the history professor did call the roll, so that was how. "I thank you for the invitation, but I have to meet with someone."

"Buenos Noches." Jarret waved good bye.

"Au Revoir," Emma responded and looked around for Professor Di Yanni. He had moved to another bench farther away and waved to her.

"Come and sit down, I have news for you," he said.

"Yes, I received your note when I arrived back."

"It's about Miss Pierce."

Emma felt her throat tightening. "What? You have a strange look on your face."

"First of all, Gerta, or your dorm mother, Miss Pierce, whose real name is Selena Klein, was arrested the day after Christmas at the dorm. She had eluded authorities for years by changing her name and acquiring fake credentials. She had made up almost everything on her resume. Obviously the college did not check her out." Emma seemed in shock. "Take a deep breath, Emma. You can forget about this woman. She won't be bothering you anymore. The story goes that Ms. Klein left home at sixteen to live with her brother, the man you met. The two were quite skilled at robbery, but she went a bit further by poisoning her husband who seemed to have some objections to her career as a jewel thief."

Spellbound, trying to absorb all the professor was saying, Emma stared, speechless. "How did you find out all this?" She finally found her voice.

"Campus police. The chief is a friend of mine, you might say, from way back. They have means of researching through the city police when they need to." He looked at Emma, whose expression was finally one of peace. "Did you have a nice break. How is your family? I bet they were glad to have you home for a while."

"Oh, yes, but my grandmother died and was buried before Christmas, and my mother is getting married this weekend but I won't be there. That was a big surprise. I guess it's true that you can't go home. They're all going their ways without me."

"Yes, and you must go yours. Just think, a schedule with no more swimming courses!"

The first three weeks of spring semester passed quickly, Emma having six new courses and a new roommate to get used to. Frances Dillard was fairly easy to deal with, except she talked too much. She was smart, a plain girl from a small town who had enough confidence to do anything she wanted to, which happen-ed to be teach English, the same as Emma. Frances had shoulder length straight mousy brown hair, wore fairly thick glasses, and always seemed to need to brush her teeth, but it may have been just the thick way she talked. Her father was a Methodist minister, who had been very strict with her. She knew all the social graces that Emma lacked and took it upon herself to help her disadvantaged roommate.

"I've been invited to a party after the rehearsal for the first spring concert of the music department," Frances announced one evening when she and Emma ate their usual soup and sandwiches at the downtown family café that closed at eight o'clock. They had a pattern of eating about five in the winter when dark came so soon after classes.

"Oh, really, I am invited also," said Emma, remembering that one of the fellows she had met said another English major would be there. What was his name?

"In high school, I was in band with Jarret Bridgewater," Frances said. "He invited me and said I could bring anyone interested in critiquing the rehearsal."

"Yes, I know him! He is the one who invited me. We were in a class together fall semester. I just happened to be at the library when Jarret and his friends were there, and he introduced himself, and invited me."

"Interesting. He's was like a brother in high school."

"Yes, he seemed quite nice."

"Well, look. It's tomorrow evening at seven. Double up on your work and let's go. You don't have a test, do you?"

"No, but an essay due. I'll try to finish it so I can go with you."

"If there is anything you can do, it's write an essay! So get to it!" Frances ordered.

When Emma and Frances arrived at Room 305 in Wainscott, there was a note on the door saying the rehearsal was being held in the auditorium with the full orchestra on stage on the first floor. Ecstatic, Frances clapped her hands. "Let's go!" She ran to the stairs, Emma trying to keep up without falling down. Emma had seen orchestras only on television. Her grandmother loved Lawrence Welk but then she also loved Smiley O'Brien.

Frances and Emma sat middle way the auditorium, the occupied seats scattered throughout, filled by parents and students who aspired to be in the orchestra as well as students who wanted to earn points to pass a music course. But this group looked peaceful, perhaps all dreamers of sorts. Frances waved to one of the musicians on stage, who waved her to come up. "I'll be right back," she said to Emma, who recognized the waver to be Jarret, all dressed in a black suit, black tie, and white shirt. Emma stared at the musicians tuning and at the audience. More and more old people came in speaking across aisles to each other. These had to be retired music teachers who lived close to the campus.

Lights dimmed as Frances returned to her seat, musicians scurried to attention, the curtains closed, and all was quiet until the curtains rose, the master of ceremonies stepped from the right side of the stage and introduced the evening's program. Emma had assumed Professor Di Yanni would conduct, but instead, none other than Jarret Bridgewater would. In fact, Emma had not seen the professor, who must be back stage. Having come in late, neither she nor Frances had obtained a program, and when the first piece began, Emma realized she had no idea what was being played: she knew it was classical; no one around her had a program. She did not want to show her ignorance by asking Frances. So she sat still and listened and watched the old people who seemed to be dreaming of past times. Indeed, it was music to dream by, too personal to share with strangers. Emma could not tell when a piece had ended, not knowing the music, and waited for the audience's applause.

Emma had always been able to lose herself in the reverie of music. When she was fourteen, her mother won a nice transistor radio for being the highest salesperson of the month, and Emma slept with it throughout the following summer, lying on a pallet on the floor, tuning from station to station to get the clearest signal far into the night. She recognized one piece being played as an Italian piece that had been popular on the radio but could not remember the title.

The thin oriental girl at the piano seemed too small to play. The girl leaned down, her face almost touching the keys. Emma had always thought she could play if she had had a chance. Once when she was about four, she accompanied her aunt and uncle to her uncle's old parents' house. There was a piano in the parlor, closed off and cold. Emma had said she needed to use the bathroom and had been taken by an older child to the parlor, where hidden under a skirted table was a little pot for children to use, there being no inside facility. Emma had only wanted to see the grand, cold room where the piano was kept. Her cousins who lived in town also had a piano, and one day one of the cousins taught her to play a boogie in thirty seconds, and she had never forgotten, often playing the tune with her fingers on imaginary keys. It all seemed a matter of rhythm, which she indubitably had.

Someone was knocking her knee. "Emma, it's over! You can applaud a long time now. They're done! See! Did you go to sleep? Boy, you must be tired!" Emma had indeed dozed off and jerked to attention, feeling drowsy and embarrassed. Following Frances' lead, Emma trudged back up to 305, where invited guests and orchestra members who cared to linger for the critics, poured glasses of wine and chattered and laughed as if they'd been drinking for hours.

Professor Di Yanni was standing in the back of the room viewing the framed prints on the wall. He was popping a piece of cheese in his mouth when he saw Emma and waved to her. Frances, preoccupied with giving accolades to Jarret for his performance, did not notice or seem to care what Emma did. Never having tasted any wine except a cheap one her father had brought home once or twice, a sickening red wine he bought at a gas station, she thought she might like the white wine better. As she approached the table, Jarret rushed up and poured a full glass for her as she put cheese on a little paper plate and picked up a napkin. "Emma, I'm so glad you and Frances came tonight. What did you think of the performance?"

"Oh, wonderful." She did not intend to say it had been her first classical concert.

"And did you approve of the pieces we selected?"

"Oh, quite appropriate for a winter concert," she said, knowing her comment must sound less than apropos.

"Well, I am so pleased to have met your approval," Jarret said in a tone Emma thought a bit mocking of her ignorance. "I thought the pieces perfect for February: Beethoven's 'Piano Concerto No. 2,' Tchaikovsky's 'Violin Concerto,' and Schumann's 'Symphony No. 4'! A splendid selection, all to my credit! Oh, I shall be another Bernstein! Come on, Emma, we are being beckoned by Frances."

"I'll be right there in a minute," she said. With that, he waltzed his way through the crowded room, holding his wine glass above heads, leaving Emma feeling quite dowdy. Once Jarret returned to the group, no one waved to Emma. Seeing

Professor Di Yanni still admiring the art work and posters in the room, Emma joined him.

"Hello, Emma. How nice to see you here. Did you enjoy the concert?"

"Oh, splendid, sir. I did not see you."

"I was behind you. Why don't you join your friends? That Bridgewater fellow will make a name for himself, I believe."

"They are already fairly drunk. Look. Jarret is already out on the couch. I have to write an essay in class for my eight o'clock class about the influence of music on my life. I already know what I will write, but I will need a good night's sleep to do a decent job. I can't flunk a course. I have only one chance."

"In that case, let's chat a while about music as a brainstorming exercise for your essay. Let's sit on the stage in the actors' chairs where we can view an imaginary audience. You know audience is important to a writer too." He led the way up the rickety wooden steps set up for the temporary stage used in last semester's classroom performances.

"Yes, I was just thinking that this old room reminds me of a similar setting from my old school that was first grade through twelfth," Emma said. "I feel safe here on this old, dark stage."

"And what role do you wish to play?"

"Maybe Anne Frank or Scout in *To Kill a Mockingbird* or Laura in *The Glass Menagerie*. Oh, or I would be Ann Margaret in *State Fair* and dance with Elvis. And I'd be Whitman and recite my favorite lines, such as 'What is the grass? Oh, maybe it is the Lord's handkerchief,' or however it goes."

"And who are your favorite artists? We cannot leave art out of our discussion of literature and music," said the professor.

"I know little about art, but Monet and Renoir invite one into a delicate mist of mystery—it is like stepping into a poem like the one by Ferlinghetti in which the girl excites the boy in the candy store where the 'jelly beans gloom in the rainy afternoon.'"

"Yes," the professor took her up, "and Childhood says, 'Too soon! Too soon!' Yes, I know the poem. Well, was tonight your first classical concert?"

"Oh, definitely, live, that is."

"And has music played a significant part in your life? I would be surprised if it has not as much as you seem to love literature, the language being so musical itself. Did anyone in your family play an instrument?"

"Oh, I had cousins who played the piano, and I always wanted to play but was just never around a piano. In my immediate family, my father did play the guitar. He was good, I thought, but his drinking diminished everything in his life. I really don't know where he got his talent. He could sing too. He loved those Hank Williams songs and a few hymns. My grandmother would cry when he played some songs."

"And you? Did they make you cry?"

"Not really, I was too young. I was somewhat transformed and amazed to see my father play and sing, more mesmerized than anything else."

"Did you sing? Did your mother teach you songs?"

"Yes, she did teach us a few children's songs, and my grandmother was always singing hymns and rocking in her chair. My cousins next door had a big radio and listened to country music, which I did not like much because it all sounded like the singers had a nasal twang. But we children did sit around barefoot in the summer in my aunt's house listening to that radio."

The professor smiled. "And then?"

"My life is boring to recount, sir. It seems strange you would be interested."

The professor looked away at Jarrett, asleep on the couch and the waning group in the room, then back to Emma. "Somehow I feel as though if I can help you, I am somehow helping my daughter. I know you cannot understand that—maybe only some-one who has lost a child can."

"I wish you would tell me more about your daughter."

"I certainly will, but tonight we must finish your brainstorm for your essay."

"You know what? I used to make my grandmother sit and listen to me rehearse my answer to a long history essay test question on Thursday night before my Friday tests, and it worked wonderfully to prepare."

"So please, continue with your music influence."

"The next phase I remember is my female cousins who lived in town. They liked rock-and-roll. They had 45 records like Little Richard's 'Long, Tall Sally' and 'Good Golly, Miss Molly.' They taught me to bop when I was about six or seven. Then the Christmas I was ten, Santa Claus brought Martha and me a little record player that played 45's and two records: one was by Jerry Lee Lewis called 'Great Balls of Fire'; the other was 'Jailhouse Rock' by Elvis. The whole Christmas vacation of two weeks at home, we played those two records and the flip side songs over and over and over. At that time, my sister and I slept in a very small, cold room that had been part of a porch my grandmother had closed in to make more space. There was a double bed and a dresser with a walkway space between, and if we pulled the drawers open we couldn't walk by. Anyhow, the record player was stored in there on the floor beside the dresser. My father got drunk during that time, and I recall that Mother made me stop playing the records because the Jerry Lee Lewis songs, especially 'You Win Again' upset my father to the point that he was lying on the floor cursing and crying at the same time."

"What about after he died? Did you go to dances during high school?"

"No, I was too shy and didn't really have a boyfriend. I did go to the proms but with a couple of girls who did not have dates —we were academic outcasts. You know, boys don't want to date girls who are at the top of their class."

"Really, let me write that down. Well, I know an attractive girl like you must have been attractive to boys."

"You have to remember that I was brought up isolated and sheltered except for school. There was a boy I liked, my bus driver for two years, but he had girl friend who guarded him. I never felt that I could compete with the social butterflies."

"So did he get married and live happily ever after?"

"Yes, well, he did get married and already has two children. I don't know about happy ever after."

"And none of the boys you liked asked you to dances?"

"We didn't have dances regularly. You must be thinking of your time and the big band dances. I have heard of those."

"Well, go on with your history of music in your life. Drink your wine. It will help you remember. You have had only two sips. I've been counting."

To show she was no prude, Emma drank the rest of the wine in the glass. "There," she said. "I guess I will remember quickly now."

"Did you enjoy church music?"

"No, I went sometimes with my grandmother, but they did not have music. They just had a man leading the congregation— no choir or special music. Primitive Baptist."

"Let's get back to the two records you had. Did you get more?"

"Yes, gradually, but money was tight. It was the era of Fats Domino and the Coasters, and of course, always Elvis. Oh, yes."

Suddenly Emma seemed to come alive. "One summer after my father died, my mother very unexpectedly bought my sister and me a big, nice Magnavox stereo that played 33 records as well as the 45s. That was a turning point for me. I think I will get more cheese and wine."

"What kind of turning point?"

"In music. Isn't that our topic?" The professor nodded and smiled at the change in her tone.

"The stereo had a beautiful mahogany cabinet and the best sound I had ever heard. It was like a dream come true. To begin with, Mother bought us two albums: the sound track from *My Fair Lady* and *The Sound of Music*, neither of which had I seen but had heard so much about and had heard some of the songs on television." Emma looked at the professor who appeared interested and amused. "Are you comparing my childhood with your daughter's?"

The professor stopped smiling. "Somewhat. She loved music, art, literature—anything artsy. She would surely have won a scholarship for her art. However, like you, she was shy. She would have needed a mentor …. And so what did you do with your newly found music?" he asked.

"That whole summer—for three months—Martha and I played our little records and danced on the front porch. Yes, I remember that after my father died, my grandmother had the wooden porch torn off and a cement porch poured. We could open the front door so that the music could be heard on the porch. The stereo was in the living room at the front of the house. And we would dance barefooted—we said "barefooted" not "barefoot" as the Yankees here say.

The professor laughed. "I guess "barefooted" means walking with no shoes in the yard where chickens roam freely and "barefoot" means walking on the sand at the beach?"

"Let me write that down," Emma teased.

"I am wondering how your grandmother tolerated the loud music."

"She did complain sometimes. Of course, Mother was always away at work, but the television had been moved to the back bedroom, where Grandmother Ila would sit for hours watching her afternoon stories; the rest of the time she was talking on the phone, which she had put in also after my father died.

"I can see us now, my sister and I. Sometimes we danced the bop together, turning each other, but mostly we danced by ourselves, often just making up steps. We had 'Hound Dog' and 'Poison Ivy' and 'Love Potion Number Nine.' Oh, yes, and on Saturdays, I think it was, there was a local TV station that put on *Teen Canteen*, where the host played rock and roll records and couples danced in the studio. Girls wore straight skirts and sweaters then and loafers with pennies in them. My grandmother loved to see the show as much as Martha and I did."

"So you played every day in the summer?"

"Well, until the tobacco was ready to harvest. Then we worked four or five full days a week, usually all day. So no dancing those days!"

"What about the movie sound tracks? They don't strike me as bop tunes."

"I sort of grew into those albums. On hot afternoons when the sun was on the front porch, I would sit by the stereo and play the songs over and over. In fact, I wrote down the words to the songs, every one of them, and learned them so that I could sing along. By that time I had *Oliver* and *South Pacific*. Eventually I started singing the songs when I went for walks alone or was looping tobacco on the harvester. The motor was so loud nobody could carry on a conversation, and usually the person opposite me on the chain was not anyone I cared to converse with anyhow. Then at times, I just made up tunes and words. They just came, different songs every time. I couldn't write music. I would dream of being an actress or dancer or both, all the while knowing I'd be lucky to get a degree to teach."

"It seems to me that you have a great deal more talent than just a love of literature and language."

"Oh, I love to write too but haven't done much."

"Well, this little session with wine and cheese, not to mention the rehearsal for a primer, has done wonders for your spirits, Emma. You must think more broadly about your goals. This is your time. You have three more years with talented young people —like Jarrett. Now, it's time, young lady, to depart to our residences and bid each other good night."

Emma had sat facing the professor with her back to the partiers. Her brain, fuzzy with the effects of the wine, she had not realized everyone was gone except Jarret, who was snoring on the couch. Even Frances was gone. She stood up beside the professor, feeling a bit dizzy and embarrassed to have talked incessantly. She felt as if she had just completed a leading role in a Broadway play.

"Let's wake Jarret and walk back together," Emma suggested.

"Oh, I don't think he would appreciate my escorting him in the shape he's in. You see, as a visiting music professor, I have to submit a report on tonight's performance, including the professionalism of the performers, and I would not want Jarret to realize my role here. I suggest we leave him to the security guards who will turn out the lights and lock up at eleven o'clock. By then, he will be okay to walk to his dorm."

"I see. I had no idea you were observing. But I am wondering, professor, why you wanted to know about music in my life, and are we finished? Did you find out what you wanted to know? I don't quite get the point."

"I don't know that one is ever finished with examining one's life, Emma, but the point is that to be happy and to reach one's potential, I believe that one must be true to oneself. However, one must know oneself to be true to oneself. You have heard that said many times, I know."

"Sure. Someone always picks that saying to go under their picture in the senior yearbook."

"But do you know what it means?"

"Well, just what it says. You have to look in the mirror and try to figure out who you are."

"But, more importantly, you must accept who you are, and seek to be the best person you can be, but not by longing to be someone you are not. You will know when you know what it means. It usually takes a while. No one can really tell you."

*****

At the end of Emma's first year, she decided to stay on for summer school, working full time typing documents for a law firm near the college and taking some of her less challenging courses at night. Martha went off to nursing school three hundred miles away, and Mother was adjusting to her new husband's family, including two teenagers who did not accept her. Emma went home only during semester breaks. Her time was consumed with work, study, and occasional attendance to free concert rehearsals, always made exciting by Jarret, Justin, and Frances, perpetual enthusiasts, no matter how lousy the performance.

After her freshman year, Emma moved into a sophomore dorm and her junior year into a brand new dorm for upper classmen. Some freshman girls told her that her freshman dorm had new house mothers and that Miss Pierce had been fired.

Apparently the reason for her being fired had been kept secret from the students.

Emma went about every day in her introversion, walking all over campus and downtown, participating when necessary, and looking forward to getting a job and teaching the literature she loved. She had isolated herself from the news of Vietnam, assassinations, protest marches, and violence. Her private war was all she could handle. If the college were bombed, so be it. It was in God's hands.

CHAPTER VIII: INTO THE WORLD OF WORK

It took three years and three summers for Emma to complete her degree with a double major of English and history. The last semester was taken up completely with student teaching and a one-night a week course to support the student teaching experience. To save a move, Emma requested a school close to the college. She had not purchased a car but had saved a thousand dollars for that purpose, knowing she would not be able to walk to work or have the conveniences of the campus. The assignment came in a memorandum from the English Office. She would report to North East High School on January 4, 1970, a rural school near a crossroads community, one with a good reputation. This was good news. The school was twenty miles from her dorm. She could drive every day.

The supervising teacher, Mrs. Turner, turned out to be a sophisticated veteran about fifty years old, attractive, with a reputation of ruling with an iron hand. She had all the college-bound students, plus drama. Emma was to observe and work on lesson plans for two weeks. She sat at a long table at the back of the large classroom, facing the backs of the students. One morning Mrs. Turner brought roses from her garden and handed the prettiest one to Emma. "Take this down to Mr. Whitman and tell him it is from Mrs. Turner." Amused, Emma obeyed, finding the principal likewise amused at the gift. When she returned to her table, she saw that Mrs. Turner had placed a silver tray filled with water and floating red camellia blossoms on the table.

There were no discipline problems in the large English classes, only a few whiners complaining about the work load of research papers, readings, and many grammar exercises. Mrs. Turner had thirty years' experience, had no children, and had devoted her life to her work. No one questioned her authority, for she had taught many of the students' parents. Her glory came from the high success of those who went off to college and from her drama productions, only the most talented students being allowed in the small drama class.

When Emma took over three English classes, she encountered no problem except for keeping up with the grueling preparation and grading papers of eighty-three students. The two morning classes were almost all strong students who took notes, answered questions, and asked few. Emma had not learned to handle discussion, but there was little time for that anyway. They were used to Mrs. Turner's knowing everything they needed to know. The afternoon class, however, was different. They were tired after lunch and not in the mood for John Donne or writing essays about the meaning of sonnets. Still, there were no serious problems. Only a few trying moments erupted.

One day as Emma was writing on the board and turned to the class, several students were snickering. By then, the afternoons were hot, their classroom facing the west. The large windows that took up the west side of the room were raised as high as they would go. Nonetheless, the students were lethargic, a few defiant, counting the days until graduation. Emma felt that the snickering had something to do with her because every time she turned around to write on the board and turned back, the snickering grew more pronounced. Finally a girl took pity on her and said, "I think your dress is pulled up in the back."

Emma had worn a dress with a straight skirt made of material that clung to her slip and made it roll up, so to prevent the rolling she had pinned the slip to the dress and unknowingly caught the hem of the dress such that one could see the hiked up section, pin, slip, and her thighs when she turned to the board. She froze, trying to pretend nothing was funny at all. Then, assigning the class to read the next sonnet, said, "I will be right back." The problem was easy enough to solve in the ladies room. She simply removed the pin, unleashing the wayward slip to roll and stick to the thin dress. The day was almost over.

When she returned to the class and started going over the Milton sonnet, one of the defiant students who knew he would not go to college but take over his father's large farm spoke up. "You think you're so smart. What does that word mean, that pamphlet that Milton wrote?"

"You mean *Areopagitica*? It was a defense of freedom of the press." The answer rolled off her tongue like fine wine from its bottle. Emma had expected someone to ask her about that work and had practiced the pronunciation the night before. The boy, undaunted, just turned his head as if he'd never asked. He inspired a couple of buddies to exhibit restlessness, roll their eyes, and make expressions that said, "Nobody will ever need to know this crap." Other than the mild revolution among the males, the only other derision came from a sweet girl who just could never make an A on an essay, no matter how hard she tried. Her sweetness soured, and she gave up, convinced Emma had labeled her a B student.

When the college supervisor came to observe and grade Emma, the only fault she found was that Emma said "okay" too much. On the second visit, it was her voice that was too soft. However, the final observation awarded her an A for the course, reporting that the class was "well behaved and would not give anyone trouble." What a masterful stroke of damning with faint praise.

After graduation, Emma began looking for a job by making appointments with principals in the towns surrounding the college, not wanting to move back home. Helen had moved into town, Martha was off in nursing school and was talking about getting married to a medical intern, and her Aunt Ophelia had moved into Miss Ila's house and rented out hers. There was nothing to go back to any more.

The second principal who interviewed Emma offered her a job for the next fall. She would have juniors and seniors. She also asked about teaching summer school because she needed the money and was eager to get started working. Although she did not expect to get the summer work, she did. Summer school for the entire county was offered only at the school where she would work in the fall. There was only a week and a half to find somewhere to live and prepare for the summer school, which would last six weeks of the three-month vacation. She began looking for apartments and shopping for a few outfits. In Belk-Tyler's department store, Emma ran into Frances, who told her that Jarret had taken a job as band and choir director at the same school where Emma would be and that he had taken a room in a house owned by a lady who rented only to teachers. In fact, the house was called The Teacherage. Emma called as soon as she could get to a phone booth. "Yes," the owner, Mrs. Camden, said, "I have one room left. Would you like to come now and see it?"

The house was within walking distance of the school, across the road from the school grounds, yet hidden by a border of tall cedar trees. It seemed perfect. Emma paid a deposit and the first month's rent. Besides Emma and Jarret, there was a third boarder, young black female, another English teacher, although neither was there when Emma arrived. All the teachers' rooms were upstairs. There were one bathroom and a large linen closet in addition to the three bedrooms. Emma's room was beside Jarret's and was the smallest of the three. The teachers could use the kitchen and parlor on the first floor as well as the garden and patio in the back yard, which was enclosed with a high white wooden fence.

Emma had the upstairs to herself during summer school, the other teachers not planning to move in until late July. There was only one other teacher teaching English to the students who had failed, a Mrs. Philyaw, who had one year's experience to her credit. The principal told Emma to seek advice from Mrs. Philyaw, but the only thing she taught Emma was that an ice cream cone from the Tastee Freeze made a cool lunch.

Emma's summer class comprised twenty students who had failed junior English, a captured group from eight until noon Monday through Friday. To her surprise, Emma had no curriculum to follow. She was on her own to do whatever she could in six weeks to make up for nine months of failure. The first day she arrived an hour early and began looking for materials, having a plan already to get her through the first day. The principal had told her the classroom would not be available until the first day because the janitors were moving books, and he did not know which room she would have. Feeling a bit panicky but sure the principal was looking out for the students and for her, Emma knew she would just have to work hard to get grounded.

When she arrived, the door was locked. At seven thirty, the principal appeared, key in hand, with a demeanor that said "Relax, the year's over. These kids don't care if you don't get started until tomorrow or the next day or the day after that." But relaxing was not Emma's style. Without materials—books and workbooks and copies of exercises—what would she do for four hours? Do without, she did, writing sentences on the board for students to correct, assigning an essay, reading the essays during break, and giving feedback after break. On the second day, she had books ready and stacks of exercises. Only Joe, a football player with red hair and ruddy face, who announced he hated English, was loquacious. He gave Emma a hard time, questioning everything she said and asking why she was assigning homework for summer school. So on Friday when she returned to her desk after break and found a bottle of coke, cap off, she did not know what to do. She just put it on the corner of the desk. Finally, Joe said, "It's for you! I put it there!" Noticing several students watching and snickering, Emma was afraid to drink it, thinking he may have put something in it. Later she noticed the boy was quiet for the next hour. Maybe his feelings were hurt, yet she could easily envision him spitting in the drink or worse.

The summer school experience was not rewarding or enjoyable; it was rather a daily grinding challenge, but a doable grind with only a few instances of disrespect. For the most part, the students were beaten down by their home environment and a school system that could not meet their needs.

During the last of July and first of August, the three new teachers renting the upstairs rooms from Mrs. Camden met on Wednesday afternoon two weeks before the first day of school. The black teacher, Eudora Grimes, who wanted to be called Dora, was a beautiful, young, tall, and slender woman from a nearby farming community. Attractive, healthy, competent in subject matter, the three had much in common and were ready to make all their students lovers of music and literature. Yet, even before school started, they established a pattern that kept them apart. Jarret came in late every night, long after the women had gone to bed. Dora ate dinner almost every night with her mother, coming in usually about seven or eight and going directly to her room and staying there with the door closed. Emma sometimes visited Mrs. Camden in the kitchen or parlor before going up to her room, but because the old lady was nearly deaf even with her hearing aids, it was hard work to communicate with her. Even so, it was a treat to get a piece of baked corn bread or an apple jack from her oven.

The first day of school Emma had thought she was well prepared, and even though nervous, was ready for the challenge. Being one of the two new members of the English department, Emma received one of the least desirable rooms and schedules. Her classroom was packed with five horizontal rows of individual tables with chairs aligned with no space between with room only at one end of a row for students to walk to their desk tables. Nothing decorated the walls other than a small bulletin board stripped of whatever it held the previous year and two large blackboards on the front wall. The teacher's small wooden desk sat in the front corner in front of the boards, facing the five rows of tables, each row containing seven desks.

Every teacher had a homeroom class for the first twenty minutes of the day. Emma's being a ninth grade group, she would keep the same students for four years until they graduated so that she could maintain their files throughout their high school years. The rest of the morning until lunch was taken up with four of her six periods, all fifty minutes long: first period, seniors; second, seniors; third a study hall of juniors; and fourth juniors. Emma had second lunch from noon until one o'clock. The two after-noon classes were fifth period, seniors and sixth period, juniors. Each group grew progressively louder as the students' body clocks ran from still sleepy to hungry to tired of sitting and hearing the noise of a teacher to it's-time-to-get-out-of-this-jail.

The three cups of black coffee before school did not provide the brain stimulation Emma needed to think by two-thirty when the last class dwindled in, pushing, laughing, and hollering at each other.

Emma was aware that it was the first year of total integration, the schools having consolidated and changed names. But it was beyond her comprehension that school as she had known it only four years before was gone forever. Even her student teaching school had been much like her own school, but she had not realized that the situation assigned to her was a utopia compared to what might have been the situation of a new teacher in that school. Yes, that made sense: give the new, naïve, idealistic teacher the worst groups, the worst classroom, and the worst schedule because she has no seniority and does not deserve any better. Then if she survives, she will be a hell of a lot better for the experience.

Students wandered through the halls after the last bell as if the last bell meant nothing of consequence. The principal, Mr. Franks, was constantly on the intercom, telling students and teachers what to do and not to do. It soon became apparent that the students felt displaced; they felt no ownership, no more than Emma felt herself. Students and their families were angry about having the names of their schools changed from the name of a person they had honored to a name that gave the location in the county. They lost their mascots, their school colors, their unique cultural events: they had been stripped of their pride and identity. Emma's understanding of the reasons for the lack of respect by the students did not render the situation any less difficult to deal with.

When Emma was in high school, there had been one token black student who started with her ninth-grade class in 1962, a quiet, intelligent girl, whom everyone assumed had been forced

by her parents and community to attend the white school. She
had seemed lonely and sad, always walking by herself at lunch.
One day when Emma was with her two lunch companions on
their way back to class ahead of the group lagging until the last
bell, Emma had gone over to the black girl standing by the
balcony wall looking out into the yard and had said hello—period
—to which the girl turned, smiled and said hello—end of
conversation. Emma and her friends went on to class. What
would the students say if she tried to be friends with the black
girl? The girl lasted only a few months before she disappeared
from the school. There was never another black student in the
school for remainder of her high school years.

But what about the white students Emma found sitting in her
class now. Had they been there when she was a student and she
just had not seen them? Had the Vietnam War that she had
ignored changed students so that they did not care about
authority, rules, and manners? Emma knew when she left high
school the boys had not let their hair grow to their shoulders or
down their backs or worn pony tails. There had been few hippies
on her college campus and even fewer blacks. She had seen the
Afro hairstyle only on television, but in her classes now most of
the black students wore tall Afros, some with large picks stuck in
the top.

In the first class a tall, pale, skinny white senior with long
black hair sat on the first row close to where Emma would stand
before the class, and beside him sat a deformed-looking white
boy with short hair and red flakey patches on his face. He turned
to speak to the long-haired boy, muttering something unintelli-
gible. The long-haired boy responded, "Thomas, you have bad
breath." Emma decided to put students in alphabetical order, a
process that took much longer than it should because some
students said they were someone else. Three boys came in late,

saying they drove a bus and had a second route to the elementary. Nothing had been said to Emma about consequences for tardiness or misbehavior. She knew in her time students were sent to the principal's office for serious offenses. She assumed she would learn the rules in the next meeting. Meanwhile she must prove herself and not start sending students to the office the first day. Someone had told her to be very strict at the beginning, so she stuck to that advice, succeeding in finally getting a lesson started with only whispering and smirks and distractions in the back. If she turned her back, students talked instead of copying the information on the board. Still the situation with thirty-three, lowest level of three levels, was under control. Some could not see the board; others could not read Emma's writing. Several broke their pencils and asked to sharpen them. Emma gave them pens she had brought and told the class to write in ink. "Ink!" They almost all said in unison. Why did they have to write in ink?

Just as Emma was about to explain, the principal came on the intercom right in the middle of the period. Without apologizing, he started announcing changes in the upcoming welcoming event, referencing white students' and black students' former school names and reminding them that the new school's name, North West, was better because it did not honor a single person. "We want to get away from names honoring people and move to geographical names." The more Mr. Franklin said the farther his foot went into his mouth. North West had previously been named for a black citizen. Emma noticed, Antonio, an alert black student wearing glasses on the second row, looking around, then standing up and moving toward the door. The principal was still talking, now explaining he did not mean leaders should not be honored. Emma had heard that there might be walk-outs and was afraid to attempt to block the black students who all walked out following Antonio. Soon could be heard the heavy, brisk steps of the principal and more students walking down the hall and the outside doors opening. Meanwhile the white students were happy that class was interrupted and they too started wandering around the halls.

The intercom came on again. "Students and teachers, this is a very sensitive time when remarks can easily be misunderstood. I will meet with the walk-out students in the front of the school with some of their parents who are coming in. Students not participating in the walk-out should go to class when the bell rings, which I will manually ring in five minutes to begin second period. Two students were still in the classroom, a stringy blonde, pock-marked girl who wore a white maternity blouse and appeared to be five or six months pregnant. "This is ridiculous," she said. "We had walk-outs about every day at the end of school last year, so I brought romance novels to read." The girl turned to look behind her when she heard a snicker. The other student left on the back row was a muscular black male who had come in late. He had a large pick stuck in his hair and promptly put his head down and slept, not hearing the end of class bell.

"Class is over, Frederick," Emma said, bending over to speak in his ear. "You need to go to second period now on the next bell. Get some sleep at home so you can participate tomorrow."

"I sleep in all my classes except band. I work late into the night."

"Doing what?"

"I catch chickens to be loaded up on the big trucks."

"Well, I expect you to do your work like everyone else." Emma thought Frederick had a quick imagination to invent such a story on the spot, but when he bent over to get his books out of his desk, Emma saw fuzzy white feathers in his hair."

Emma found the blonde's name on the roll. "Sally, let me

know if I can help you with your work. Be sure to bring some loose-leaf paper, a black ink pen, and your books tomorrow." She had noticed the girl had nothing with her except a large pocketbook with a paperback stuffed in the top.

During the five-minute break, Emma ran into Dora in the teachers' restroom.

"How does Frederick Whitfield get away with sleeping in every class? Do you know him?"

"Everyone knows Frederick," she said. "He's twenty-two and has a reputation for cutting people who bother him with a knife. He will graduate this year. Lucky you. I'm glad you got him instead of me."

"He won't graduate unless he does the work," Emma declared. Dora smiled and pushed open the restroom door.

Second period seniors were more alert, some showing a desire to do the work; only a few were purposely obnoxious. Three pretty, well-mannered black girls sat together in the middle of the room, dressed as if going to church. A fiery red-haired, wiry boy on the front row mumbled under his breath, just low enough that Emma could not hear but loud enough to keep the neighboring black male smiling and giggling. Finally Emma reprimanded Gary, the mumbler, who exclaimed self-righteously that he had done nothing. The next day the principal told Emma that Gary had come to tell him that she singled him out for misbehaving but never said a word to the black students. "Well, I'm sure he said that as a defense mechanism," she said.

"I'm sure he did," the principal responded, in a tone that seemed indicting to Emma. However, he left without further comment.

Then, in third period, when a cute, short, sandy-haired white boy used an expletive in class, Emma told him to get out of class. She was so angry and shocked that it did not matter what the rule was. No one had told her the rules anyway. Shortly the principal appeared asking Emma what the student had said, and she told him indirectly, not wanting to say the word. He told her that this time he would keep the boy in his office but that students got two warnings before a third offense of being sent to the office. At least she had made an impression on the class with her action, and hopefully news would spread.

Third and fourth periods went by fast, the students becoming progressively louder as the hours passed. By this time, students could not be still, especially the boys. It was as if they could not control the tapping of the desks with their fingers or the twitching of their necks. The girls could not stop rummaging through their purses. Emma told one girl to put away fingernail polish to which she said indignantly, "I've got a run in my hose I have to stop." Most of the white girls had long hair which every five seconds they flipped behind their ears and then back in front of their ears. They thought nothing of combing their hair or putting it up in a ponytail during class lecture or certainly they considered it fine to primp during class work. Thus, to Emma's surprise and disillusionment, she spent more than half her time correcting behavior.

By the time she got a class settled, called the roll, tried to learn the names—a daunting task with three Karens, plus Caryn, Karin, and Carin, all pronounced the same, with three having the last name Smith in one class—half the class was over. When on the third day of class, Emma still did not know a black student's name, he said, "Well, you know we all look the same." The same student told Emma he was disappointed in her for not walking out the first day to support the black students.

Whatever happened, Emma believed she must handle it herself from now on. Her main weapon was a highly structured lesson plan with more planned than could possibly be done in fifty minutes. Fifty minutes went by so quickly that by the time she had finally gotten the students focused, it was ten minutes before the end of class, a signal to students to sign off and start packing up. Gradually Emma got the students in the habit of following rules she now knew she should have given out the first day in writing. Yet when she finally did get time to type up rules and directions, she found the papers she had handed out on the floor or wadded into a ball and left in the desk.

The key to achieving anything close to a lesson was reading everything aloud in class. Yet this technique did not work for the last period, a low group who acted as if no one had been expecting anything from them, so why start now? They were juniors, tired, ready to go home, and offended by being expected to read or listen. Nothing worked to keep the group settled and quiet. An older male teacher said to Emma, "Sometimes you have to holler at these students." The next day deciding to take his advice, she did holler at the students to be quiet. They stopped talking and looked up for three seconds as if they were hoping someone had stuck her behind with a needle and then seeing she was just hollering at them, started talking again. There was no one in this class who could read aloud, so Emma had to read everything they studied. During tests, students, having not even elbow room, had no problem comparing answers and copying. Keeping one's eyes on one's paper and using a cover sheet was as important to them as swatting a fly on one's desk. As one student who received a zero when Emma caught him cheating said, "It's only a grade." And Emma knew he meant a zero was nothing compared to not getting a soda after school. The students had been passed every year for warming the seats.

The third week Emma had lunchroom duty and the fourth week hall duty, duties that were scheduled for one week of every month. Before her duty week came up, she spent the first ten minutes in the lounge eating and the next twenty minutes making copies, putting notes on the board, and looking over her plans. Lunchroom duty, according to the principal meant staying in the cafeteria all period, looking for students throwing food or fighting and picking up paper on the floor as well as emptying any trays left on the tables. Emma did not mind the tasks as much as the noise and smell of food. Some of the T-shirts she felt were obscene, such as "Don't mistake me for someone who gives a Sh__," a boy was wearing, or one a girl wore with a lollipop on the front with the words: "Want a lick."

The fourth week's hall duty made Emma feel like a policeman, a role she abhorred. To prevent students from walking the halls during their lunch time but to give them access to the restrooms at the end of the halls next to the outside doors, wooden gates had been erected, which she must lock at the beginning of lunch and unlock at the end of lunch. Meanwhile as the hall monitor, she was expected to stand in the halls throughout lunch; hence, there was no time to eat.

One day when Emma thought she had made some progress in the hellish last period class, Mrs. Murphy, a veteran teacher, asked her in the hall just before the last class to switch rooms with her because her room did not have a pull down screen. Emma agreed and entered her class room with the intention of telling the students to go to Mrs. Murphy's room. When she walked in, the students were laughing, one in particular smiling as if he had just hidden a copperhead in the teacher's desk drawer. Then she saw her desk splattered with broken eggs that dripped onto the students' desks on the first row. The student who must be the culprit had been the most devious, smart-assed white boy in all the classes. Emma, too shocked to respond, told the students to move to Mrs. Murphy's class, and as she turned, books in hand, to go out, she met Mrs. Murphy at the door.

"This is just for today," she said to Emma, "and I'll tell any of your students who come in to go to my room."

Emma wanted to burst into tears and walk out of the building and drive away. But something made her go to Mrs. Murphy's room and somehow held the class until the bell. No student mentioned the eggs, and neither did she. What irony and what a disappointment for whoever broke the eggs. It was Mrs. Murphy who had to deal with the scene. When Emma returned to her room after the dismissal bell, she dreaded walking in, knowing she had to clean up her desk and wondering what Mrs. Murphy had thought. Someone had wiped the floor, her desk, and the two student desks, leaving a now dried, sticky glaze of egg whites with clumps of yellow yolk. Emma found several rags in her desk drawer, went to the restroom to wet them, and returned to scrub the mess. She threw the rags in the trash, gathered her books, and walked out of the building. By now most students and teachers were gone.

She had walked to school that day and was glad to be alone for she could not hold back any longer. She burst into tears, sobbing as if someone had broken her heart, the way she cried when her father died. Maybe she wasn't going to make it. Emma had to walk past the middle school parking lot to get to the Teacherage, and as she approached the large parking lot in front of the school, she saw a man in a suit and tie, walking toward her. Not wanting to meet anyone, knowing her face was red and streaked with black mascara, she walked briskly to a foot path students had made between the border cedars, a shortcut that led to a store, where they bought drinks and candy at lunch.

The worn path led a few yards to the edge of the campus and then through a field of corn. Emma paused at the sight of the dried corn stalks, beige, burdened with heavy shucks bursting with golden kernels on red cobs, graced with tangles of morning glories, still open as if waiting for Emma, lifting their purple, pink, white, and cornflower blue heads. What was that poem by Cummings about nature making perfect a scene and the Bible verse that said Solomon in all his glory was not arrayed as one of these. She remembered when she was a child and young teenager asking God to show her a sign. The field was like a Monet painting. Surely it was a sign. She cried again. "God, help me," she prayed.

"Hello, hello there," a man's voice called from Emma's back. She turned to see Professor Di Yanni. She dabbed her eyes with a handful of wadded Kleenexes from her purse and was speechless.

"Emma, is that you? I thought I recognized you before you turned off the sidewalk. What is the matter?" he said smiling in his way that made her feel he had never had a failure.

"Professor Di Yanni! Where did you come from? I saw someone but had not the foggiest notion it was you?"

"I'm here to meet with some department heads and central office coordinators about changes in the music programs for middle and high schools. It starts in fifteen minutes, but I just had to see if it was you I saw. You look as if something has done a good job of upsetting you. Can you tell me what it is?"

"Just some students that seem to be sent from hell. I'm tired of working every night and weekend and then not being able to teach because of some students who have no manners, no desire to learn, and seemingly only want to keep everyone else from learning anything."

"Sit here a minute," he said, seating himself on the trunk of a fallen tree beside the path at the edge of the field. She sat facing him. His face looked like that of an old man in the afternoon sun even though he could not be more than fifty-five. "Don't you have some good students?"

"No, well, in homeroom, I do. This year, I have the lowest

groups. But, yes, in homeroom, I have a mature girl who keeps roll and reminds me of what the bulletin says we have to do. There are some other good people in there but I don't teach them; they're ninth graders. There are some good people too in my classes but not good students. I can't give the sweet, quiet ones any attention for the few that are obnoxious and loud."

"When I look at you, I see a smart, determined, healthy, strong young woman, well dressed, well mannered, commanding a presence. Try to remember that you are older and more mature than the children you are working with. Next year you will have better groups. You cannot let the hellraisers win. When they see they cannot drive you away, they will get tired of trying. But you must respect them all. Some are dealing with horrendous home situations. Of course, that is not your fault. Think of one each day whom you have helped, one student who has a better chance because of your attention and care and teaching."

"It will be hard to find one every day. It's true that it is like a war to see if they can get rid of me." The image of a nervous boy with a speech impediment who brought her a black red rose from his mother's garden came to her mind. And there was the plain, bumpy faced Irene, whose mother was a maid at the school. Irene had told Emma that her mother said her English teacher was the hardest working teacher at the school and that she better not hear of Irene misbehaving or not doing her work. To quote her mother to Emma was the highest compliment Irene was capable of giving. "Yes, there are two or three students that I would beg, borrow, or steal for."

"Try to find one everyday, even the same one will do. By the way, I stopped by the Teacherage, thinking you would be home, and I left a package for you at the Teacherage. Be sure to get it— and I think it is something you can use tonight and share with a friend. You do have friends there?"

"Yes, a couple, but we don't share much."

"Well, promise me you will share my gift. I need to hurry now to the meeting! I will be checking on you! Remember, you ain't going nowhere! That would ensure their victory over you!"

Emma managed to smile as the professor hastened towards the high school.

She walked back to the street and was home in five minutes, stopping to look in on Mrs. Camden, who stood by the table rolling dough for apple jacks. "Did someone leave a package for me?"

Mrs. Camden looked up, adjusted her hearing aid and asked Emma what she said, then understanding at the same time, said, "Oh, I haven't seen anyone." But when Emma went upstairs, she saw it outside her room door, a decorative yellow bag with handles stuffed with purple paper. It was a bottle of red wine labeled Doudet Naudin Chambolle Musigny, 1966." That was the year she graduated from high school. There was also a handwritten note that read: "This is a special wine to be drunk, along with a large salad and dark chocolate, and to be shared with a friend after you have done your lesson plans for the next day and graded all your papers! Hope you enjoy it! Dr. Di Yanni" The last thing Emma felt like doing was sharing her day with a friend. Besides she had none. She put the bag in her closet.

Emma had not mingled much with the other two teachers staying in the Teacherage. By the time Thanksgiving approached, Emma had seen Dora with students, usually white, outside her classroom door, talking with them about their behavior. There were also rumors among the students that Jarret was gay. The rules of the game seemed to be to contain one's own classes. The administration and even veteran teachers battled the unrest among students forced to leave their community for the sake of integration, of students smoking marijuana instead of tobacco in the smoking areas and bathrooms. Certain students came into Emma's class everyday smelling of the sweet weed, looking spaced out, and either talking nonsense or immediately going to sleep. At first she had been outraged that students slept in class and tried to stop them, an effort she soon relinquished, realizing that when troublemakers slept, she could do more teaching to those awake. Besides, there was nowhere to send them. She never woke them and at least got some revenge when often they would not hear the bell and woke up to the laughter of the next class, embarrassed and fuzzy headed. Once a girl who wore a wig fell asleep and woke up when a fat boy leaving the class jerked off her wig, arousing her into a spitting fury.

Once in a while a day would pass when only one student said one unkind thing, and yet, Emma took it to heart, such as the morning she had done a good job with the lesson, saying at the end that everyone has a talent and that she was still looking for hers.

"Yours is Teaching," said Janice on the front row, setting off a boy behind her to grimace at the absurdity of that remark. It became a daily catharsis to cry after school, to visit the local bookstore to pick out a card for her mother or sister, to gain strength from her youth, to feel the spring in her booted feet, to breathe deeply and walk faster as she passed old people hobbling along or slowly shuffling their feet.

At Thanksgiving, Emma accepted an invitation from Aunt Ophelia and Uncle Milton, her mother having gone to visit her new husband's family and her sister spending the holiday with her boyfriend's family. They ate in the kitchen where The Last Supper hung high and dominant, the table laden with turkey stuffed with homemade dressing, creamed potatoes, corn, lima beans, and fried corn bread. The only company besides Emma was her aunt and uncle's grandchildren, who were in elementary grades. Most of the banter centered on the children, but the attention turned briefly to Emma. Her aunt wanted to know about her job. Emma shared the good things she could think of. "Do you have any colored students?" her aunt asked.

"Yes, I do have some." Emma did not say half.

"I can't believe what the world's come to," her aunt sighed.

"Some people will do anything for money," Uncle Milton said instinctively as if Emma was not in the group of humanity.

Stunned and hurt, Emma said nothing. The children, busy eating chocolate pie, listened. At five- and seven-years-old, they were getting lessons, the same lessons her students had been taught. One of her black students had said in class one day that her mother had once said she wished all white people could be put in a pit and burned but that her mother didn't feel that way anymore. But, for Emma, the only goal was to make all the students behave and pay attention and want to learn. She had gone into teaching because of her love of the language and literature, but had found that that love had almost nothing to do with reaching the students.

Monday morning after Thanksgiving the bulletin announced an assembly to be held at nine o'clock. Emma was busy during homeroom having students fill out forms due back to the office before first period, and later when a trusted girl in first period interrupted the lesson to remind Emma of the assembly at eight-thirty, Emma said she thought it was at nine. No, the assembly was at eight-thirty agreed a group of the students who usually kept on top of important things like assemblies. Falling for the dupe, Emma stopped the lesson and led the class to the gym. When the first students poked their heads in the door, they encountered the principal, who turned them around with vicious venom, "It's not until nine o'clock. Those damned stupid teachers." Emma heard the remark as the students coming out the door faced her. "I didn't know principals could talk to teachers like that," said one boy, a rare specimen of manners. Unnerved by the episode, Emma took the students back to the classroom and held them until nine o'clock when once again they sauntered out. It was too early in the day to cry.

It seemed an eternity from Thanksgiving to Christmas. Students became more and more restless. Emma bought a collection of Christmas plays and typed several on her manual Royal elite typewriter on the weekends. Plays sometimes had the power to bewitch students to listen as the few good readers read aloud, taking on several characters at times. One day the principal came in and motioned Emma to the hall. She told the readers to keep going. Mr. Franklin wanted to know if Emma had made an assignment of writing a suicide note. No, she had not. Stunned, she tried hard to think if she had done such a stupid thing. She had resource books that described even more bizarre creative assignments to get students to write. A student named Boyce Davis had left a suicide note in his room at home, and when his mother found it, he told her it was an English assignment from Miss Applewhite's class. "No, that student is not even in my class," Emma told the principal, breathing again, sure she was not guilty.

The last week before Christmas break Emma accomplished nothing academic in classes, holding wards for pent-up energy. The students had signed off, waiting for Wednesday, December 18, their last day. Third period was about to begin, Emma standing at the lectern, ready to check the roll, most of the students seated, when Sally Hendricks, whose baby was due, entered with a paper in her hand, handing it to Emma, without speaking. It was a withdrawal from school report, listing end-of-term grades, including a sixty in English. Sally had done no work, and Emma had not begged her to do her work. Sally had sat, making no trouble, talking a little to those beside her, her body language as an unwed expectant mother saying poor pitiful me will pass because teachers feel sorry for me. Only once had Emma gone out of her way to coax the girl to do her work. Sally was the least of her problems when there was Carl, who was on drugs, and lay down on the carpet in the back of the room about half way through the class Sally was in. Emma signed beside the grade of sixty for her class and handed the paper to Sally, who snatched it, suddenly showing more life than she had in four months. "You God damn bitch!" she said, and walked out. Emma looked up into the staring eyes of an effeminate little boy who sat in front of the lectern. Neither said anything. Emma breathed deeply as the last bell for class rang and started calling the roll.

The rest of the day passed with the inevitable recursive path forward until the end of the day when thirty minutes before the bell, students started laughing and looking toward the back. Carl once again was curled in a fetal position, asleep on the carpet, his long, stringy brown hair across his face. This time Emma went to get the principal, and of course, when they returned he was up, red eyed, with a halo glow on his face. "I think you were over reacting," Mr. Franklin told Emma in the hall.

After school, Emma had to pick up a certified letter from the post office and happened to get behind the bus that let off Carl. There he was, wide awake now, jumping from the bus and swinging his arms as he walked with his sisters to his house just three miles from school. Suddenly, adrenalin flowing, Emma turned into the driveway and saw Carl looking at her, pale and rabbit-eyed. He disappeared inside. The front wooden door stood open to the glass storm door. Not seeing a door bell, Emma knocked on the door, not peering in, although she could hear a television. A woman said, "Come in." As Emma pulled open the door, she saw a small, wiry woman sitting up from her reclined position on the sofa. A soap opera played out on the television in front of the woman.

"I'm Carl's English teacher, Emma Applewhite. Are you Carl's mother?"

"Yes." The woman looked a bit startled and frazzled.

"I have been wanting to talk with you, and when I saw him get off the bus just now, I thought I should stop. I have been having a problem with Carl not doing his work and sleeping in class. Almost every day he lies down on the floor and sleeps for the last thirty minutes of class. So I wanted to see if you could help me with this situation."

"You have my sympathy," the mother said strongly. "His father is in Germany, and I can't do a thing with him."

Emma couldn't believe what she was hearing. There was nothing else to say.

Carl had won again. She excused herself and left. More than anything else she felt naïve. There was no fix beyond her wits. No one wanted to be bothered. It was her job to take care of her students. She was a babysitter, policeman, psychologist, and psychiatrist. No one asked what students were learning. The principal was too steeped in racial issues to worry about a white boy asleep on the floor. Just the day before he and the football coach were drawn into a fight between players after a game.

The next day, Emma walked the half mile to the Teacherage. She had just started out, a book bag in each hand, when Jarrett called out to her from behind. "Hey, you don't really take all that work home and actually do it every night, do you?" She turned and glared at him. His smile changed to mock her indicting frown, and she knew he was teasing. "I sure as heck do out of necessity to survive since I lack the talent of those like you whose art can be hammered out. I'm sure your drummers think of me each time they beat!"

"Why so touchy? It's not as bad as all that, is it?"

"I'm sorry. That was rude. I just get tired of hearing students say the only class they enjoy is music."

"Sure they love the music, and for those who are talented, it gives them an identity. Well, even for those who are not talented. It gives them an identity. Everybody has to have a niche where they are successful, and most of my students are lousy in academics."

"I'm envious."

"Don't be. Trying to get them ready to perform is like training animals for a circus act, except for a few who really love music. It would be ideal if we never had to be heard and seen outside the classroom. Have a nice survival day."

Emma smiled and walked into the building. It was a test day. Besides the usual attempts at cheating, and Emma knew who to watch by now, there were no incidents to speak of. By four-thirty, she was ready to leave, having made copies of handouts for five classes for the next day. She started on the walk back to the Teacherage. It would be a typical night grading papers and recording them in the gradebook.

"Hey, Emma, you're really tired, aren't you? You're walking slumped. Stand up straight!" Jarret was not close behind her but yelled out loud enough for the neighborhood to hear. He ran to catch up with her. "Don't let the bad apples get to you. You have to roll with the punches. They have just had no one to model respect to them, not for themselves, let alone others. Remember, they do not think teachers are human. They are in the me stage, still babies, but with the body of adults."

"How did you get to be so wise?" Jarret's wisdom did not make Emma feel better.

"I know who I am and I know who they are. I like myself better. I don't take what students say personally as you seem to do."

"Good for you, Jarret. We all cannot be as wise and mature as you are."

They had reached the Teacherage. Emma went inside, and Jarret went to his car. The house was quiet, Mrs. Camden having gone out and Dora not in yet. Her goal was to force herself to get ready for the next day by seven-thirty. She had three hours.

Unloading the book bags, sorting the rubber-banded stacks of papers into five piles, one for each class. Emma felt the task unbearable. She was tired. The energy she had left should be put into a new lesson, not marking up yesterday's assignment, but if it was not graded, the students wouldn't do the next day's work. She would lose any credibility she had been building. A cup of vanilla almond coffee would get her through, along with the classical music on the radio. Mrs. Camden would not mind if she brewed a pot of coffee. She had offered Emma and the others the use of the kitchen and her special teas and coffees.

Armed with a perfect shade of purple felt-tip pen, instead of red, her brain charged with Irish cream coffee and soothed simultaneously with Mozart, she read and marked first-period's twenty-seven essays. That took two hours. There were four more stacks and still tomorrow's plan. The coffee was making Emma sick without food, but if she ate, her brain would die for the day. She went downstairs to brew another small pot. This time she would add plenty of milk. This was the fourth cup, first of the second pot. As she climbed the stairs once more, she thought of what to do: she could record the remaining essays as homework with a check for 100 for completeness, a lower grade if not complete, or a zero if not turned in. Homework counted twenty percent of the course. She had indicated the essays would be marked, but it was only Tuesday; she would have more stacks to grade. There were always more stacks to grade. Recording the remaining papers took thirty minutes. Now there was an hour to do a plan. The topic was already determined, a continuation of *Macbeth* with the seniors and *Julius Caesar* with the juniors. The first step was to read the pages to be covered and make notes in the margin of the texts. That done, Emma looked at the clock on the radio: it was seven forty-five p.m. What could she do besides another writing assignment? Perhaps the library at the college would allow her to check out films on the plays. Students made fun of the film strips in the school's collection.

Even though she knew she should not walk, she needed the exercise to relieve the built up stress. It took twenty minutes to get to the front door of the library, the windows on all floors brightly beckoning passersby. What a haven the building was to her. She had not known how safe she had been here among books that were like friends, her favorite cubicle, beside the stack where Melville's captain Ahab slept. Nothing seemed to have changed since Emma left. Students lingered outside smoking and talking. It was exam time. Inside, Emma sought out the media resource librarian she knew well. Mrs. Lawhorn, glad to see Emma again, asked her about her job as they walked to the section where the films were housed.

The trip was not in vain: films on both plays were in, and Emma could have them for three days. She could finish the week before the holiday break with the films. Her treasure under her arm, thinking ahead to reviewing the plays in January and then testing, Emma thanked Mrs. Lawhorn, and turning quickly to head out, bumped into someone, the film canisters hitting the carpet with two thuds. At the same time she realized she was jittery, not having eaten all day and having drunk nothing but coffee and coke, she also heard a familiar voice say, "Excuse me. Are you all right?" Then she stood up to face Professor Di Yanni.

"Emma, I should have known it was you!" They both laughed. "How in the world are you anyhow? You look thin."

"I have not eaten today. I think that's why I am a klutz."

"Well, I was just on my way to get a sandwich at the coffee shop. Let's go sit and chat for a few minutes."

"Sure. I would like to get a bite before heading home."

"Are you all right? You seem quite tense."

"Just tired," Emma's voice quivered and then the tears rolled just as they had years before when the professor had noticed that she was troubled and had been kind. As before, she turned her head as they walked the short distance to the shop. The professor said nothing until he opened the door.

"Well, something smells good like baked bread. What will you have?"

"Let me order. You have bought me too many dinners." He did not protest but let her in front of him.

"Just coffee, I think, after all. I'm on a diet," said the professor.

As they sat, Emma eating her usual grilled cheese, she relaxed, smiling and waving to a group of old classmates passing by the window.

"So you are just tired, you say? Are you up late?" The professor asked.

"Yes, usually midnight. That's when my mind seems to be fully alert. Then at six-thirty in the morning, I'm dead, like a truck has run over me."

"I believe if you can hold out this year next year will be better. You'll know the tricks of the trade, as they say, and will get some of the better students. You won't be the one with no experience or seniority. Teachers are not the only professionals who have a tough first year."

"You almost make me believe you're right." Tears floated in her brown eyes, not spilling this time. "It is strange I should run into you because I came out tonight to clear my head. Did I conjure you up?"

"No, I come to the library most week nights. It is my favorite place. "Where is your car?" the professor asked as they walked out the coffee shop door.

"I am afraid I walked. I really needed a stress reliever, but I know I should not walk after dark alone."

"I won't say a word. Let me walk you home."

"No, really I will follow those folks there ahead. They live in apartments close to the Teacherage."

By the time Emma arrived at the Teacherage at ten-thirty, she felt calmer, thinking about how the last two days before break would go as smoothly as possible with the films to view and discuss. She would get a good night's rest. She could make two more days, and then during two weeks of break, she could make plans for a month ahead.

The last two days before break went miraculously well, the troublemakers having begun their holiday early, the others lethargic, drawing, writing notes, or sleeping during the film. The discussion and test on the film were nothing to them except another lecture and a grade, another F for the term. They had long ago learned how grades were determined by who they were. If parents expected A's, something none of Emma's students' parents did, they came out and so lobbied. They were somebody or were trying to be somebody and put pressure on the administration and school board members.

Emma was invited again to Aunt Ophelia's, her mother and sister also having been invited, and she spent a hundred dollars of her savings to buy gifts for everyone who would be at the Christmas Eve gathering. They would sit around the same table where Emma had sat eating chicken and dumplings when her little cousin came running in to say her father had died. Everything since seemed like another life, a freeing of fear of someone she loved into a reluctant embracing of fear of the unknown adult world.

It snowed on Christmas Eve, making the evening perfectly festive for the children, cursed for the arthritic aunt and uncle, and inconvenient for Helen and Martha, who were driving together. Emma arrived first, even though she had to drive slowly on the icy patches. She was eager to see her mother and sister, Mr. Willis not being able to travel because of a bout of bronchitis.

Approaching the house was like entering Wuthering Heights, the turn off the main highway led to the familiar dirt road, one house, and then nothing on either side but icicled pines and black gums, snow strewn shrubs, the road cut with hard frozen tracks one must stay within or slide into the ditch, the air thick with cold and silence. The wind had died, and Emma heard only the cracking of the ice under the tires until she turned into the driveway and aroused the mangy pack of dogs, mostly hounds that ran out barking in deep voices at her car. Only one was brave enough not to run back when she opened the door and spoke. "Black Jack, you know me, old boy. What are you barking at?" Her tone calmed the old friend she grew up with, blind now, but recognizing her tone, and wagging his tail.

There was no door bell and no reason to knock. They would not hear her until she knocked her knuckles red, Uncle Milton having the television loud and Aunt Ophelia busy mixing and stirring. There were three cement steps leading to the back porch enclosed in recent years with a bathroom on the right. A pot of wild wandering dew sat on its table creeping toward the light, and under it sprawled on a ragged rug, a black cat and four black and brown kittens, one of which ventured forward in time to meet Emma's boot. They both screeched. Emma gasped and the kitten spat and clawed the boot.

The kitchen door opened into the warmth and glow of weeks of preparation even more elaborate than that of Thanksgiving, every spot on the table covered with plates and covered dishes, waiting until all the hugs and greetings were done. Her mother arrived seconds behind Emma but without Martha, who had not been up to the trip. Disappointed that her sister did not make the visit, Emma wondered what could have kept her home. Mother was vague as they sat relishing the country cooking Aunt Ophelia was known for. John, she said, was getting better but did not need to be out in the snow and ice. It was not until everyone had finished eating and Uncle Milton had returned to his television that Helen told what had happened to Martha.

Two days before, Martha had received her Christmas bonus, cashed it, eaten at the cafeteria at the mall, and done some Christmas shopping afterwards, staying until closing time at nine-thirty, and leaving through the front door of Penny's, having parked in the parking lot in front of the store. Just as she was about to cross the street to get to her car, someone called to her from behind saying, "Are you Martha?" She said yes, turning around, but did not see anyone. Then, sensing danger, she started to walk fast when someone jumped her, snatching her purse from her shoulder, wrenching her arm back, knocking her down, and scattering packages.

"She never saw the person," Mother said, "but a security guard saw a tall, thin man wearing a coat with a hood pulled over his head running through the woods with a package. An employee at the mall found Martha lying on the street when she went out to go home. The police have no clues as to who the attacker was. What they couldn't figure out and what I can't either is why the attacker called Martha by name."

Emma's chest tightened, her breathing stopped until she caught a short breath. Gerta, she thought. It must have been Gerta putting someone up to it. Even from prison, she was threatening Emma.

"Her arm was broken in two places, and some ligaments were torn," Mother said. "She'll be in a cast at least six weeks. But the worst part is she's scared to death now to go out alone."

"What is this world coming to?" Aunt Ophelia wrung her hands. "Don't even tell Milton. His heart is bad, and you know how he loves Martha."

The rest of the evening was a blur to Emma as she went through the rituals of opening gifts and having dessert and coffee afterwards. When she did not eat any of Aunt Ophelia's Japanese fruit cake, Mother declared she must be coming down with the flu. The plan had been that Emma and her mother would both stay overnight and go home in the morning. Aunt Ophelia had already borrowed an extra cot and a little kerosene heater for the bedroom, empty now the children were gone. For hours Emma lay under layers of quilts, scared, wondering if she should go to the police the next morning.

At day light, Emma was up, dressed, and ready for the long drive back to the Teacherage. The drive would settle her mind and give her time to think what to do.

She left her mother and Aunt Ophelia enjoying a breakfast of ham, eggs, homemade biscuits, and homemade pear preserves. The dirt road was still covered with snow, the car tracks hard frozen, but once out on the highway, Emma found it had been scraped. Nine miles out on the main road, she came to a crossroads town with a family restaurant and Quick Mart.

Deciding to fill up her tank so she would not have to make another stop, Emma pulled across the main road to the opposite corner to the Quick Mart gas pumps. After paying, she smelled freshly brewed coffee, and although she had had a cup of Aunt Ophelia's, she wanted to take some with her on the road. When she walked to the counter to fix her coffee, a man, bundled up with top hat and overcoat, turned to face her. It was Professor Di Yanni.

"Hello, there, young lady. And Merry Christmas to you! My, you are out early on a cold, cold morning!"

"We do meet in the most unexpected—I stayed with Aunt Ophelia—you remember her, and I'm on my way home."

"So early. You must have another gathering to attend."

"No."

"I'm just on my way to visit mother in the nursing home," he said.

"Oh, do you have time to talk? Maybe in my car?"

"Oh, surely, I will be glad to do so."

Professor Di Yanni followed Emma out and got in the passenger's side of her car. She started the engine and turned up the heater.

"What is it, Emma?"

The tears that always sprang so easily in his presence dropped without her blinking. "My sister was attacked and hurt."

The professor stared, not blinking either. "What happened? When?"

"Two days ago. Mugged as she left a store at the mall." Emma whimpered, almost incoherent. "He knew her! He knew who she was!"

"Have you talked with her?"

"No, I'm too upset. I wanted to wait until I calmed down. I thought the drive home would help me."

"Was she robbed?"

"Yes, her purse snatched off her shoulder. He broke her arm but got away, but he called her name—as if seeking her out. Don't you see? Gerta is still after me and now my family."

"Well, I just can't believe this has anything to do with Selena Klein, aka, Gerta. I am still waiting to get my report on her from my contact with the law, but I will speed it up. You call your sister and try to find out who knew she was going shopping that night. At this time of year, there are many muggings unfortunately. You just hold tight until after New Year's. I'm sure by then I can give you a report. As I told you, the chief of police on campus is a good friend. I can get a report to you. Ms. Klein should still be at Central Prison. It may take a couple of weeks after we return from semester break."

"That's a long time."

When Emma arrived back at the Teacherage, Mrs. Camden was playing Christmas music on her stereo and singing along. She invited Emma to have dinner with her. Jarret and Dora were gone for the holidays. Accepting the invitation for six o'clock, Emma went to her room, wrote down some notes, and called Martha. To Emma's surprise, Martha was cheerful, saying her arm was expected to heal and be as good as new in six weeks. She said it was not smart to be the last person out of a store at closing time. When Emma asked who knew where she was the night of the attack, Martha said that before work, a group had discussed the bonuses they received and what they would do with the extra money. Then, of course, her boyfriend knew and their mother. Martha asked Emma to come to stay with her on New Year's Eve.

Emma spent the week after Christmas making lesson plans, ordering materials to integrate literature, art, and music with reading, writing, and speaking skills. On New Year's Eve, she drove to Aunt Ophelia's again, this time to be with Martha. The weather was clear, the meal simple—ham, black-eyed peas, and sweet potatoes. Martha's arm was mending, no longer causing pain. The police, however, had not caught the assailant but had told her they had a witness, the security guard, who was helping by looking through files of photos. When Emma left to go home, she hoped she would find some word from Professor Di Yanni in a couple of days.

CHAPTER IX: A CRISIS

The first day back at school after the holidays was Tuesday, still a holiday for many students. Introducing a unit of work she had worked on for two weeks was exciting for Emma, and she hoped her excitement would be contagious. The Romantic Period for the juniors, and The Age of Reason for the seniors. But the students, overwhelmed, saw only endless assignments. And then she remembered, they couldn't read well, some not at all. "We're going to do the work together," she reassured them. "We're going to do it step by step. This is just the plan. I'm going to walk you through the lessons. You can do this."

At the end of the second day back, Emma realized with astonishment that she had not had a single incident to greatly disturb her, the troublemakers not back in school yet. She made detailed plans from the unit for the next day and then tackled five sets of papers. The seniors had gone to the library just to be able to spread out and have more room to think and write an essay on their concept of The Age of Reason based on the previous day's class discussion. The handwriting, so varied, some in pencil still, although Emma had asked for black ink for five months, made her eyes burn. Then she came to a paper that was neatly written and even made sense. Jubilant, she put a big A on it and a comment of "Good work!" Then the next paper was not neat, but, still, in black ink, and making good sense. As she read page two, something clicked in her tired brain: this sounded familiar.

She looked back at the paper she had just read. Except for the first sentence, where the student misspelled two words and had a comma splice, the two papers were identical. And these were two of her sweetest girls, so pretty, chic, and well mannered. They had sat together in the library with a third friend, the threesome inseparable when left to themselves. Emma pulled out the paper of the third student and compared it to the other two. All three had written an original first sentence, all with errors, and had copied the remainder of three pages from some book in the library. It would be easy enough to find. She wrote "See me about this paper" on all three and went on to the next.

At nine-thirty, she started the last set. Halfway through, she came to Hiram Schlipf's paper, one of the most difficult to read, yet original and always cynical. He always signed his name at the end, instead of putting it at the top of the paper as directed to do. This time he had added a post script: "You had better watch your back. Someone is out to get you!" His face rose in Emma's mind. Hiram was tall and skinny, his face thin, his black hair flying as he swept into class at the bell, taking his seat in the back. He had not been any trouble and thus had not received much attention. Emma thought he was bright judging from his papers, when she could decipher them. If he spoke, it was to make a sarcastic remark; thus, she avoided calling on him. He seemed harmless, but bored. She had seen him reading a paperback when the other students struggled with the assignment, his work completed, all he intended to do.

Making herself read the final nine papers, she put a grade and comment on each, and stood up to look in the dresser mirror. Her brown hair was limp with unruly strands sticking out, her oval face, thin and pale. Although exhausted, she was tense, now allowing herself to think about Gerta and Dr. Di Yanni. She had hoped to hear from him by now. She decided to go to the Stop and Go about a quarter of a mile away to get some ginger ale. Professor Di Yanni had never given her his phone number. The only phone in the Teacherage was in the parlor, where there was no privacy. Descending the stairs, Emma did not see or hear anyone. Dora and Jarret came in late usually. Mrs. Camden's reading light that hung low from the ceiling by her recliner shone dimly on the old woman, who appeared to be asleep. Emma decided not to wake her, but opening the front door roused her.

"Emma? Is that you?"

"Yes, ma'am, I'm going to the store to get some ginger ale. Can I bring you something?"

"No, I have some Coca Cola. You are welcome to it."

"I need to get out and get my blood circulating so that I can think and figure out a couple of things before I go to sleep." She did not wait for any motherly advice but walked out into the cold air.

From the front steps, Emma could see the lights from the store. The crisp, chilly air felt good after sitting for hours in her stuffy room. In the fall she had often walked at night to the store for exercise and had met a few neighbors who were walking or jogging. When the time changed in the fall, she started driving if she went out. But there was something about walking that helped her to reflect and dream, often coming up with solutions and new ideas. The Teacherage and school, located on a secondary road, were part of a rural community. On either side of the Teacherage were fields and several tobacco barns. Across the road was a subdivision of families with school age children. As she walked, Emma wondered how she could handle the three girls who had copied so as not to turn them against her. She had found that a number of her students had received A's in their former schools for reports containing information copied from encyclopedias, usually *World Book*, which they had at home. Did their former teachers not read the reports, didn't care, or what?

A bicycle whizzed by, breaking her thoughts. She hadn't even heard it coming, but the biker came so close she felt the handle bars bump her coat. Crazy people. Now she had to watch out for bikers. The biker looked back as if to see whom he had almost run down, his form a black silhouette, soon out of sight.

Several customers were inside the store, one young man obviously flirting with the attendant, who was making him a hot dog to go. Emma waited her turn, glancing at the clock on the wall. It was ten forty-five; the store closed at eleven o'clock. She paid for her bottle of ginger ale, and walked out, eager to get back. The air seemed colder than when she set out. She stopped to pull her gloves out of her coat pocket, setting the cold bottle on the road. She walked facing traffic, stepping onto the shoulder of the road when she met a car, the bottle of ginger ale stuffed into her coat pocket. As she passed the field and tobacco barns next to the Teacherage, Emma heard a whiz again and turned around to see the biker, but this time he stopped beside her. He had a mask over his face, but when his eyes met hers, the steely grey penetrated her whole being. As he leaped from his bike, she started to run, almost stumbling, thinking if she could just get to the Teacherage yard only a short distance now. But he grabbed her first around the waist; then one arm was around her neck, pulling her back, cutting off her breath, and dragging her across the field into one of the tobacco barns. He flung her down and she could feel sand shifting; an image of her Uncle Milton shoveling white sand in his tobacco barns flashed in her mind. The attacker started kissing her with dry lips and fondling her breasts but he did not speak. Then as he covered her mouth again with his, she could not breathe.

Finally her brain got the message. She had never been in this kind of danger. He braced one of her legs with his knee and started to pull down her hose. He paused to loosen his belt and trousers, looking down and away from her. Suddenly with more quickness and power than she would have ever believed possible, she raised up, her leg still braced, and lunged forward to the right side of his face and bit his ear as ferociously as a bobcat grips a rabbit. He screamed, grabbing his torn, bloody ear, emitting a stream of curses while she freed her leg and flipped on her side, rolling in the sand. But he caught her, this time slamming her on her back and pulling her skirt up. God, help me was all she could think of. She scratched him in the face, trying to gouge his eyes. He raised his body to pin her arms, freeing one of her legs enough to hit his groin with her knee. But nothing stopped him, and she was tired. Maybe if she just gave up, he would rape her and not kill her. As she lay still, he pulled a piece of rope from his pocket and a handkerchief, first gagging her and then tying her hands together behind her back. She watched knowing she would not live to tell and that she did not want to live to tell. With her bound, he started to undress, curiously putting his clothes and shoes in a neat pile, still wearing the torn black mask and knitted cap pulled down to conceal his hair.

Again a superhuman strength surged her blood, and she pulled one hand through the rope knot. She had just enough time to fill her hands with sand, and when he knelt down in front of her like the beast that has stilled its prey and is ready to tear it at leisure, she hurled two fists full of sand into his eyes. Surprised but not stunned, he knocked her back, this time hard enough that she lost her breath. He would have to tie her hands again. But she had slung the rope with the sand, sending it into the dark corner of the barn. Still he had time to look, she not able to fight any more. Emma lay still, trying hard to breathe, but her chest hurt when she tried. God, help me. Please, help me, her mind prayed.

The attacker was on the ground feeling in the sand, searching for the rope, his back to the barn door. He cursed as he felt for the rope, and then his cursing was interrupted by a swooping and cracking like breaking a coconut. She tried to turn but a pain like a knife in her chest wouldn't let her breathe when she tried to move. There was more swooping, this time, she could tell someone was hitting someone else with a heavy instrument. Then someone called her name. "Emma! Emma! I've knocked his brains out! It's all right. It's all right now!" And someone slipped his arms under her and gathered her up. She knew the voice and the touch. It was Professor Di Yanni. "God sent you," she whispered and lost consciousness.

*****

Emma dreamed she was dead in the barn but no one was concerned with her. She saw Professor Di Yanni, looking wild, a bush blade in his hand, still, even though her attacker lay dead, blood from a deep cut on the side of his head seeping into the sand.

"How did you know?" Emma was able to ask even though she knew she was dead.

"I had attended a meeting with several school board members, art teachers in the county, and their principals there at your high school. It had run much later than we thought, but our report was needed for the next day's board meeting. Anyhow, I needed to see you on a matter we had discussed, and I drove to the Teacherage parking lot and parked. I went to the door, rang the bell, and the landlady opened it, startled at seeing me. She said she thought I was you, that you had forgotten the key. She said you had gone to the store and had had time, she thought, to be back unless you went somewhere else. I told her I would go looking for you. I drove to the store. The clerk said yes you had been in and had been gone about ten minutes. I asked her if other customers had been in at the time. Yes, some folks who

lived in the subdivision. But the clerk had noticed a guy on a bike ride by on the road several times earlier in the evening."

"So that was your tip?" Emma asked.

"Yes, I left my car at the store and walked quietly in the dark, listening, pausing, and waiting. Then, maybe a few hundred yards from the Teacherage, I saw a bike lying in the field, abandoned near a tobacco barn, so I walked in the dark, waiting and listening. I heard struggling and sneaked closer to the barn, very cautiously, slowly, waiting to determine what was going on. Then I could see two figures and knew a man was attacking you. I had to find a weapon. The only thing around was a bundle of tobacco sticks, but when I picked up some of the sticks to use as a weapon, I saw a bush blade behind the sticks. I figured he had a gun, so I wanted to surprise him from behind, hit the back of his head. And that moment came when he was searching for something on the ground and had his back to the door. I just could see him and came down with the bush blade on the side of his head with strength I didn't know I had, and he dropped without a flinch. Then I picked you up and ran out to the road. I laid you on the grass near the road so that I could run to the store for help. And just as I reached the store, I saw a man flag down a truck. I saw him pick you up and get into the truck, which sped away."

*****

When Emma heard voices again, she thought she was still dreaming. She could not speak or move. A man was talking in a low, serious tone.

"We've identified the attacker: Benjamin Earl Daughtry. He's not a student. He dropped out. He's nineteen and has been in trouble before. This time his luck ran out."

"I know him; he's called Benjie." Another voice, this one familiar, was Hiram's. "He's been in trouble before. He dropped out of school last year. He lives right around the corner from me, and he told me he had been, as he put it, 'watching the new teachers in the Teacherage.' I think he's been planning this attack. It's like he wanted to do something bad enough to be put away. You know what I mean?"

"Yes, Hiram, I'm afraid I do know what you mean. But I sure wish you had told someone before this happened. This girl is lucky to be alive."

"I did tell someone, officer. I told her, Miss Applewhite."

"When?"

"Well, in a paper I handed in two days ago. I wrote that she had better watch her back."

"Next time, son, don't be afraid to tell somebody in authority."

"You don't know the guy, sir; he would get me if he found out I snitched."

"He won't bother anyone now, son. He's dead. The hook of that bush blade you sunk into his temple. Now I need for you to tell me what happened. How did you happen to be on the scene?"

"I didn't kill him!" Hiram screamed in disbelief. "I been watching Benjie since he told me he'd been watching the teachers in the Teacherage—Miss Applewhite and Miss Grimes."

"What do you mean by watching?"

"Well, since Benjie lost his license about a year ago, he rides his bike everywhere and usually goes out after he eats supper. He rides by my house to get to the main road, and every night when I see him go by, I go out a few minutes later on my bike and tail him until he comes back home."

"Did your parents know that?"

"My old man is in the pen, and Mama works at the hospital at night. She don't get in till one-thirty in the morning. Most times Benjie was back in by eleven 'cause his old man would beat him and throw him out if he stayed out too late after he got in trouble with the law."

"So, describe exactly what happened tonight."

"Well, I was watching television after supper and facing the front living room windows that look out on the street. I seen Benjie about seven-thirty ride by on his bike, and after five minutes, I got on mine and went out. Usually he goes to the pool room and plays with the guys and eats hot dogs and drinks beer. Sometimes I go there too and hang out. There's a television in there, and they watch games while they shoot pool. Some of the guys gamble in a back room. I don't stay if I see the trouble-makers. Some of the guys are okay, but some are mean as snakes, just looking for trouble."

"And so did Benjie go to the pool room tonight?"

"Yeah, he did, but when I went in to see who was there, someone said Benjie was in the back room. So I stayed and played pool until about ten-thirty; then, I decided Benjie was going to stay back there, and I was tired of pool, so I left and decided to ride around before going back home. You might say I had a funny feeling. I mean, Benjie had never stayed in that back room that long before."

"You mean, the pattern was different?"

"Yeah, I guess so. Anyway, I decided to get a soda at the Stop and Go, and while I was in there, who do I see but Benjie, hanging around outside smoking. He was walking back and forth, like he was agitated or waiting for somebody. Then I saw him get on his bike and light out on his bike. So after a minute or so, I lit out after him. There was nothing but a straight strip of the road between the store and the Teacherage and, of course, our subdivision street across from the Teacherage. So I circled around the Teacherage and didn't see him. I even got off my bike and looked in the back yard. No sign of him. Then I circled real fast to Benjie's house and didn't see his bike where he always parks it under the carport. So I started to go back to the store. Then I happened to hear some noise. I couldn't tell what it was, so I stopped. I seen something on the side of the road like a bundle, and when I got to it, it was Miss Applewhite. I thought she was dead, so I started to run for help, but just then I saw a truck. I waved the driver to stop and he did. It was a man I have seen at the store before, so he helped me load Miss Applewhite and drove to the hospital. I told the police I seen Benjie's bike out there near the barn, so Sergeant Newell drove with me back out to the site. By the time we got there, two patrol cars were already there. That's when I seen Benjie lying there in the sand in the barn. There was blood still oozing from the gash in his temple. I seen what looked like brains. I turned to walk out before I threw up. Sergeant Newell asked me did I do it, and I said no and told him the same thing I just told you. That's all I know."

"All right, son. You'll be okay. You go call your Mama."

Emma tried to open her eyes, tried to speak, tried to raise her hand, but could not. She felt she was paralyzed. The voice of the officer was farther away now, droning so that she could barely hear it.

"Hiram killed him, all right, but he won't admit it," the officer who interviewed Hiram commented to a second officer. "He's scared he'll get in trouble. He claims he found Miss Applewhite on the shoulder of the road and flagged down help and didn't see this Benjie, the attacker, just his bike, until the sergeant took him back to the scene. The kid needs a night's rest. He'll tell me the truth tomorrow. I'll tell him he won't be in trouble for saving the girl's life. I say he's done this community a good deed by killing that bastard."

*****

"Emma, Emma. It is I. How do you feel this evening?" Professor Di Yanni squeezed her hand. The first squeeze felt like a butterfly opening and closing its wings in her hand. She heard him, dreaming she was resting finally after a long struggle. She knew everything was all right. The butterfly in her hand grew stronger as it opened and closed its wings. It was black with yellow spots, and it wasn't afraid she would close her hand and squash it.

"Time to check your vital signs, dearie," a cheerful feminine voice said. "Wake up! You've slept a whole day!"

The nurse's uniform rustled around the bed. The head of the bed was raised and a thermometer was stuck in Emma's mouth. Emma turned her head and saw Professor Di Yanni sitting in the corner. He smiled and nodded, waiting for his turn to speak.

"I'll see you get some soup and juice. I think your stomach is not ready for much yet." And the nurse left, leaving the door slightly opened.

"Hello, Emma, how do you feel?" Professor Di Yanni pulled his chair closer to the bed.

"Not so hot. Nauseated and a bit dizzy. What day is it? What happened to my classes? It's a school day, isn't it?"

"Yes, but all is taken care of. You have a substitute."

"How would she, or he, know what to do?"

"It will be all right. The world has not stopped. Well, just yours temporarily. The doctor told me you have three broken ribs and several bad bruises. Only time will heal them. But still. I was afraid it was worse … physically, I mean. Of course, psychologically, one never quite gets over trauma, although my mother would say you were given a warning."

Emma smiled. "Yes, so would my mother. This is not my

farm community where I roamed night and day unharmed for eighteen years."

"Well, I see you have figured it out. Now I wish you would share that revelation with your sister. Your grandmother's farm on that isolated dirt road with only relatives as neighbors was idyllic and sheltering. You were chained to innocence. What is that line in "Fern Hill"?

"You saved my life—again. Are you really real or an angel?"

"Oh, no! It was your student, Hiram, who saved you."

"Hiram? The irony is I had just read the note at the bottom of Hiram's paper saying to watch my back. When the biker first stopped, I thought it was Hiram, but when he grabbed me, I knew the person was much bigger than Hiram."

"Yes, the attacker was not a student but a young man, nineteen, I think, living right across from the Teacherage in that subdivision. But don't you think the student who wrote that note was trying to warn you? Maybe your student knew the attacker. The sheriff says the attacker was a dropout and had been in trouble several times already."

"I had not taken Hiram's note literally because the boy is so smart and doesn't seem mean, just wanting attention and not by being good. You know what I mean. It's not cool to get the teacher's attention by being a good student."

"Yes, I know. And, I see you have a note here that your principal and department head are coming at six o'clock, so I need to finish and get out of here. I have some news for you. Remember our little research project? Well, I finally got some answers. Let me clarify because you are woozy with pain medication. Remember the woman you first met as Gerta, who then showed up as your new dorm mother as Miss Pierce, and who I found out through campus police was really named Klein?"

"You've received a report on Klein?"

"Yes, and also on the mugging of your sister. First, that mugger worked as a janitor for Martha's company, so he may have known she had cash or that she had bought expensive presents, which he attempted to take with him. So I don't think he had any connection to Gerta, or at least there is no record of a connection between them that my source found. He was a drug addict. Now to Ms. Klein. She has cancer, diagnosed over a year ago. The report I got was that she is trying to save her soul by going to Bible classes as well as helping other prisoners with reading skills. Miracles do happen. It is amazing what facing death can do for the soul."

"I can't believe it. You mean, all I have to worry about now are my students. Wow, I feel as light as a feather. And you think one of them was on my side?" Emma's voice was full of sarcasm and hurt and thankfulness all mixed up.

"Come on. This is not the Emma, I know. Look, here, you have this kid, whom, you said yourself you had not given any attention to, and he saves your life. I think you are lucky! Obviously you are doing something right. The student who wrote that note to warn you was not one of your few good ones that, to use your words, you 'would beg, borrow, and steal for.' So my point is you must be reaching many who are reacting in negative ways because peer pressure or their own needs will not allow them to do otherwise."

Emma listened. The professor would not give her the pity she wanted. She knew what was next. She had her health, and that was everything.

"Emma, you're becoming a woman and a professional in a tough world. It is scary, and you were so protected compared to some kids raised in the cities who came home to do nothing after school but get into mischief. I believe you need to do your very best this first year and just mark it up to initiation to adulthood. Then if you don't want to try another year, find another job in the summer, and pay back the remainder of your scholarship working in a field you like, something that would nurture your love of literature and the fine arts. I know you are a good teacher. I have heard good things about you from the committee I'm serving on. But you must find out for yourself, and it takes time."

Someone knocked on the door, and Mr. Franks and Mrs. Murphy entered smiling, carrying a vase of cut flowers. The twosome did not seem to notice the professor, who said hello in passing and slipped out the door.

When Emma returned to school, she found she had been elevated in the minds of students to have survived the attack described in the paper as having "fought off her attacker until help arrived." Many of the students had known the attacker. In short, she was something of a celebrity and a heroine. Hiram actually started to do some work, most likely because he feared reprisal. She reaped such praises as "I'm shore glad you're back, Miss Applewhite. That substitute was worse than you!" But the welcome back mood wore off in a few days, and they were all back to their normal selves, saying they hoped she would be attacked again soon to give them a break.

CHAPTER X: PLEDGING SUPPORT

The third week in January Mr. Franklin called a meeting of the Junior-Senior Prom committee. While Emma was out, there had already been two meetings, and she had been put in charge of raising the extra money needed to fund the prom. Mr. Franklin had thought there was enough money from the magazine drive, but he had forgotten to give funds to several clubs he did not know existed. Emma had heard her seniors say that the year before they had shown films the last two periods of the day in the gym and sold tickets to students who wanted to go. Others stayed in class.

The idea had sounded preposterous to Emma, but when Mr. Franklin said, "How will you raise the money?" She had answered that she had thought about showing movies in the gym and selling tickets. He said okay. So, without any guidance, she asked students what kind of films had been shown the year before. *Frankenstein* and other horror movies, they said. Dora and Jarret, the other members comprising the prom committee, did not have a clue about fund-raising either. They would support whatever Emma wanted to do. So she set about finding a film catalog through the central office. She scheduled the first film for the first week in February, a film based on a Poe short story about a man buried alive. No one approved the film, which Emma paid for via her personal check mailed to the company. She scheduled the showing with Mr. Franklin, and her juniors started selling tickets. Any student who had the seventy-five cents bought one. Through the students, Emma found a student to operate the projector and put up a big screen in the gym.

When the film did not arrive the day before the scheduled showing, Emma broke out with a rash on her arms. Standing before her fourth period class, she rubbed her arms, pushing up her long sleeves. "Miss Applewhite," the bespectacled girl in front of her said, "You are turning into a monster, just like in a movie I saw." That remark broke up the lesson, and with only ten minutes before the bell, the class never refocused. Emma made a mental note to buy some good body lotion. The winter weather was drying out her skin. Examining her other arm, she saw that it too had red blotches. By the end of the day, her neck had broken out with the rash. In the hall, she saw Dora. "If that film doesn't come in the morning mail, I don't know what I'll do."

"It will," said Dora. "We've sold out the tickets too! A couple more films, and we'll have enough money for the prom."

After school Jarret and Emma walked back to the Teacherage together, discussing the logistics of the film showing. "Emma, you look like you have a fever or something." He felt of her forehead.

"I have this itchy rash. And if I scratch it, it just itches more. I need to get something for dry skin."

He opened her collar and looked at her neck. "That's hives, the mad itch, Emma! I had it once in college when I had to conduct my first concert for a public audience. It's your nerves, dummy! You are letting this school drive you crazy! I keep telling you: you have to roll with the punches! Look, go get a shot to knock up this itch, so you won't scratch yourself to death tonight! I know you; you'll just worry all night because that film hasn't come."

There was something about Jarret that made Emma feel like

his little sister. She envied his nonchalant, dare-devil attitude. Arriving at the Teacherage, she got into her car and drove to the nearest doctor's office, six miles away. She had never been there but knew that Dora came here regularly. Not having an appointment, she had to wait to be worked in. The doctor wanted to know how long she had had the rash, how fast it had spread, and if she knew anything she was allergic to. He gave her a shot of cortisone and told her to take a tub bath in hot water and to rub salt on the rash, and to come back the next day if it wasn't better. The next morning the rash had calmed down.

At ten thirty the mailman brought the film to the school's office. Emma saw him coming in and took the package. At ten till two, after all lunches were over, students with tickets filed into the gym and filled the bleachers. Right away, Emma saw that the light from the uncovered windows on the opposite side of the bleachers made a glare that would greatly impede the viewing. Luckily the afternoon was cloudy. Next time she would need to get the windows covered. Nervous as a mother hen, Emma walked from the gym door, where assigned juniors took up tickets, to the projection manager, who seemed to be having difficulty threading the film. If they didn't soon start, time would run out before the film was over, and students had to catch the buses.

Finally the film started. There were no teachers in the gym besides herself. Finally Dora and Jarret came. "I have a parent who has come unexpectedly," said Dora. "I'll be back."

"Looks as if you have everything under control," Jarret remarked and left.

Luck was with her this time. Except for talking during the film and some traffic to the restrooms, all went well, the film ending thirty-three seconds before the end-of-day bell.

Having no other strategy and no input from anyone with

experience, Emma scheduled two more film showings. During the second, she noticed some students leaving before the film was over. By the third showing, many students who had tickets did not go to the gym but stayed outside and smoked, and those who had cars or lived close by headed out. Alarmed at the procession to the parking lot thirty minutes before the last bell, Emma walked out of the gym to view the exodus in time to see Mr. Franklin sprinting across the parking lot to close and lock the gate before any more students escaped. That ended the film showings. But the films had made enough money to get by if no unexpected expenses popped up during the preparation of the prom. Mr. Franklin, however, knowing the unexpected always happened, suggested selling doughnuts to raise more money. Each homeroom in the school had a goal of selling thirty dozen. On the last day of the sale, Emma's class had sold only twenty-one dozen. Her roll keeper and beloved confidante, Hannah, a freshman with more wisdom, common sense, and maturity than most adults Emma knew, told her the sad news. As the teacher spearheading the fund-raising, she felt her homeroom must not set a bad example. "I'll buy nine dozen," said Emma. "But will you take them home and put them in your mother's freezer?"

During the weeks of fund-raising, Emma had depleted her lesson plans. It was day to day now, every night staying up late and not getting all her papers graded. On Sunday night as March blew in a bone chilling rain, she couldn't face Monday. She needed to plan the rest of the year for the juniors and the seniors so that when the time came to put on the prom, she would be able to survive. She had heard the stories about the long hours of preparation into the early morning the week before the prom. The whole gym had to be transformed from the ugly, smelly facility it was to some fairytale land that awaited princes and princesses, whom, she had been told, would not attend school on

Friday that week. The more she contemplated the prom the more she felt the need to prepare for the rest of the year. She could not face the upcoming week.

Teachers had to arrange for their own substitutes. Emma had a list of names and phone numbers. She had met a Mrs. Rathbone, a doctor's wife, one day when the woman came in for Dora. She was a sweet lady, petite, soft spoken, well educated, and meticulous to a fault. Emma had wondered how such a demure person survived as a sub. Perhaps it was her respect and good manners and taking the students at their word. What did it matter as long as no one was killed or injured. Mrs. Rathbone agreed to go in for Emma on Monday, and Emma worked out detailed plans for both the juniors and the seniors and then went out in the pitch black night of wind and rain to drive seven and a half miles to deliver the plans, texts, and work sheets. Feeling guilty because she was not really sick, just exhausted, she had trouble looking Mrs. Rathbone in the eye, feeling that she would know she wasn't sick but slipping into a black hole of failure.

Monday Emma started planning for the juniors for the rest of the year. By noon she had just become immersed and become grounded in a vision. She had gotten up at the usual time but felt so guilty for not going in to school that she could not bear to watch the clock, visualizing her homeroom coming in for twenty minutes with nothing to do. On her desk, she had purposely put a big red vase with vivid blue flowers with yellow centers painted on its sides, and out of its mouth flourished red and blue silk flowers, fragile, flamboyant, silent, yet flaunting their color and courage to be in a room where their defilement was a matter of time.

It was only after school was out that Emma could turn the clock's face up. She needed some books for her planning, but instead of going to the school, she drove ten miles to the public

204
204 ∞ *Mi Mi Roberts*

library, checking out the maximum and picking up a hamburger on the way back. Avoiding others in the house, she locked her door and did not answer when Mrs. Camden knocked and called her. By seven-thirty she knew she needed more time to really get these units of plans together. She called Mrs. Rathbone, asking how the day had gone and if she could finish the week for her. The day had gone okay, and Mrs. Rathbone agreed to go in the rest of the week. Emma dictated Tuesday's plans and promised more the next night. Mrs. Rathbone asked no probing questions, quietly accepting Emma's directive.

In some ways, it was a perfect week to stay in to read, reflect, and make creative lesson plans, for the rain that had begun in torrents on Sunday night did not let up. When Emma took a break from her work and looked out her front window, she could see the houses in the subdivision across the road. The house directly in front of her window had a dog tied with a chain to an iron rod in the ground beside the house. It had no place to escape the beating rain and stood barking all Monday. Tuesday morning started out dark but not rainy until mid-morning when the heavy clouds could no longer hold their burden. The dog stood, his short hair matted to his skin, not barking any longer. Someone had to help the underdog, Emma decided. So when Mrs. Camden was busy in the kitchen, her counter top TV blasting *The Price Is Right*, Emma sneaked out the front door. Looking in all directions for anyone about, and, not seeing anyone, she dashed across the road to the prisoner's yard and unchained the poor dog, which looked at her as if to say "I can't believe someone if freeing me." Running back to the front door, where she stopped to catch her breath and look back, Emma realized the dog had blue eyes. She had never seen a dog with blue eyes before. He still stood in the rain, looking at her, not knowing where to go. There was no dog house, no carport, no big tree, or shrubs. He was saying, "What now?" So, without thinking, Emma ran back again, looked around, and not seeing anyone, picked up the dog and carried him dripping to her room. When the rain stopped, she would take him back. Mrs. Camden would most likely not hear him bark, but Dora and Jarret would, so she had to get the dog out before they got home. She would wait until dark, but by then the owners would be home. Oh, well, she would figure something out. She gave the dog a peanut butter cheese nab and let him go to sleep on an old sweater she didn't wear. The dog slept the rest of the day, not bothering Emma as she continued her work, not distracted by any pitiful thing. When the day light waned enough she thought school was out, she turned the clock face up.

A little after five, she heard Jarret come up and go into his room, waking up the dog, which barked for the first time. Before Emma could quiet him with more crackers, someone knocked on the door. Emma did not answer. "Hey, it's me," said Jarret. "I heard at school today that you were sick, and I thought I heard a dog bark in there just now. What is going on?"

Emma opened the door. "Shh. Come in. I need your help." She pulled Jarret in by the arm and pointed to a chair.

"Where is the dog?"

"In the closet." Emma told Jarret what she had done and asked him how she could get the dog back home.

"Wait a minute. Are you home because of this kidnapped dog?"

"No, I was at my rope's end. You know we have the prom coming up, and I had run out of steam with no more plans beyond the end of the day last Friday. I spend most of my time being a policeman instead of a teacher. Your students love you, on the other hand. You have a subject they choose. Dora and I have to teach everybody."

"Yes, I have it made. That's right. I get all the good students.

Like the one who just today delivered a love letter to Mr. Franklin from me."

"What?"

"Yeah, one of your favorites, Anthony Tillman, drew a picture of Mr. Franklin and me in … well for your delicate ears … in a compromising position and signed my name to it. So here comes Mr. Franklin, all hot and bothered to my room, interrupting my rehearsal without apology, thrusting the drawing in my face. When Mr. Franklin left and the class ended, Margaret Forehand, being the intuitive angel she is, stayed to tell me she had seen Anthony slip a note under Mr. Franklin's door when they changed classes from history to my room. I asked her if she would mind going to tell Mr. Franklin because the note had said something untrue about me. She did, and Mr. Franklin came back to let me know. Now you see that I have no problems, unlike you."

"Well, I apologize. Just help me get this dog back to the house right across the street without being seen."

"Don't take him back to those damned Bolsheviks! I know that family, dumb as bricks, every one of the four. They lived beside me when I was growing up, and the father was a hunter. He taught his son such noble rules of deer hunting as blinding the deer with a light and shooting them just for fun. There were always buzzards swarming and a pack of dogs running on our road to tear and pull away the flesh of those poor creatures. That dog is smarter than anyone in that house, so it would be inhumane to take him back."

"Well, what do you propose we do with him?"

"Oh, so it's we now? This is the friendliest you've ever been to me, but I won't let it stop me from coming to your rescue. Actually what I propose is that we call Dora at her mom's and tell her we need her pronto."

"I don't want the whole world to know I've stolen a dog. I could lose my job over this blue-eyed mutt."

"Blue eyes? A weimaraner? Oh, we must save him." Jarret got up to examine the dog. Yep, he is one. "Hey, Mr. Blue Eyes." The dog licked his hand. "I'm going downstairs and call Dora. Her mother still lives on a farm and could take him, and would, if Dora asked her to. So we just need to let Dora see him. Maybe we could get Mr. Blue Eyes out there tonight."

Jarret returned so quickly Emma was sure he didn't get Dora. "Well, she's coming. I told her you and I were having a party in your room and that we were celebrating an unexpected surprise with a bottle of champagne, so she said, "I'll be there in fifteen minutes.""

"You are truly crazy, Jarret!"

"But you are in a jam and need a crazy person to help you out of it!" He rolled out of the chair onto the floor to play with Mr. Blue Eyes. Then standing up, Jarret said, "I must be true to my word and go get some champagne, for Dora will be expecting it, and I am a man of my word; just ask my students who got expelled today for telling lies about me to their parents!" He left smiling and waving his arms as if he were conducting a concert. Gone only twenty minutes, he returned with an ice bucket and three bottles of champagne.

"Jarret, what in the world? Where did you get all that so fast? I hope Mrs. Camden didn't see you."

"I have connections in high places, and she never does."

"Seriously, where did you go?"

"You know those new apartments just down the road on the right?" Emma nodded yes. "I have friends who live there, and they keep our refreshments since I don't have accommodations here in this dump. If I put a liquor bottle in our garbage can, Mrs.

Camden would have it all over school before homeroom was over the next day that I was an alcoholic."

"Does she really look at our trash?"

"Hell, yes, a teacher who lived here last year got fired for throwing away beer bottles every night. You know what the old lady told that teacher one night when they were talking?" Emma waited for the answer. "She told him that when Kennedy got shot she was quote 'afraid he wouldn't die.'"

"What did she have against him?"

"Think about it, Emma. You are smart enough to figure it out. There's Dora. Let the party begin. I'll get my guitar, dearie!"

Jarret returned, guitar clutched under his right arm, his left arm around Dora's shoulder. Her face was swollen, her eyes red. Usually composed and beautiful, Dora looked strangely wild.

"Dora, what's the matter?" Emma thought it must be her mother.

"Oh, nothing, just another happy day at North West High. I haven't seen you around this week." Dora slurred her words.

Before Emma could decide how to answer, Jarret did for her. "You see, Dora, dear, our friend Emma has taken it upon herself to save a wretched weimaraner from its abusive owner across the road, and we have to help her find a home for it tonight." He opened the closet, picked up Mr. Blue Eyes and set him in Dora's lap. The dog looked up at Dora as if he understood her sad eyes. "Voila! Look, he's taken to you already, and he acknowledges only blue bloods."

Picking up the big puppy, clutching him to her chest, Dora snuggled Mr. Blue Eyes like a baby. Emma had the impression that Dora never let down her professional mask, but something was wrong. "I like animals so much better than I do people," Dora said, sitting down on the carpet, still holding the dog close.

"Dora, what's the matter? You look green!" Emma said. "Here, let me take the dog."

"Help me to the bathroom," Dora said, reaching her hand out to Jarret, who pulled her up off the floor and guided her to the bathroom door.

"Do you want Emma?" But Dora was down on her knees vomiting in the commode. She closed the door, but Emma stood by the door to listen. In a minute, Dora flushed the commode, washed up, and came out. Her complexion was its natural light brown, no longer greenish.

"I'm all right now," said Dora. "I took something on an empty stomach."

"Sit down," said Jarret. "We have to get you straight quickly because we need you to convince your mother she needs Mr. Blue Eyes tonight, and we have to drive out and deliver her new boy."

"What are you talking about?" Dora asked. "I thought you were in trouble. Are you telling me this is all about a dog? I had planned to be asleep by now."

Suddenly Jarret looked as if a light went off in his head. "What did you take?"

"Some Darvocets that Mother gave me."

"How many?" asked Jarret and Emma at the same time.

"I'm not sure. I think fifteen, but I just vomited them up."

"Good God!" Jarret was putting on his coat. "Emma, let's get her checked out."

"What are Darvocets?" Emma asked.

"Some kind of pain pill, but fifteen of anything might kill you. We don't know if she vomited them up or not," Jarret said, looking at Dora, who had lain down on her side on the carpet.

"Let's take her to the emergency room. I'll drive," Emma said, pulling Dora up to put on her coat. "Jarrett, I'll go down and tell Mrs. Camden that the three of us are going to a meeting. While I am distracting her, get passed the parlor door with Dora, and bring the dog! He is our second emergency."

Mrs. Camden, deeply engrossed in her favorite television program, the sound blasting on her deaf ears, said fine and thanks for telling her. She did not notice the doorway.

Emma drove with Mr. Blue Eyes up front with her in the foot, Jarret and Dora in the back so he could monitor her. "Hey, Emma, step on it. She's passing out, I think." Emma did speed, until hitting water on the road, her slick tires hydroplaned the car and spun it across the road into oncoming traffic. She shut her eyes bracing for a collision, then heard the screeching of tires. In the dark, Emma made out the form of a man coming towards her side of the car.

"Lord, have mercy! Miss Applewhite!" It was Mr. Franklin. "Is this a suicide squad?" He glanced at the dog and then suspiciously at Dora and Jarret in the back.

"I didn't know you had a dog."

"Oh, Mr. Franklin," said Jarret, "are we glad to see you! Dora is ill, food poisoning, we think, from that infamous Jake's Grill. We are taking her to the emergency room. We'll give you a report, but we need to get on."

"Well, do you want to take my car? I see Emma's tires are as slick as my head.

"No, we need to go on. The rain has stopped. But thanks for your kind offer, sir," Emma said. "I'll slow down," and rolling up the window, drove on, leaving Mr. Franklin looking as if he just remembered that Emma had been absent for two days.

"Emma, pull over and stop," Jarret said. "I think she has to vomit again, and that's what we want." But the stop was too late. Dora vomited on Jarret coat, which he had placed in her lap for that exact purpose. "Well, go on now."

In ten more minutes, the three arrived at the emergency entrance of the hospital, Jarret getting out with Dora at the door, and Emma driving to park. The only space she could find was in a remote corner of the farthest lot. Bands of rain started again, and she fumbled in the trunk to find an old umbrella. Running through the lot to the lighted walkway toward the ER entrance, holding the umbrella in front of her face bracing the wind, she felt her big black tattered umbrella snag something as it blew out of control. The torn umbrella of a passerby caught Emma's and locked ribs, the owners pulling in opposite directions. Then Emma jerked free, sending the unhooked umbrella flying in the wind. Stopping finally to retrieve her victim's umbrella, she looked up, "I'm so sorry!" But the man was bending over to capture his wounded umbrella from the shrubbery.

"Well, it is fitting that her umbrella should die too!" the man said seemingly to an invisible person. Emma knew the voice. It was Professor Di Yanni! Who else would she ever lock umbrellas with?

"Professor!" Emma thought he looked disoriented. "It's me, Emma! What's wrong?"

"Oh, Emma, Emma! So it is you! Of course, who else! What are you doing here?"

"One of my friends, a teacher at the school, is sick, and another teacher and I brought her in."

"Nothing serious, I hope."

"We hope. But what are you doing here?"

"Mother died about an hour ago, and this was her umbrella. She always bragged that she had kept it for twenty years when most people lose theirs in two months."

"I'm so sorry, but she was sick for so many years. My grandmother would say she is better off."

"Yes, no more suffering."

"Well, it's so good to see you."

"Oh, Emma, I was going to look you up soon anyway because I just found out some news yesterday and was delayed by Mother's sudden turn for the worse."

Emma forgot Dora for an instant, eager to hear the news.

"I received word through my sources that Gerta died in prison a few days ago. She really did have cancer and was on large doses of morphine at the last. You can forget her forever, Emma. No more nightmares on her account." Speechless, Emma sighed. "Now be on your way to your friend, and I will be in touch soon!"

He left her standing under her torn umbrella, and she watched him walk toward the parking lot, rain drops dripping from the brim of his hat.

When Emma found her way to the admission desk, the attendant told her Dora had been taken right away and Jarret was with her. Emma was not allowed back. She knew news of the two coming here together would be all over the school the next day, and all kinds of rumors would start about an interracial relationship between two new teachers. It was also likely that the real reason for the emergency would get out. Emma waited two hours before Jarret appeared. The doctor had pumped out Dora's stomach and said she was in no danger, having vomited up most of the pills. Dora would be ready to go in thirty minutes. She needed something to eat she could keep down.

It was fifteen past eleven when the three left the emergency room. Dora was talking like herself. "Stop at Mother's," she said to Emma. "I'll tell her to keep the dog until I come back. She can give me some of that soup she tried to get me to eat at supper, enough for all of us." Dora's mother lived down a dirt path off the main highway. The lights were out, but as the car pulled up, shining lights, the porch light popped on. "You two stay put while I go in for just a minute." Dora got out of the back and opened the passenger's door in front, stooped to pick up Mr. Blue Eyes, who looked questioningly back at Emma.

"It's all right, puppy. Someone wants you. Someone has a piece of cold ham for you and a rug," said Dora as she shut the door.

Emma and Jarret watched as the front door opened. "What's the matter?" they heard Dora's mother ask. Dora went inside carrying the dog.

"It's nice to know I'm the only stable new teacher at North West," said Jarret, pulling a bottle out of his soiled coat's pocket.

Emma turned back to look at him. "Can you put that coat in my trunk? The smell is making me feel queasy."

"Sure," he said, getting out with the key she handed him. Through the rear view mirror she saw him turn up a bottle and drink. She wondered if he drank every night or just in emergencies. She decided not to say anything. After all, he had orchestrated the night's events rather well—so far.

The front door opened again, Dora backed out, still talking, then turned to walk to the car, carrying a small container in one hand. "Well, folks, this is all that's left of the homemade soup. We can share it with lots of crackers. Mother's tickled to death with the dog. I wouldn't be surprised if she keeps him in the house at night."

Jarret took another swig from his bottle, this time in plain view of Emma and Dora. "We still haven't had our party, ladies. I've always maintained the view that homemade soup, champagne, and eighty proof Old Crow go splendidly together. In fact, you can have only soup, Dora. And you, Emma, can have the champagne, while I, not among the dilettantes with whom I otherwise find myself in the most intellectually appealing company, will have the crow.

"I need to go back to school tomorrow," Emma said, worried that she had no plans and had not called the substitute."

"When we get back, all three of us will get subs for tomorrow," Jarret said. "It is precisely the hour of midnight that teachers get sick. Ask any veteran sub. It's not only common; it's damn well expected. Actually it could be that we all get food poisoning from the soup! We must watch over each other throughout the night. Just look, the rain still coming in torrents. Why it's not a fit night for man nor beast."

"Are you drunk?" Dora said turning around to look at Jarret in the back.

"Ho! Ho! I perceive thou art much improved! Oh, how quickly thou forget thy comforter! But, being thy faithful servant, I will not desert you even now though thy words pierce my heart like a sword. I will assist both of you with getting substitutes, having already procured my own, before we have our party in Emma's room, it being the farthest away from Mrs. Camden's room below."

"I already have one but she doesn't have a plan for tomorrow yet." Emma said. She was exhausted, nervous, and worried. The three made their way quietly to the front door. All lights were out, and Emma fumbled for her key. Jarret, seeing Dora was wobbly, held her up. Once in Emma's room, Jarret asked Dora for a plan she could use for an emergency and said he would go down to call someone to go in for her. Meanwhile Emma strained to focus on what she could tell her Mrs. Rathbone, her sub, and prayed silently for strength. When Jarret returned, mission accomplished, Emma went downstairs in the dark with a flashlight to make her call. It was almost as if Mrs. Rathbone was waiting for the call. She understood about Dora's food poisoning and the emergency room. She would make do somehow. "I will make it up to you—somehow," Emma promised. "And thank you so very much."

It was done: all three would be absent the next day, already in its infancy. Returning to her room, Emma found Jarret perched on her dresser stool, playing "Edelweiss" on his guitar, Dora sitting on the carpet where she had held Mr. Blue Eyes, her back cushioned to the wall by one of Emma's pillows.

"Notice we have not violated your bed or desk, knowing both are sacred space," said Jarrett without interrupting his tune.

"You play so lovely; no one hearing you would guess you are such a juvenile, a sweet juvenile, of course." Emma said. "I give up on this night."

"Give up! No, never! We shall overcome! This is the time to screw up our courage. The fates are on our side." Jarret grew more dramatic as he started over his song. "It is the time for Mademoiselles to tell their tales of woe and be baptized in the spirit of redemption."

"I love all the songs from *The Sound of Music*," Dora said, as if remembering something magical.

"Oh, so do I," said Emma. "I learned all the songs when I was fourteen and sang them every day of that summer."

Jarret stopped playing. "It is now time for you to eat your soup, Dora."

"No, I couldn't keep it down. You eat it."

"No, it would interfere with my delusions about life. You eat it, then, Emma."

"No, this is soup from a Mother's heart and hands." Emma pointed out. "It would be sinful for anyone but Dora to consume it."

"Now, let us begin." Jarret joined Dora and Emma on the floor, leaning his back against the hall door, nestling his guitar in his lap as if it were a boxy baby. We will each make our confessions and be forgiven by the other two and hopefully God, if he is still awake at this hour. And afterwards, we will make our vows to stick together in this hellish place until our scholarships are paid off, or until the Millionaire visits us, or until I go to Vietnam and take you two with me. Oh, by the way, what happened to make you take fifteen Darvocets?"

"It's nothing you would understand," Dora said.

"Emma, you look too anxious and sad," said Jarret, diverting his attention away from Dora. "Have you ever tasted champagne?"

"No, but I had some wine at your rehearsal party. Remember?"

Jarret opened Emma's small refrigerator and took out the champagne he had brought earlier. He poured two small cups, handing one to Emma, the other to Dora. "I know you pure bred country girls have never tasted champagne, but tonight is the night. It is good for the spirit and good for confessions."

"Do you think she should?" asked Emma, looking at Dora.

"Oh, she will vomit it up if her stomach is not ready, but I predict it will be just the thing to settle her."

"I did have champagne at my cousin's wedding once when I was sixteen and went to New Jersey with another cousin," Dora confessed. "Of course, Mother wasn't there. She trusted my older cousin to look after me."

"And there's our first confession. Now, Emma. Why are you here hiding in your room this week, not facing the enemy? And don't tell me you're sick."

"I told you already. I just ran out of steam, out of plans, out of spirit. I want to make plans for the rest of the year so that I can put some energy into the prom we have to put on. You two know it is next on our plates."

"Why did you want to be an English teacher, Emma?" Jarret took control of the discussion.

"Because I love literature and thought I could make my students love it."

"And, you, Dora?"

"Ditto."

"And me? Ditto for music."

The champagne seemed to go straight to Dora's brain, Emma noting Dora's serious countenance changing into a relaxed smile. Emma was slow to feel the numbness creeping over her. She wanted the soup, remembering she had not had anything except crackers she shared with Mr. Blue Eyes at lunch.

"This champagne tastes just like that I drank at my cousin's wedding," said Dora. "Give me some more. It's is settling my stomach after all."

Jarret played a song now that Emma tried to recall. She knew it from a movie. "What is that you're playing?"

"As soon as you tell me the movie it's from, I will tell you the words, and we'll all sing it together until we believe it and make it our anthem."

"I know it too," said Dora, waving her cup for more. "Just give me a minute and I'll tell you the movie and the name of the song."

Emma could see a group of children and the actress with short red hair leading the children in song. And then she saw Cary Grant come into the room.

"It's the movie about the woman; what's her name, who was supposed to meet Cary Grant at the top of the Empire State Building and she was so excited she ran in front of a car and was paralyzed and couldn't walk. She never tells him and he tracks her down and finds out at the end."

"Yes," said Dora, "what a love story, it is. *An Affair to Remember!*"

"And the song title?" asked Jarret, still playing his guitar.

The women hummed and drank champagne. "Tomorrowland!" said Emma.

"And that's where we're headed, all together. Here's the words. I'll sing it once for you:

Tomorrowland
There's a wonderful place called tomorrowland
And it's only a dream away
And the moment you get to tomorrowland
You'll forget about today.

You'll be walking on clouds,
You'll forget every care,
And your troubles, like bubbles, will vanish in air
Ask me how do you get to tomorrowland
Close your eyes; make a wish and you're there.

Jarret stopped when he saw Dora crying. "What! This is a happy song! What's the matter?"

"When I close my eyes, I see only more of yesterday, all the mean, hateful, ignorant people. We haven't moved beyond the time of Frederick Douglass."

"Frederick Douglass, eh? Well, I must say I have not thought of him lately," Jarret said. "Well, the laws have changed."

"But you can't legislate attitudes and principles," Emma added.

"Damn right! Just look at the conscientious objectors who have fled to Canada. The only reason I'm not in Vietnam is that I'm here teaching in this poor county where they need me to stop fights and drive buses on field trips and stand in the rain during bus duty. Still, I'll take it over risking my life every day in muddy rice fields. This is my honorable way out without disgracing my family and of course paying back what we all owe to the gov'ment for our teaching scholarships."

"I was taught I could be anything I wanted to be if I worked hard, harder than white kids," Dora said. "That's what my mother taught me. She took me with her to Washington when King made his dream speech. I knew I had what it takes to conquer the world. I knew I could make a difference. I knew I could make all students love to learn and all white students love me because I was a good teacher who wanted a good future for them. Could I have some more champagne, please?"

Jarrett opened the second bottle and passed it to her. "Emma," he said, "what do you make of Dora's confession? Did you want to make all students love you?"

"Not after the first class the first day. But I am too thin-skinned. I take every little comment they make personally. I know they don't see teachers as human." By now Emma felt as if nothing mattered except the bonding of the three. Dora was such a beautiful, sensitive, quiet spoken girl, and Jarret, tall and handsome, not intimidated by authority and rules, tackling life head on, not turning a blind eye to anything he did not like or not want to deal with. Jarret continued to play "Tomorrowland."

"Dora," said Emma, "why did you mention Douglass?" She sensed she'd hit on a nerve as Dora grimaced and leaned back on the pillow to her back.

"Well, as an English major, you have read some of Douglass, no doubt, but there is never any of his writing in our text. I wanted to try to get the students, black and white, really to see that reading and writing can empower them, that these skills are weapons against ignorance, against those in power who would feel more secure if they never became literate. So I typed a couple of long passages from Douglass's *Narrative* where he relates how his master's wife taught him the alphabet and was going to teach him to read until the master told her not to teach him because he would become dangerous. They wouldn't be able to keep him in his place. So Douglass devises strategies to learn to read from white boys and later how to write from white boys. He was hungry for knowledge and found a way to educate himself because he wanted to be free, to become a leader, and make a difference."

"Why did you type all that? To make copies?" Emma asked.

"Yes, and that was my mistake. All that work. I thought we had a good lesson. I told them they were spoiled and lazy to have such an opportunity and not soak up all they could learn like sponges. I told them if they got home and the television was on, they should tell their parents to turn it off and read while they read and did their homework."

"That is sacrilege!" Jarret shouted. "Don't you know that nothing interferes with the soaps from one o'clock to four thirty? Then mother fixes supper if she's home. If she's working, the television is on as soon as she gets home. Also, it's part of the working poor's social elevation to go to work and talk about last night's sit-com. You know these families don't have newspapers and magazines in the house. Students don't see their parents reading unless it is to find a Bible verse to back up the evil of something." He never stopped playing as he talked, now "Edelweiss" again. Emma marveled that he had such concentration.

Afraid Jarret would suppress Dora's confession, Emma made stern eyes at him and frowned. "So you had a good lesson?"

"I thought so, but yesterday Mr. Franklin came to homeroom asking me about the lesson. Someone had given him a copy of the passages I handed out. Well, a parent I should say. Some white student had gone home and told the parents that I said white people did not want blacks to be able to read and write because as long as they couldn't whites could keep them in their place."

"I'd say that student was correct!" Jarret stopped playing.

"But that is not what I taught! That was not the objective of the lesson!" Dora raised her voice louder than Jarret's.

"Then Mr. Franklin said he knew I had not meant to make that point, but that he wanted me to stick to the literature in the text. You know what that is for blacks: the Uncle Tom stuff, like Booker T. and Langston Hughes."

"And don't forget that black Colonial poet," Emma said. "What's her name? The one that was raised by whites and lived in luxury?"

"Phyllis Wheatley," said Dora.

Suddenly they all started to laugh, silly giggling. Jarret took the last drink of his pint of crow and opened the third bottle of champagne.

"If you just go through the proper channels, use the judicial system as it was meant to be used, you can effect changes and bring justice to all," Emma said in her best dramatic voice. "If a student is disrespectful or impedes the learning of others, just bring it to the attention of the parents and the principal."

Jarret joined Emma in her theatrics by standing to deliver his speech. "Yes, the parents will whip their wayward urchins for disgracing them by being troublemakers as did their parents, and the principal will back you unconditionally as the authority in your own class and bring out his hickory stick for ten whacks." They all laughed again, uncontrollably.

Then Dora started to cry again even as she laughed. Emma thought of the eggs splattered on her desk and of the drawing

Jarret described to her of him and Mr. Franklin, and she started to cry too.

"It is time, my dearest friends to make our pledge to support each other, to pledge our hearts, our superior intellect, our resources, our courage, our loyalty to one another, and our mutual dream for a better future once our debt here is paid. Let's drink to it. Give us liberty or give us death."

Emma and Dora raised their paper cups to meet Jarret's: "I pledge to all you said," they said simultaneously and drank the last of the third bottle of champagne.

Now to prove your devotion, you must sing with me all the words to "Tomorrowland." Jarret played and started to sing as the girls joined in where they remembered or guessed the words. "Again," he said.

They laughed and cried at the same time and sang the song over and over until they collapsed one by one and slept until Mrs. Camden knocked loudly on the door at eight-thirty the next morning. Emma conversed with her without opening the door, telling her that Dora had been sick and spent the night with her and that neither of them was going to school. When Mrs. Camden asked if Emma knew where Jarrett was, she said he had gone with her to take Dora to the hospital and that he had gone to his room upon returning. That much was true, but she did not say that Jarret had joined the girls and spent the night and was now sleeping on the carpet at the foot of her bed.

While Mrs. Camden prepared scrambled eggs for Emma and Dora, Emma woke Jarret, helped him to his room, and locked the door behind her. If Mrs. Camden decided to invade his room with her master key at least she would find him in his own room. When Dora woke up mid-morning, Emma told her to go down and let Mrs. Camden know she was all right so that she wouldn't spread any rumors about her being sick. Meanwhile Emma cleaned up her room and worked the rest of the day and night on plans. The next day Jarret and Dora went back to school, but Emma did not return until the following Monday. Armed with weeks of plans, a rested body, a rejuvenated soul, and a bond with Dora and Jarret, she was ready to take on the system.

It was not until second period that Annie, a gossipy girl who lived in the subdivision across from the Teacherage said, "I know why you, Miss Grimes, and Mr. Bridgewater were out yesterday. I heard you all got drunk and had an all-night organism." Shocked and angry, Emma counted to ten silently. "Annie, someone has told you lies."

"Miss Applewhite," said Clarence, who sat beside Annie, "I think Annie means *orjee*, but she wouldn't know what it means anyhow."

The rest of the day Emma thought about the comment and where it must have come from: Mrs. Camden, of course. Then Emma remembered that she had put Jarret's empty bottle as well as three champagne bottles in the garbage can outside the building. Mrs. Camden must have examined her trash and said something to a neighbor. The rumor would have reached the principal by the next day.

Emma was selfishly thankful when Jarret caught up with her walking to the Teacherage at the end of her first day back. Mr. Franklin had confronted him about the rumor that he, Dora, and Emma had consumed a large amount of alcohol after taking Dora home from the hospital. What kind of sense did that make he had asked Jarrett, who caught off guard, simply said the three were at a point of needing a catharsis and that the champagne for the girls had made it possible for them to share their anxieties and vow to support each other as neophytes in their profession. Jarret said he told Mr. Franklin that he had drunk the bourbon. Mr. Franklin didn't buy the story. He reminded Jarret that the community was comprised of good church-going folks who did not tolerate such conduct from teachers, especially unmarried teachers living right there in the Teacherage. Mrs. Camden's husband had been chairman of the school board for twenty years, and she still felt it her duty to monitor and report the conduct of teachers when she thought it inappropriate. If Jarret would warn Dora and Emma, Mr. Franklin said he would not embarrass them by calling them in, but that if he heard any more, he would and that they should remember they needed a recommendation wherever they worked.

That evening, the fates on their side, the three were able to meet in Emma's room, Mrs. Camden having been taken out for her grandson's birthday party. From Emma's window they could see any car that drove up. Jarret led the meeting, histrionic, waving his arms wildly and shouting and then dying to a whisper. "We must find a secret place to meet to renew our pledge of support and devise strategies to survive until our four years are paid, and by then we will know if we can stay or go."

"My mother's farm is the place. No white folks would dare go down that woody path at night unless they were prepared to shoot to kill. My mother has a pistol and a shot gun, plus two German shepherds.

"Well, my dear, I wouldn't rule that out," said Jarret, his big brown eyes shining in the room lighted only by the dying light in the window. "Yet, I believe you are correct that it is the best place: close, secluded. But how about your mother?"

"We could meet on Wednesday nights while she's gone to church. My uncle and aunt pick her up every week. We would have a couple of hours at least and often they eat at the church before the service. If I told my mother not to say anything, you could count on it."

"And your aunt and uncle?"

"No, besides we could park behind the old barn, and they wouldn't even see us. In fact, the old tobacco barn would be a good place to meet. There is still a kerosene heater in there from when my bachelor uncle lived there until he died."

"This is sounding spooky," said Emma, "but I have fond memories of tobacco barns where we had tobacco tying parties and where corn was stored for the mule."

"No," said Jarret. "I thought you were a bona fide country girl. You mean pack houses. Tobacco tyings were held in pack houses, not tobacco barns!"

"We were not prosperous enough to have a pack house, but I do remember a mule shed with a shoulder high trough for ears of corn." The banter was interrupted by headlights of a car turning in the Teacherage driveway. "So when's the first meeting?" Emma asked.

"This Wednesday night," Dora said, "at seven-thirty at the barn. Park behind it. I'll explain everything Mother needs to know."

They scattered like Robin Hood and his band, Jarret kissing each sister on her cheek. Emma thought he should be on the stage. He seemed always to be acting, his brown hair waving in tempo with his wide gestures. Life was a concert to conduct, something he could direct if only others would hear the music and follow.

CHAPTER XI: THE PROM

The first meeting of the threesome was cancelled when Dora, on lunchroom duty, slipped on spilled soup and broke her leg. She was still able to do her work and did not miss a day at school. The accident, however, threw the prom work on Emma and Jarret while Dora nursed her leg and supported them by making phone calls and sending her best juniors to the gym to help clean up and transform the place into the scene of Jay Gatsby's elaborate parties designed to allure the beautiful and wealthy Daisys of North West High. The week of the prom Jarret took his afternoon band classes outside to the field beside the gym and left his best student in charge with orders not to interrupt him unless a fight broke out or someone tried to leave. He did not say anything to Emma, who noticed his classes outside after lunch and realized the prom was only five days away. She worked Monday and Tuesday after school with her students until ten at night. Jarret's crew was there also, cleaning, decorating the ceiling with tarps and colored lights. His students put down a sea of grass, a fountain, a gazebo with a winding walkway leading to it, an exquisite painting of a garden on the wall behind it. As one entered the gym, one was greeted by a gigantic painting of Jay Gatsby, standing by his yellow Rolls-Royce, art work by the most talented junior at the school. Oh, thought Emma, if only I taught art or music.

Emma was in charge of decorating the bathrooms, setting up

tables, getting flowers, ordering food, and launching a hundred balloons to the ceiling. Jarret had retained several college buddies to provide music free of charge with his band students. They often played at events for each other's schools without charge. Emma ran out of money after making a deal with a caterer. Instead of asking for Mr. Franklin's help, she spent her own money to finish the work, spending ninety-three dollars the last two days. Dora said she could get fresh flowers free from her mother's garden and rode out to the farm with Emma the morning of the prom to cut gladiolas, zinnias, spider lilies, phlox, gardenias, tulips, and chrysanthemums and to pull armfuls of ivy growing under the crepe myrtles and camellias. So integral a part of the garden was Mrs. Grimes that, donned in a green dress and straw hat with streaming yellow ribbons, she appeared as one of the sun flowers in the mesh of unwieldy stems and blossoms tossing their heads in the morning breeze. Emma sensed that Mrs. Grimes was proud of her donation of flowers she had grown to adorn the tables as well as the gazebo for the prom. Watching Dora sitting in the car, the passenger's door open, her leg cast extending out, her mother, knife in hand, turned to Emma, who pointed to the flowers she wanted cut.

"Dora really appreciates you and Jarret, and I also appreciate the support and friendship you all have given Dora. It's a tough time to enter the teaching profession. You three are playing a role in what we will look back on as a critically important time in history."

"We have pledged to stick with each other through this year and the next three. And we haven't given up our idea of meeting here on Wednesday nights, as soon as we can get out here. It seems as if there is always something going on at the school."

Once the flowers were placed in smoke-colored vases to adorn the tables covered with black cloths with pink fringe,

Emma and Dora left Jarret in charge of assisting the photographer's setup and the stage for the band. Emma hoped she would not fall asleep standing in the dim lights until midnight. In a long purple dress borrowed from Martha, Emma arrived at the prom without fanfare just as the food was being brought into the gym, and as she entered the façade of an Italian chateau, she would not have been surprised to see Gatsby standing by the gazebo. Instead, she saw the photographer, who looked amazingly like Emma imagined Tom Buchanan, a strong brute, mustachioed, and already sweating in his long-sleeved white shirt. Jarret, arriving just as the students with their dates stepped from their newly waxed, mostly borrowed cars, sprinted with occasional stumbles through the grass and gravel parking lot in front of the gym. He provided the closest image of Gatsby that anyone was likely to see. Setting up his guitar on stage with his fellow musicians, he looked cold sober and clean, his white jacket and black bow tie more immaculate and fitting than the attire of his friends, who struggled clumsily with their instruments, tuning and testing, asking Jarret for assistance. Emma thought him so handsome and talented. She wished she had his courage not to care so much, not to let her emotions get the best of her.

But for one night, all the students behaved, acting the part of the prince and princess come to the castle to eat in tiny bites and dance slow dances at first and then, once the photos were taken, to let go and line dance, some right out the side door and into the moonlight, where unknown to them, Mr. Franklin had twenty fathers with flashlights milling around the building. Inside, the atmosphere was perfect. Despite her broken leg, Dora slow danced briefly with the handsome black math teacher, Harold Reed, a single man with six years' experience at the school.

The president of the senior class, one of Emma's favorite students, asked her to dance, but citing her duties as punch server, declined. The night passed quickly. The worst Emma heard was that a few boys smuggled in liquor and that fathers found condoms in the glove compartments of their borrowed, unlocked cars. Emma did overhear a whispered exchange between two chaperones in the ladies' room about eleven that the fathers had found pantie hose under a shrub and were frantically trying to determine who on the dance floor was naked under her shimmering gown, for all who had arrived by car were accounted for. Perhaps the locker rooms, thought Emma, but no one thought to check those smelly quarters, not part of the prom's domain. But realizing that if something happened, she would be partly blamed, she squeezed behind the photographer's setup and wedged herself between the gazebo and the hall door leading to the locker rooms. As soon as she found a light and turned it on, she heard scrambling and rustling sounds. "George and Alma, if you come on out and dance, I won't tell on you," Emma said in a calm voice, making the accusation based purely on intuition.

"Miss Applewhite, we weren't doing nothing but kissing," a terrified, high-pitched Alma Bailey's voice echoed from a dark corner.

"Just do as I said. Be out here in two minutes!" Emma was angry and amused at the same time, all the time wondering how buxom Alma ever got through the small space behind the gazebo. Emma waited, pretending to be interested in the photographer's work. In less than a minute, George appeared, literally pulling Alma through the space. She looked thinner as if she had held her breath to get through and was afraid now to breathe.

"Just move leisurely with me to the punch table, my handsome couple," said Emma. No one seemed to notice the three except Mr. Franklin, who made it his business to approach Emma. "What's going on? Anything I need to know?"

"No, sir. Everything is fine. I just asked George and Alma to serve the punch for a while. My arm is getting tired."

"Good experience for them," he said, giving them a big smile.

Well, there were two Emma wouldn't have to worry about the rest of their days at North West High. Officially the prom was over at midnight. The last half hour Emma noticed the band played slower songs, couples clung to each other on the dance floor, and the others sat at their tables, most somehow drunk on pineapple sherbet and gingerale punch. On her second visit to the ladies' room, Emma heard two students gossiping. "I've heard he's gay too," the girl in the stall beside Emma said to the other refreshing her makeup. "But he sure is sweet and handsome and a devil if you make him mad in class."

"Well, everybody in school knows about the drawing of him and the principal that was delivered to the office. Too bad I never got to see it."

Emma did not leave the restroom until the girls had time to return to the dance floor or their tables. Who would believe these rumors? Jarret was no more gay than she was. Something in her heart felt that she was in love with him and that it had taken those vicious words to make her feel it. She, Dora, and Jarret needed to meet in their secret place without the refreshments. Emma wanted to protect Jarret. It was because of his audacity that they targeted his sexuality. He was not one of the Southern gentlemen who put their white women on pedestals in public. Sometimes he scolded girls, telling them they were spoiled and made them cry. Spreading these rumors was their way of getting back at him.

The plethora of praises heaped upon the prom committee precluded any reprimands or citations of shortcomings to that bedraggled threesome, the brief remainder of the school year passing without calamity, the secret meeting place never used.

Emma applied for teaching summer school again and won the job, veteran teachers considering teaching summer school unconscionable. Dora went to New Jersey to stay with an aunt who had offered her summer work in her beauty shop while Jarret left for, in his words, "travels to broaden his intellectual horizons."

Emma received a brief letter in July from Dora, who was managing the books for her aunt; neither had heard from Jarret. Except for two visits to Aunt Ophelia's, where Martha and Helen gathered, Emma did not leave the Teacherage all summer. Once summer classes were over, Mr. Franklin needed Emma to help develop fall class schedules. He scheduled her and Dora with all sophomores for their second year.

No teachers having been hired, Emma, Dora, and Jarret continued to be the new teachers and were the youngest by at least five years. Dora, arriving a week before school started, bubbled over with stories of the wives of black attorneys and successful business men who patronized her aunt's shop. She had fallen in love with a self-described rising star in an accounting firm and lamented that if she did not owe her state scholarship, she could get a job up there. Jarret arrived just two days before teacher workdays, as brown as if he had cropped tobacco without a shirt all summer; instead, he said he had worked all summer at the beach in South Carolina, in a hot dog and ice cream stand on the boardwalk by day and in a bar in the pavilion at night. Emma thought he looked more handsome than when he left, yet rugged, his complexion like overdone toast, his hair streaked blonde and red. Yet he had lost none of his aggressive nature, cursing when he found out the new instruments he needed for band had not arrived.

The first day with all sophomores Emma thought they were all angels and wondered that there could be so much difference between them and her last year's students. By the second day, however, the illusions became reality: they were the brothers and sisters of last year's students. Having all one grade level did provide Emma the time to plan richer, more in depth lessons, and such was her forte. She ordered materials with her own money, studied the professional journals, soaked up all the new ideas, never tiring of searching for the food she could serve that would charm the beasts.

The first week a farm girl in her first period class brought her a biddy in a shoe box, the ultimate compliment, a bribe, and cry for help all in one yellow downy chick. The gift was unexpected, bestowed by a shy, stringy haired girl who never said anything and never caused trouble. She said it was an Easter biddy even though the month was September. Emma did not know how to refuse it, so she simply thanked Molly, who said the biddy would be all right until after school, having put a cup of water and some feed in the box. She had also put a small plastic bag full of biddy feed in the box and had punched air holes in the top. Emma asked her landlady what she should do with the biddy, knowing Dora's mother no longer raised animals on her farm. Mrs. Camden said to put the chick in the kitchen where the floor was linoleum and where she could take care of it until they figured out someone who would want to raise it. One evening when Mrs. Camden was out to dinner with her daughter, Emma decided to fix spaghetti for herself and leave some for Dora and Jarret if they came in hungry. Hearing the beep, beep of the chick in the box, she decided to let the prisoner out while she cooked. Emma forgot the chick as she darted from the stove to the cabinet to the refrigerator to the table until glancing down, she realized the chick was following her, sometimes losing traction and sliding on the waxed floor. The downy chick was also growing brown wing feathers. He or she was now a teenager. Something had to be done before the chick started flying. When Dora came in about

234   *Mi Mi Roberts*

seven-thirty, Emma, cleaning up the kitchen, called to her to have some spaghetti. "How did you know I did not have supper?"

"I just have a way of knowing these things," said Emma. Dora had just left school, having had a meeting with a parent and Mr. Franklin. Emma decided to let Dora figure out the dilemma of the chick while she ate at the kitchen table.

"Am I just tired, or is that a biddy following me to the table?" Dora did not sound amused. The homemade spaghetti worked wonders on Dora's heart. She said her mother would know someone who could take the chick. She figured he or she was still in a malleable stage. Dora also said her mother had fixed up the old tobacco barn behind her house for storage of some antique furniture. "It has not only a kerosene heater but tables, chairs, candles, and kerosene lamps. Let's meet on the Wednesday, Halloween, while Mother is gone to the church program for the kids. Tell Jarret," she said.

Emma had her story ready for the first meeting, one that overshadowed the normal cheating, disrespect, sweet innocents ignored for being good, handouts left in the desk or on the floor, gum stuck under the desks, obscenities scratched on the desks, her constant attempt to transfer students' destructive creative energy into constructive energy by turning them into leaders, for the troublemakers were usually those with the highest intelligence. One student, however, presented a dilemma she needed help with, and having learned that taking a problem to the administrative staff made her feel weak and inept, she wanted to find out Dora and Jarret's ideas. Shortly after school had started in late August, a sophomore named Edith Munden, had grown obsessively clinging to Emma to the point that Emma felt something was abnormal. The girl was bright, but shy in class, watching the scene to support Emma if she needed help when no one would volunteer to take a grammar problem or go to the board or read a poem. English came easy for Edith, her papers some of the best Emma had from all five classes.

Edith volunteered to come to Emma's study hall to grade papers, saying she wanted to be an English teacher and wanted the experience. The girl ran errands and recognized tasks that had to be done before Emma assigned them to her. Emma found Edith competent and easy to get along with, but after about three weeks, Edith became a burden and a nuisance. She returned to Emma's room after school, a time Emma wanted to be alone. The day's end was always like the official end of a six-hour hurricane, passing sometimes intense, sometimes lulling in the eye. It took at least twenty minutes for Emma to focus on what she needed to do, what to pack up, what to make copies of for the next day. The duplicating machine was always tied up in the early morning, a line waiting to use it. On her way out each day, Emma checked her mailbox in the office for the third time. Today she had a note from the secretary saying she had a gift on her desk. Seeing several students waiting in the office, Emma tried to sneak in unobserved, looking on Mrs. Tillman's desk for a box; instead she saw a dozen long-stemmed roses with her name on the small white card pinned to the red ribbon. "Thank you. I can't imagine..." Emma muttered and took the huge vase out. She had driven to school because of the rain and put the flowers in the car. There was no name or message inside the card. Emma wracked her brain, but could think of no one. Who would send roses on the day before Halloween? Oh, Lord, no. It might be Edith!

On Halloween a cold rain set in, predicted to last through the night. Students decided to play their tricks during the day. Just as Emma had gotten the worst class working after twenty minutes of directions and reprimands, she sat down in her desk chair, producing vile sounds of flatulence induced by a device hidden under the cushion of her chair. The ensuing uproar of laughter gave those who did not know test answers ample time to copy their neighbors' papers. It took ten more minutes to get the class settled again. The test was important, and most students were doing their best. Emma, taking the joke good naturedly, suspected the culprit was Jerry, who had put his felt hat on as if to heat his brain. Almost unconsciously, Emma, feeling lighthearted and sympathetic to this, her lowest class, walked up and down the rows, stopping by Jerry, who uncharacteristically concentrated on his test, and on a whim picked off Jerry's hat, setting off a small snow storm of small notes falling from the top of his head. Stunned, the boy stood up, looking at Emma as if she had supernatural powers. "How did you know!" he said.

Emma could not help laughing because she had had no inkling he was hiding cheating notes in his hat but did not deny her powers to the class. "Well, one less paper to grade, Jerry. You really shouldn't go to such lengths to make my life easier." Unfortunately Emma knew that a zero did not much matter to Jerry Sykes or to his parents. What concerned him was whether he would have any supper or whether his mother's boyfriend would beat her up that night. He was the same boy who during a writing assignment had asked in a flurry of attention from his pals if he could use a four-letter expletive in his essay. Emma had already checked their dictionaries to see if such words were entered and knowing they were not, had nonchalantly answered, "You may use any word in the dictionary."

"All right!" the boy had said, excited that he might use a dirty word in his writing. But, alas, none of the three whose heads bobbed over the intimidating dictionary could find the word they so longed to use.

Halloween night was wet, the rain still misting. Clouds raced through the sky intermittently, hiding the low-hanging orange moon. Dora rode with Emma to the farm, arriving at seven-thirty. "Something smells like a funeral home in this car!" Dora said, looking in the back seat. "What kind of fragrance do you use? Whatever it is, you should change to vanilla."

"I do have something to show you and Jarret at our meeting, but I want to tell it only once."

The old farm house was lighted with warm white candles in the windows as if it were Christmas. "Wow, the candles are pretty and inviting on a night like this," Emma remarked.

"She keeps them on all year. In July they make me so hot I can't sleep here. Stop here, and let me make sure my uncle has picked her up already." Dora used her key to unlock the front door, called her mother, and not getting an answer, returned to the car. "Drive to the barn, just keep on the path that circles around to the back and goes down to the fields." The tobacco barn was about a quarter of a mile behind the house. Jarret's Mustang was parked in the path just past the barn. When Dora and Emma opened the door and stepped over the high door, they heard a grunt. Jarret was chinning on one of the tier poles.

"I bet you ladies can't chin like this," he said between grunts. "I used to do this all the time growing up. It was something to fill in while I waited for the next stick of looped tobacco to poke up to the hangers. I was always lucky enough to be the poker."

"Bet I can," said Dora. She was five-feet seven inches and had no problem pulling her chin up to the first tier pole. When Emma, five foot three, tried, Jarret came to her aid, picking her up by her waist and hoisting her up to chin.

"We are all hereby initiated into the brotherhood—and sisterhood—of all who have toiled and dreamed in this sacred barn, the equalizer of landowner, tenant, and day laborer." Jarret had a way of articulating thoughts that, once said, Emma realized were hers also but never so well put.

"Can you remember the wet tobacco leaves dripping on your head on rainy days when you worked in the barn?" Dora asked, looking around as if seeing herself in younger years working in the barn.

"Oh, sure," said Jarret. "Not only on my head but, as poker, into my eyes as I looked up to find the hand of the hanger."

"So can I," Emma said, "and I remember picking up the scrap leaves strewn like a pallet and gritty with sand. My aunt wanted every stem and ragged leaf saved. It was my job to pick them up and loop them."

"The women around our barns were apt to hear some sassy talk," said Jarret. "It was mostly a man's job with us, and if a woman helped hang, she might get embarrassed if we forgot she was there."

"You just made me recall a funny thing that happened to me one day when we were hanging and carrying heavy sticks to the barn to hand to the poker," Emma reminisced. "I must have been about thirteen and had on an old cotton bra, which I really didn't need. Anyway, as I carried those sticks, too heavy for me, one strap worked its way down my arm and broke. I felt it when it broke but I had a jacket over my shirt, so it didn't matter except for feeling awkward. Well, a black man and his wife were helping us work that day. They were very quiet folks, and as we passed each other going back and forth from the looping racks to the barn where I handed each stick to someone inside, my bra slipped down my arm and hung naked on my arm and hand. The black man and woman saw it, but made not the slightest expression as I looked at the bra and then at them. I stopped, bent down, dropping my stick of tobacco, pulled the bra out of my jacket's sleeve, and put it in my pocket. I was just thankful they were the only ones who saw what happened because you know how humiliating that would be at thirteen."

"And now women are burning their bras!" Jarret exclaimed. "I once went to such an affair while visiting my cousin in Los Angeles."

"Did you have a good time?" asked Dora.

"Yes, a blast, but we didn't have any bras the size you would have contributed unfortunately!"

Emma thought Dora a beautifully balanced girl. She seemed to have everything, including brains and an unpretentious sweetness. Dora motioned Jarret to a table in the corner, and they pulled it to the center while Emma brought up three chairs. Jarret pulled up another for his guitar, which was leaning in a dark corner, and picked up the kerosene lamp he had lighted and put it on the table.

"We will sing our song at the beginning and the end of this meeting. I hope you two have not forgotten the words!"

"Oh, I have something to add before we start," said Emma, jumping up and going out to her car. Returning with the bouquet of roses Edith had sent her, she plopped them down on the table. "Oh, they need a table of their own beside ours; otherwise, we cannot see each other." Dora rummaged in a dark corner where old furniture was stacked and returned with a fern table for the bouquet, placing it beside the round table between Emma and Jarret and placing the flowers on it. Seeing the card, Dora asked, "Who sent them you??

"That is my story for the evening, one I need advice on."

"All right, let's get started, then," Jarret demanded, "and you may go first, Miss Emma Applewhite of Northwest High. Tell us, Miss Applewhite, just what is going on in your life that this group of the best and brightest can help you with?"

"I am assuming your story has to do with these flowers?" Dora said, lighting her face with a beautiful smile.

"Don't get excited, folks. The flowers came from a student, and what's worse, a female student."

"I've been meaning to ask you," Jarret said. "Didn't you ever have a boyfriend?"

"It's not time for you to be clever and philosophical," said Emma. "I need some practical advice."

"Well, answer my question then. You'll see the relevance."

Dora rolled her eyes, doubting Jarret's wisdom.

"I was in love with a boy in high school. He was my bus driver actually and four years older. He married a girl at our school a year younger than he; I think he liked me, but he was already taken by the time I found him."

"Okay, so you have pined ever since?" Jarret asked.

"No, you know how shy and introverted, I am. I just never got out—as my grandmother used to say—amongst them."

"Well, what can I say?" Jarret could not help sounding high minded. "Here we are, all three of us misfits in many ways when most of our high school and college associates are married and have children."

"We're not exactly over the hill," Dora said. "We're just twenty-four! I've had boyfriends, but I'm looking for somebody who speaks standard English and who puts me before basketball and football!"

"Don't hold your breath, Miss Shakespeare!" Jarret cried out, jumping up and waving his arms like a cheerleader. "I need some refreshment before I can solve any problems."

"Mother has some homemade scuppernong wine. Shall I get some for the three of us?"

"Your mother makes wine and you never told me?" Jarret said as if he were going to cry.

"My uncle makes it and gives it to the whole family. Mother drinks eight ounces every night at bedtime. She says the doctor recommended it, but I think that is just because she gives the doctor some of the wine."

All three walked in the dark to the house to get the wine and glasses. The house was a log cabin with a large dark birch paneled kitchen. Dora insisted on using crystal wine glasses. "Now how would it look to the roses if we insulted their presence with wine in paper cups?"

On the way back to the barn, Dora said, "Emma, was it Edith who gave you the roses?"

Emma was completely surprised. "That is what I am wondering. I can't think of anyone else, and Edith is a bit strange. There was no name on the card."

"Well, I've noticed that girl following you around like a puppy," said Dora.

Jarret, ahead of the ladies, did not hear the remarks, preoccupied with placing the glasses on the table and pouring the wine. They sat down and tasted the wine.

"I don't know anything about wines, but this tastes good, Dora. Your uncle should sell this."

None of them having eaten dinner, the wine encountered no obstacles on its way to their brains. Jarret said it would be sacrilegious to start the discussion before singing "Tomorrowland," with his guitar accompaniment, and they sang.

There's a wonderful place called tomorrowland
And it's only a dream away
And the moment you get to tomorrowland
You'll forget about today.

You'll be walking on clouds,
You'll forget every care,
And your troubles, like bubbles, will vanish in air

Ask me how do you get to tomorrowland
Close your eyes; make a wish and you're there.

"So, what's the story behind the bouquet?" asked Jarret, putting his guitar down.

Emma began: "There's this sophomore named Edith Munden, who is in my class and study hall. She is a good student —well, with an aptitude for English—and she told me she wanted to be a teacher and asked if she could help me with marking objective type papers and recording grades—that type of thing. She really has been helpful, accurate, reminding me of things, thinking ahead for me. I think she would make a good teacher. But there is something about her that makes my skin crawl at times and then I feel ashamed for feeling that way about the child."

Jarret had listened pensively as if analyzing as Emma talked. "What exactly disgusts you at times about the girl?" He asked.

"Well, she has such a shiny face and fat cheeks that look as if they are going to pop open. And she giggles at everything and sort of bounces around. I can't quite articulate what it is about her that at times is obnoxious."

"I don't know the girl except for seeing her in the hall. She does sort of smile like a big cat," Dora said.

"And the flowers worry you?" Jarret inferred.

"Well, that is going too far. Don't you think?" Emma said.

"And you are wondering if she is a lesbian? Is that it? Are you afraid of her?" Jarret sounded sincere, Emma thought.

"Emma, you're so nice and kind to all the students who will let you," Dora said. "I don't see anything to get upset about. Just ask her if she sent the flowers and if so, tell her you don't want her to do anything like that again."

"Well, I have listened patiently to you two before interjecting my opinion," said Jarret. "You see, Edith is in the band. She tries to play the clarinet, but has no talent. I can tell you though. She is not a lesbian."

Emma was amused and already lightheaded from the wine. "And how did you determine that? Because she has no talent as a musician?"

Jarret laughed and poured everyone a second glass of wine. Dora looked at Emma in a strange way and then looked at Jarret. Emma thought they shared something she was not privy to. She drank the rest of her second glass of wine and pictured the grapes it was made from. Emma was familiar with scuppernongs on her grandmother's farm cultivated by Uncle Milton, the grass knee high around the arbor, serious bees buzzing their fill. She knew some farmers made wine, but Uncle Milton never did.

"What is at times obnoxious to you about Edith, Emma?" Jarret continued after the pause, jolting Emma from her daze. "Is it that Edith at times looks at you, wanting you to show some sign of loving her, and because you can't, you feel disgusted that someone wants what you cannot feel and deliver?"

Dora looked from Emma to Jarret. "Kids go through weird stages. She'll snap out of it in a week or so," she reassured Emma.

"Okay, I'll get Edith reassigned to help you!" Emma offered.

"That's kind of you, but I have my own little darlings and their parents. You have noticed that I am black and that most of my students are white. You know I have that one accelerated class with only two blacks in there. Thirty-five sharp sophomores, some base brats who have lived all over the world and consider Huntersville a third-world country. They were talking about Strawberry Hill the other day as I passed out papers, and I thought it was odd that they knew about Horace Walpole's Gothic estate. Boy, was I impressed until Joanie, my one loyal student in there, sensing my ignorance, said, 'Miss Grimes, Strawberry Hill is the name of a wine.'"

Jarret fell out of his chair and rolled on the floor with laughter and the effects of wine. "I'm sorry, Dorie," he said, laughing hysterically. "Everybody knows Strawberry Hill is a cheap wine sold in every Quick Mart."

"I didn't know that," said Emma.

"I rest my case," said Jarret. "Of course, you wouldn't know, Emma. You two are the epitome of ignorant, educated girls."

The next day at school as Edith graded a matching vocabulary quiz she said casually to Emma, "What do you three do at your meeting in the tobacco barn on Halloween? Have a séance? Boil a witches brew?"

Emma, astonished, said, "What are you talking about?"

"I saw your car and Mr. Bridgewater's out at the farm parked behind the old tobacco barn."

"What on earth are you talking about?" Emma looked at Edith, whose face was so shiny it looked greased. She wore makeup that did not hide her pimples and no powder. Her tone insinuated something Emma did not like. "When did you think you saw my car?" Emma was sure Edith was lying.

"Oh, it was you all right, you and Miss Grimes? Last night."

Emma thought Edith must live out in the direction of the farm.

"I live on Fireman's Road," Edith said, grinning in her catlike manner.

"How did you happen to be in the vicinity? Are you an undercover agent for the school board?"

Edith giggled, delighted now that she had Emma's full attention.

"Are your parents aware that you trespass on private property?"

Still reveling in Emma's agitation, Edith said, "It was Hallow-een night. Most kids go out. It's not like it was late or anything."

"But Miss Grimes' mother's place is down a private road, a quarter of a mile off the public road. You couldn't have seen any cars unless you drove down the wooded path to the farm. Have you been talking with Mr. Bridgewater?" Yes, thought Emma, Jarret must have talked with Edith. But why would he?

"Oh, I didn't know that was Miss Grimes' mother's place? It's nice. I love the big, old trees and all the shrubs. I bet she has tons of flowers in the spring!"

"So, how did you happen to see us?"

"Actually I followed you from the Teacherage to the farm. Well, once you turned off the road, I went on down to that Quick Mart, parked, went in and bought a hot dog in case I needed to make friends with a mean dog, and walked back down the path. I didn't hear any dog, so I kept walking close to the woods out of the path, and after ten minutes, I saw the house but no cars, so I sneaked around until I saw the two cars near the barn. I could see a dim light through a crack in the barn door, but I couldn't hear what y'all were saying, so I decided to split before I got caught."

The last bell for class rang. "I need to talk with you more about this after school, Edith, about ten minutes after the final bell." Emma's tone was icy but she knew she had played into Edith's hand.

During study hall, Edith reported to help Emma, who had written out directions for her work assignments, not even want-ing to have to speak to Edith. The girl worked the entire period without taking a break. She knew Emma was not pleased.

After school, Emma checked her mailbox and went back to her room to wait for Edith, who appeared promptly at three-thirty, wearing once again her best Cheshire grin.

Emma got right to the point: "Did it ever occur to you that someone might shoot you or that a dog might maul you during such excursions?"

"I'm sorry. It's just that it was Halloween. You know, you get caught up in the excitement. Everybody is up to something." Edith dropped her smile but was not contrite.

"Yes, everybody is up to something. Why weren't you out with your friends, instead of doing personal surveillance?"

"Because my dad had said when he got home that I couldn't go out unless I went to the church function, and my little sister was going to that with my dad's girlfriend. That was the last thing on earth I wanted to do. So, about six-thirty when he was about three sheets in the wind, he fell asleep, and I took his keys and car. He was still asleep when I got back about eight-thirty, and my sister wasn't back yet. I knew Dad would sleep on the couch until his girlfriend brought my little sister home after nine o'clock. So, you see, no one knew I even left the house."

"So you are clever, huh? Outsmart everybody, don't you." Edith grinned but Emma didn't. The story was getting convoluted. "And what about your mother?"

"My mother is gone."

"What do you mean, 'gone'?"

"She left during the summer. About four months ago."

"What happened?" Emma was almost afraid to ask.

"Well, she had a boyfriend. She got tired of Dad's drinking every weekend. It was a long, drawn out thing, but she finally left for good."

"Were you close to her?"

"Yeah, I was. We used to go shopping a lot. Stuff like that."

"Do you talk with her and see her now?"

"No, I wrote her a letter once, and she answered it. Her nerves are bad. She said Dad was driving her crazy and she had to leave. I can see why, but now he is good to me and my little sister. We can get anything we want out of him. And every Saturday night he takes his girlfriend—he just started going out with her a few weeks ago—dancing at a bar in Maysboro. They wear hats and boots and look like Roy Rogers and Dale Evans. She moved in with us about two weeks ago."

Emma wondered how Edith knew Roy Rogers and Dale Evans. Her Dad, of course.

"Here's a picture of Mom," Edith said pulling a photo album out of her large book bag.

The woman looked to be in her early forties. She was pretty and looked nothing like Edith except for the color of her hair. Emma hated her for leaving Edith, but smiled and said, "She's lovely," she said, handing the album back.

"Oh, there's more if you want to look."

"Oh, I didn't realize. Oh, yes, these are nice. Who took them?"

"I took the ones of Mom and Dad and Margaret, my little sister, and Dad took the ones that I am in."

"I thank you for sharing these. Now it's getting late. I have to get ready to go, and I'm sure you need to get home."

"I'm in no hurry. If you have anything for me to do, I can stay and do it and lock your door when I leave."

"That's kind of you, but you don't need to be here alone. So go ahead and let me think what I need to pack up. See you tomorrow."

Edith whirled around and was gone quickly out of the room and out the hall door. Emma put her elbows on her desk and rested her chin in her hands as she watched Edith bounce down the sidewalk to the student parking lot. Her eyes stinging, her throat hurting as though she had swallowed a hard-boiled egg, Emma tried hard to focus on which papers to pack.

Chapter XII: The Epiphany

The remainder of the second year, Emma felt that she regressed. She played games to review for tests, dividing the class into two teams. The students loved the competition. All the sleepers woke up to see the score kept on the board by an honest student and the extroverts leading each side. The method worked well for a fifty-minute class except the last two minutes when the teams almost rose up to fight, and Emma, the perpetual referee, knew they could start fighting any time. But, somehow, the year ended without their coming to blows. There was a God.

Emma's third year was no easier than the first two. She had learned some tricks of the trade, but each year there were new challenges: new rules, new materials, new colleagues, new students, new parents. With all juniors this year, Emma found enthusiasm in presenting plays, letting the actors in each class read the parts, even bringing props and walking through some of the actions. She bought class sets of *The Birds*, *Flowers for Algernon*, *Butterflies are Free*, and *Splendor in the Grass* to supplement the text. In February, she wanted to do something special for Black Literature Month and bought a class set of black poetry paperbacks and ordered *A Raisin in the Sun* with Sidney Poitier. The two-week long unit was an enrichment she was excited about and felt her enthusiasm would be contagious. However, none of the students, not even the blacks seemed excited. She wondered if they were afraid or distrustful. Then on Monday of the second week, a white student came in about twenty minutes after the class had started. He went to his desk but did not give Emma a note. "You're late," she said. "Do you have a note?"

Standing by his desk, which happened to be in the center of the class, he said loud enough for everyone to hear. "I didn't think I'd miss anything important: All we ever do in here is black literature."

Emma couldn't believe her ears. Mike was a good boy or had been up until now. They studied white authors all year and because she presented two weeks of black authors, he had the nerve to say that. Never mind, all her preparation and personal funds invested, she just wanted to slap his stupid face, and she wanted to cry for all the stupidity in the world.

During her lunch period, she stayed in her room if she did not have hall or lunchroom duty. Emma could hear the teacher next door, who had first lunch, lecturing to her class. The teacher's voice projected so well between the thin walls that Emma could hear most of the teacher's words but not the students'. Emma knew which teacher this was and knew she was already a veteran. Emma was enthralled with the interaction of the class and the generation of discussion, the laughter, and yet the lesson sounded academic. One day she heard a student ask, "What was Romanticism?" The teacher replied in a tone that seemed to invoke the gods to help her answer such a mysterious subject, "It was … a movement in which the critical criterion for genius was imagination." And Emma was hooked. She decided then and there without realizing it that she would study and lecture and stop spoon feeding her students. She would present the information and let them digest it or choke. It was all the same to her. She was tired of thinking for them and repeating everything ten times.

At the end of the year during a teacher workday, Emma took

Dora and Mr. Quinten, the black assistant principal, to lunch; that is, she asked them if they wanted to go to lunch. Everyone besides the three of them seemed to have already gone. They agreed to go, and Emma drove them to a nearby country kitchen restaurant. They were seated at a table in the center of the room where all could inspect them. Not long into the meal, Emma could feel the eyes on them. White men, most in their twenties or thirties, wearing their caps as they ate, looked at the racially mixed group as if they were on exhibit in a jar of formaldehyde at the fair. Well, now she knew where Mike got his views. My God, Emma thought; this is 1973, but here it was more like 1873. Emma wanted to turn toward the men and scream, "We're teachers, trying to educate your children who are growing up to be just as narrow-minded as you."

The third year ended without a single meeting at the barn. Dora had been preoccupied with taking care of her ailing mother, and Jarret's musical talents were tapped by folks all over the county for charitable work. Still, he was rough with the lazy and untalented students. Still they spread rumors of his being gay. Emma knew students could be vicious. Most did not even know what gay meant.

Emma, Dora, and Jarret had been busy battling but growing, gaining confidence. The summer separated the three, Emma teaching summer school again and visiting her mother and sister, Dora working on the farm with her mother, and Jarret traveling to wherever he desired.

The fourth year began with the three reuniting in Emma's room the night before the first teacher day back, a Tuesday night. Emma thought Jarret had never looked more handsome. Again he had worked at the beach, and he had endless stories of his friends' little band playing at the pavilion every night except Sunday and Monday nights. His dark tan contrasted with his perfect white teeth and large grey-brown eyes, complementing his blonde-streaked sandy hair. Dressed in a long-sleeved white shirt and tan trousers, he talked on and on, not dulled by drink this time, Emma noted. Dora also looked robust, having assisted her mother in her vegetable and flower garden all summer. It was the start of the last year of paying off their scholarships.

Emma had all juniors, one of whom was the principal's son, a sweet teenager who had some type of disability. No one talked with Emma about him, and she was surprised when he showed up in third period and sat right in front of her lectern. She noticed he had trouble writing but he did not ask for any special help. Emma wondered why the principal had put him in her class when there were several more experienced teachers in the school that she thought he would have preferred for his son. She had already made up her mind that she would demand some critical thinking: no more true false, multiple choice, and matching tests. She would present the literature in chronological literary periods and give essay tests. Grammar and writing would be taught through essay writing. The approach would most likely kill her with paper grading but at least she would not go quietly into that good night. She felt strong and was thankful for being thin and strong and enduring, thankful she could walk and stand lecturing five hours every day, not missing any note passed, any smirk, and whisper, any hint of gratitude or malice. She had accepted that students did not perceive teachers as human beings with feelings. Teachers were part of the system that their parents had taught them tried to control and push them around.

And so Emma started the year with the Colonial Period, to be followed by the Revolutionary Period, the Renaissance, the Romantic Period, the Age of Realism, and the Modern Period. Students were interested in the Puritans and witchcraft and read the *Crucible* with more interest than Emma had expected. For one thing, she had better students. Most could read, if not well. Emma studied and researched the music, art, architecture, and other literature written during the periods. Preparing activities to bring alive the historical backdrop of the literature, she lived the periods as she taught them. By the time she taught the Trans-cendalists, she realized she had always been one. She had always listened to her own heart, the spark of divinity that lived within she had never doubted. And she had found it not so much in her grandmother's church as in the tobacco fields and corn fields and in the wild flowers growing along the path to the back fields, in the long walks during her college days, in the eyes of certain students who understood she loved them, in the kindness of Professor Di Yanni, in the camaraderie of Dora and Jarret. Emma ordered posters out of her own money and filled her classroom walls with pictures with quotations from Emerson, Thoreau, Hawthorne, Whitman, and Poe.

From "Self-Reliance," she chose:

"Whoso would be a man, must be a nonconformist."

"A foolish consistency is the hobgoblin of little minds, adored by little statesmen and philosophers and divines."

Her favorites were from *Walden*:

"If a man does not keep pace with his companions, perhaps it is because he hears a different drummer. Let him step to the music which he hears, however measured or far away."

"I learned ... that if one advances confidently in the direction of his dreams, and endeavors to live the life which he has imagined, he will meet with a success unexpected in common hours ... If you have built castles in the air, your work need not be lost; that is where they should be. Now put the foundations under them."

Some students shared their beliefs and opinions, drawing parallels between the Salem witch trials and the Mc Carthy era, which they studied in history. Above all, Emma wanted to empower them to think for themselves. At first they made remarks such as "Why would they print it in the newspaper if it wasn't true?" and "What can I learn from studying people who have been dead a hundred years?" Emma realized she had no concept of how some of them thought or rather did not think. The greatest hurdle was to break the white or black mentality, the right or wrong mentality, the we and they, the my parents said, the who-ever-heard-of-that syndrome. Shades of gray to them meant You don't know the answer, do you?

If a student said he or she was bored, Emma said, "You are the one who is boring. With all the interesting things in the world to study, how can a thinking person be bored?" The students had not learned to read for pleasure or to observe people or nature. Most had not ever had to sit still and be quiet. They had not memorized nursery rhymes and poems. They did not know they had an imagination that could free them from boredom. Television had nursed them into oblivious sponges. They ate by the TV. They did not see their parents read or, if at all, it was the local paper while the TV was still on. They did their homework by the TV or more likely did not do it at all. How many parents had told Emma that their child had said she did not give homework or that they finished it at school.

One day Emma reprimanded Joseph, a black student who was the son of the head of the janitorial staff at the college Emma had attended. She had gotten to know Mr. Swinson the first summer when she was a college student. Knowing Joseph was from a family who cared, she had pushed him perhaps too hard. When she was critical of his work, he crumpled the paper he had worked on and threw it towards the trash can at the corner of Emma's desk. He missed, and she walked to pick up the paper. She opened it and read at the bottom: "When the teacher talks to me as she did, I want to bash in her face with a chair." Surprised and hurt, Emma saved the note and mailed it to Joseph's father with a note of her own, simply saying she found the note after telling Joseph his work was not acceptable. Joseph was lazy and she knew he was capable.

Days passed and Emma did not hear from Joseph's father. She had expected a call as soon as he received the note. Perhaps Joseph had intercepted it, but she had not told him she had contacted his father, and, indeed, had never told Joseph she even knew his father. After a week, the father appeared unannounced in Emma's classroom after school. He looked the same as he had five years before when she saw him every day on the college campus. He had never appeared to be in a hurry, taking time to chat about how things were going with the college students in general. He was smart and philosophical, sharing his observations and principles.

Emma asked Mr. Swinson to have a seat. He had the envelope and notes she had mailed. In his presence she felt immature for having mailed Joseph's note. There was something so calm about Mr. Swinson that she felt she had made a big deal out of nothing.

"I see you received my letter."

"Yes," he said. "That's what I came to see you about." Still he waited for her to talk.

"Joseph is bright, but he seems not to want to do his work or at least not up to his potential. When I read his essay and saw how little thought he had put into it and how little time—he was the first to finish—I told him it was not acceptable and to rewrite it. After a minute or two he crumbled his paper and threw it across the room toward my trash can but missed. That's when I walked over and picked up the paper and decided to open it. Of course, he had added that little note about me at the bottom. It hurt my feelings but also scared me a little." Mr. Swinson listened intensely as if he were the counselor instead of the father. "Anyhow, maybe I have been too hard on him. I guess I thought he would be like you."

Mr. Swinson smiled his slow, easy smile that lighted his black face. "I'll talk with Joseph about this. I wanted to hear from you first. I don't think you will have any more trouble with him."

"Well, thank you for coming. I was just trying to get Joseph to do his best."

Mr. Swinson left as quietly as he had appeared. Emma wondered why he didn't say more about Joseph. He had not said Joseph was smart. Maybe he was not as capable as she thought. Maybe he was not like his father at all. Whatever the truth, Mr. Swinson was right: Emma did not have any more trouble with Joseph.

The big project for Emma, Dora, and Jarret during their fourth year, the team having worked together successfully for the previous three, was a talent show to be given near the end of the year. All year the three had talked about the project and looked for talented students to participate. It was to be primarily musical, a salute to the 50s and 60s, the inception and rise of Rock and Roll with Little Richard, Elvis, Fats Domino, Marvin Gaye, and many more of the big names. Jarret's band was to be the center piece, and Dora had volunteered to lead several dance numbers with the history teacher and a group of enthusiastic students, mostly black. The chorus, mostly white, directed by Jarret, would sing several songs also. In addition, the show would feature the individual students who made the cut to perform. Emma would not be on the stage but did everything behind the scenes from organizing, managing, and directing. Jarret was purely the entertainer and that was all he needed to be. His students knew not to make a mistake. Dora flourished among the talented students like a brown long-stemmed black-eyed Susan.

During rehearsal, which started as early as March for the mid-May show, Emma was transformed by the music she remembered from early childhood, teen years, and college, the music she danced to on her grandmother's front porch until warts grew on the bottom of her feet. She had the rhythm and soul in her bones and had learned that some had it and some didn't. She remembered that as young as ten or eleven she had wanted to be an actress and dancer, second a writer, and third a teacher.

One afternoon during rehearsal as the students danced to Marvin Gaye's "I Heard It by the Grape Vine," "I Ain't Got Time," and Elvis's "Hound Dog," Emma remembered summer school during college when she stopped by the cafeteria where the servers took their breaks in the basement. One day Emma had heard music and asked Mr. Swinson, who was working in the cafeteria building, where it was coming from. He told Emma it was fine for her to go down and watch the staff play pool or play if she wanted to. The routine, according to Mr. Swinson, was that each day ended with the last hour being spent in the basement where cafeteria staff, and curious students, played pool, danced, and talked. Emma had ventured down to watch and was captivated by the scene. There were two pool tables where players concentrated as if oblivious to the loud music and dancing around them. Record after record played loudly on the intercom, facilitated by a mysterious hand. Most days during this wonderful hour from three until four, an old black female employee entered and was greeted by everyone with affectionate hugs and smiles. She was called Miss Eva. Her small body was toned and shapely, but her face showed her to be in her late fifties or early sixties. Emma heard that she was going to retire in a few months, having worked at the institution for almost forty years. It was evident that Miss Eva was revered, an icon and a legend. She smiled at Emma, who, being shy, had simply smiled back but had not

258   SO   *Mi Mi Roberts*

approached her. Yet she observed Miss Eva who inevitably would begin to dance with the college students. Miss Eva wore her hair up on top of her head woven in plaits, one long one trailing her back, dressed in a pants suit of floral blue, yellow, and red design. She moved as if the rhythm of "I Ain't Got Time" came out of her body, as if she were Marvin Gaye's mother come to honor her son and share the spiritual release of all the day's cares and worries.

Dora had that same rhythm, innate, oozing from the soul like sap from a Massachusetts maple on a sunny morning after a freezing night. Emma watched every second of the rehearsals of the school's talent show, excited, performing vicariously through Dora and the students. The principal had been so pleased with the praise heaped upon the team of three for the past three years that he did not question anything about the talent show. Emma, Dora, and Jarret had proved themselves. The best dancer was Emma's weakest student, Damon Hedgepeth, a black student who stuttered and who endured teasing from other students every day of his life, but who on the stage controlled the show; consequently he was in the beginning, middle, and grand finale. Damon and Dora danced together and with other students in all the dance numbers.

During the first week of rehearsal, four white students and fifteen blacks participated in the dance numbers, but by Monday of the second week the whites had dropped out. Emma heard her students say the parents did not want the two white girls dancing on the stage with all those blacks, and consequently the two white boys had dropped also. However, whites made up more than half of the individual performances.

On Monday before the talent show on Friday, Dora came to school and couldn't talk. Not only did she have laryngitis, she was too sick to teach. The doctor said she had a virus going around the community and she could expect it to last about a week. Jarret asked Emma if he could talk with her after school that day. Rehearsal was at five-thirty so Emma did not leave the school. As soon as the last bell rang, Jarret showed up. "You gotta help me, Emma!" he said.

"Sure, what's the matter?"

"You know Dora's sick as a dog!"

"These viruses don't last long. She may be out two days. She doesn't need any more rehearsals and even if she's not well, Damon is a one-man show anyway. He can dance with the other students and it will be fine."

"No, Emma. We have to have a teacher in the group, and a white teacher would be even better to alleviate the tension we have in this school."

"To intensify it, you mean?"

"Seriously, Emma. I went over to the Teacherage at lunch and went up to Dora's room to talk with her. She said just what I had been thinking, which was that you are the only one who can take her place. She knows you have the rhythm and know the songs and the steps. I mean, we see you dancing on the side of the stage behind the curtain every day and having a ball!"

"No, I think it's too late for me to rehearse enough to be smooth in the group."

"Come on, Emma. This is just a high school talent show, not a Broadway performance!"

"I'm not good enough!"

"I thought you might do this for me. Of course, you're good enough! Don't be so self-centered. You take yourself entirely too seriously. I mean, who will be watching you? The parents come to see their children, and that's it!"

"I'm sorry. You know the show will be fine anyway."

"Okay, okay, my prudish princess. Forget it! Just forget it!"

Jarret turned to walk out. He was already in the hall when Emma called him back.

"All right. I'll do it for—for you because I love you."

Jarret smiled as if his psychology had worked once again. "You'll be the star of the dance numbers taking the spotlight away from Damon!"

"No one can do that," Emma said.

"Well, rehearsal is at five-thirty as you well know. I can't wait to tell the students! This will clinch your reputation as cool!"

"I've never wanted to be cool."

At fifteen past five, Emma showed up in the auditorium as she had every rehearsal. There were only three rehearsals left before the show. She had watched the dancers. Dora had danced with Damon. Both were tall. She pictured herself as looking really odd being so much shorter than Damon, plus white as milk in contrast to his dark face. In fact, she would be the only white dancer. Well, she had to do it for Jarret and for Dora. They would do it for her.

When Emma arrived at the auditorium, the students were a buzz, she assumed about her taking Dora's place. They seemed serious and didn't notice her when she went on the stage. A few were talking about the show, but others were in huddles whispering. Suddenly she felt that they must not want her in the show taking Dora's place. She had not considered this possibility, being concerned only with her own feelings. But as she walked around speaking to the students and listening, she kept hearing Jarret's name. Turning her head aside, as if observing the band instruments, she listened to one of the conversations.

"He's in trouble, I think, now with Mr. Franklin and probably a lot of parents," said one of the band members.

When Damon arrived, Emma called him aside. "Damon, has

Mr. Bridgewater talked with you about any change in the numbers?"

"Oh, yes, ma'am. He said you would take Miss Grimes' place. I couldn't believe it, but I sure am glad. I need a partner to make the numbers look good. I think you and me will be a great team. I know you feel the music. You usually dance along with us anyway behind the curtain. So, no big deal to be on the stage instead of behind the stage. Right?"

"Oh, yeah, sure. No big deal. Hey, Damon, what is everyone buzzing about? What's going on?"

"I ain't real sure, ma'am." Damon seemed embarrassed.

"I know about rumors. Usually they are just that—rumors, but tell me what it is."

"Well, I heard this morning on the bus that Mr. Jarret was caught with a student in his room at the Teacherage."

"Oh," said Emma, stunned and afraid to ask any further question.

Jarret came whisking in, cheerful and smiling. He got the students' attention and announced that Emma was taking Dora's place, and everyone applauded.

"You might want to wait on that applause," Emma said, encouraged by the support."

The first dance she did with Damon and other couples was the bop to "Slippin' and Slidin'." She was a little self conscious for a few seconds but all she had to do was evoke the images of dancing with her sister on her grandmother's porch. After that, she felt she did as well as the others besides Damon, who was like a dancing black panther. They went through "Josephine" by Fats Domino, "Love Potion #9" by the Clovers, "Hound Dog" by Elvis, and last, Marvin Gaye's "I Heard It by the Grape Vine" and "I Ain't Got Time." The more they danced, the more energy they had and the more they all improvised their movements until they were on a high and could have danced on through the night.

Jarret and the band played all the songs with perfect rhythm. Jarret jumped up and down as he conducted and sang along. Everyone on stage seemed transported as if they really were at the Kennedy Center performing to honor the icons whose music they performed to. During "Hound Dog" Damon had picked up Emma and whirled her around when she least expected it, set her down like placing a china doll, and never missed a beat.

"Hey, give me a warning, when you're going to do that!" she said blowing her breath. Her skirt had flown up over her head. She must remember to wear slacks until this shindig was over.

"You doing great, Miss Applewhite. Maybe better than Miss Grimes."

"Sure," Emma said. "You're very kind, Damon."

"I ain't just saying that! You doing great! We gonna bring the house down."

"That's what I'm afraid of." Emma laughed, and Damon pulled her and slid her between his legs this time.

After the practice, Jarret drew Emma aside after most of the students left.

"I need your advice on something," Jarret said. "Do you think maybe we could meet at the barn? It is Wednesday. Have you had dinner?"

"No."

"Tell you what. I'll pick up some burgers and drinks, and we can eat at the barn while we talk. I just need someone to talk to, and there's something so calming about that barn."

Emma hesitated, thinking about the papers she needed to grade and return the next day. It was already seven-thirty. It would be eight by the time they drove to the barn. "Sure, I can do that. What time do you want to meet? Let's go as soon as we can. I need to grade some papers."

"I think I can be there with food by eight," he said. "Dora's mother will not be back until nine or so, and she won't mind the cars leaving later. She knows it's us."

Emma drove back to the Teacherage and called Dora on the phone from the parlor, Mrs. Camden being out for dinner with her daughter. Dora had told Emma not to come into her room for fear Emma too would come down with the virus. Emma wondered if Jarret had talked with her on the phone or visited her room at lunch.

"Emma, thank you so very much for taking my place. I just think it's wonderful for the kids that you stepped in. They need your support for the dances. They really don't have much confidence, but what talent!"

"It's nothing," Emma said. "The show will be fine but not as good as if you were in it. Anyhow, I wanted to ask if you knew what was wrong with Jarret. There are rumors today about him and a student. Have you heard anything?"

"Yes. I heard it from Mrs. Camden. She came in here, although I warned her she might get the flu or whatever I have. But, she had rather die of the flu than miss a chance to gossip. She said she saw Thomas Morgan—you know him, one of the seniors in the band; he's actually nineteen because he failed ninth grade—she saw him coming out of Jarret's room at five in the morning yesterday. Now you know she must have called Mr. Franklin and the board members she knows as soon as they would answer their phones. I just hate it so bad. She said Mr. Franklin said, quote: 'This is the last straw.'"

"Jarret asked me to meet him at the barn at eight and I dread going. Do you think it's okay to go out there?" Emma asked.

"Oh, yeah, Mama knows our cars. I've told her any of us might go on Wednesday nights, and it sounds as if he needs you."

"Are you sure you're not well and just playing hookey?" Emma asked, laughing.

"I just got my stomach settled today with chicken and rice soup that Mama brought. I still feel weak and shaky."

"Okay, dearie, I'm off to meet Jarret. Take care."

The drive was easy with little traffic. Once past the school and stoplight, Emma could see the full moon, white as a man's face, and white winking stars, and Venus shining bright and steady. She rolled down her window when she came to the streak of woods where in the spring she could always smell honey suckles. She must go out early one morning and pick some for her classroom. They evoked images of sitting on a large front porch in late May, drinking lemonade and eating tea cakes with no papers to grade and with Dora and Jarret there to amuse her and make her think dreams come true. Jarret played his guitar and they all sang "Tomorrowland."

She started to sing:

There's a wonderful place called tomorrowland
And it's only a dream away
And the moment you get to tomorrowland
You'll forget about today.

You'll be walking on clouds,
You'll forget every care,
And your troubles, like bubbles, will vanish in air
Ask me how do you get to tomorrowland
Close you eyes, make a wish and you're there.

As Emma turned into the long path leading to Dora's

mother's house, she longed to have Dora with her. It would be difficult to talk with Jarret without her. Dora had a sense of things that Emma lacked. She was not as naïve. Perhaps it was because she had older brothers. Emma saw no cars at the house when she drove past and on to the tobacco barn. The moonlight bathed the field beside the barn where corn was just getting a good start. Suddenly something flew over her shoulder frightening her as she jumped back to see a crazy bat soaring lop-sided. "Hey, you! It's not Halloween!"

She saw Jarret's car but there was no light shining under the barn door. She called out to him but there was no answer. He must have gone to the house looking for candles or a lamp, but the house would be locked. Maybe Dora told him where to find a key outside. She would go in the barn and wait. When she opened the door, she smelled an unfamiliar bad odor, which diffused with the outside air. It was dark. She had a flashlight in her car. She had to go back and get it. Light in hand, dim thought it was, she went inside the barn to sit down and wait. Finding the table and chairs where the three had sat before, she saw the kerosene lamp and matches on the lamp just where they had been left over two years ago now.

She lighted the lamp. Where was Jarret? She stood up. She called again, louder this time. Hearing a rat scurry under the furniture piled in the corner, she walked to the center of the barn where the space was clear, bumping into something over her head. She looked up and saw Jarret's black shoes and tan trousers. She screamed and jumped away. "Damn you, Jarret! You scared me to death! I hope you are amused, but I'm not!" She wondered how he could play games when he was in jeopardy of being fired. He didn't answer. Reaching up, she pulled on his leg and felt something sticky. She looked up. The legs swung freely. And then, standing aside and looking up again, she saw his face, white, his head turned crooked to one side, and she screamed like a wounded animal, screaming and running out of the barn, screaming and running as the bat flew over her head again. Her legs weakened and shaking about to give way, she ran to her car and drove to the house, still screaming. Maybe Dora's mother would be home. Finding no one there, she tried to think between emitting screams rising from her throat, not her lungs. She could hardly breathe. The front door had glass panes. Before she thought any further, she picked up a wrought iron chair on the porch and broke the glass. She reached in, cutting her hand on the glass, and was able to unlock the door.

The phone was in the kitchen at the back of the house. She dialed emergency and was giving directions when Dora's uncle entered the kitchen, pointing a gun. Emma was crying and trying to talk. The uncle knew something was wrong. When she hung up the phone, he said, "Who're you?"

Then Dora's mother, who had recognized Emma's voice, came in. She and Emma spoke at the same time. "That's Emma," she said as Emma said "I'm Emma."

"What's happened, child?" Dora's mother asked.

Emma opened her mouth and tried to speak but could only make the little screaming sounds in her throat. "He's in the barn." She cried uncontrollably. "He hanged himself."

The police questioned Emma and before releasing her gave her a copy of a note Jarret left in his pocket. It read:

"Dear Emma and Dora,

You two mean so much to me. I couldn't have stuck it out this long without you. I apologize for letting you down. I do have a couple of requests.

Emma, you must carry on with the talent show tomorrow night. The band can do the songs without me now. Tell them they must do well for me. I taught them well and they must show the community. And Emma, you must lead the dances. You don't seem to know it, but the kids love you and need your approval. They will fall apart without you. And Dora, you must get well and help Emma make the rest of the few weeks left in this fourth year. The scholarships will be paid off then. Tomorrow belongs to you!

My love,

Jarret"

The young policeman who drove Emma home told her he would get her car to her the next day. It had to be examined. She stayed up late, going into Dora's room and hugging her until they could speak. Emma gave the note to Dora. Tears streamed down Dora's face as she read. Emma stayed in Dora's room and slept on the couch. The next morning Mr. Franklin caught her when she walked in the front door of the school.

"Emma, I'm so sorry about Jarret. I know he was your friend —and Dora's too. I need your advice on some matters. I know your study hall is fourth period. Would you please come to my office then? I will send someone to take your place for that period."

"Sure." Emma was still in shock. She half expected to see Jarret in the hall in his immaculate white, long-sleeve shirt, waving his arms and shouting to students to get to class. "You'd better not be late for my class!" He would shout.

Emma's twenty-five minute lunch period came just before study hall. No one in her classes had dared to mention Jarret. They apparently read the dull terror in Emma's eyes and let her alone. They even behaved. Luckily it was a test day, and she did not have to talk much. She had brought coffee in a thermos and poured a cup now. It was still hot and good. She watched the students who were outside in the courtyard not eating lunch. She wondered if they were hungry. They were certainly skinny. A light knock at her closed door caught her attention. She rose to open the door, hoping it was not Mr. Franklin. No, it wasn't. It was Professor Di Yanni!

Emma hugged him without speaking and then pulled him inside and closed the door. She looked into his face. "He's gone. He's gone" was all she could manage, afraid the animal sounds would enter her throat again.

"I know," said the professor. "I actually got a call last night from one of my colleagues who lives over this way, and I made the trip early this morning really just to see you."

"Let me show you the note he left," she said reaching in her book bag on the floor behind her desk. "I don't think I can honor his request. I really don't think I can do it."

"Well, how about Dora?"

"Dora is sick. Well, she's getting better but not able to be in the show. It's tomorrow night."

"Emma, how about putting off the show for one week? That way Dora would be well enough to help you. I know you're not going to let Jarret down and all those kids."

"Let him down! He let me down! He's gone! He's gone!" She sobbed again as if Jarret had hanged himself just to hurt her.

"He was a troubled young man. He just couldn't make it, Emma. The police report says he died instantly of a broken neck. He dropped twelve feet. So he did not suffer like some who slowly choke."

"Yes, he would have done it with perfection."

"I must go now, Emma. You are stronger than Jarret. He was never quite of this world. I've seen what you've been through. You will prevail. By the way, there is a new master's program in

English at the college. I know you want to get your master's at some point. I had thought it might not get approval, but it has and will start registration for the fall immediately. And a real drawing card for some prospective students will be that they can, if they so choose, teach two college classes while they are full-time students as well as earn extra money helping in the Fine Arts Department, which includes dancing and drama. They put on shows during the fall and spring semesters as well as produce a summer theatre. Just something to think about."

He left walking quietly but quickly out the side door into the courtyard and on toward the parking lot.

At study hall, Mr. Pinkney, a biology teacher, came in and told her he had been directed to take the period so that she could go to see Mr. Franklin.

"Emma, help me out. What should we do about the talent show?" Mr. Franklin got right to the point.

"Well, I have a suggestion. If you could postpone the show for one week, I think I can carry it out. By then, hopefully, Dora will be able to help me. This was Jarret's last request, and I would like to fulfill it."

"Done deal, Miss Applewhite! I'll get out a memo right now and put in a call to the paper. I thank you for your help." He rose from his chair, done with her.

I'm not doing it for you, she thought. I'm doing it for Jarret and the students.

Dora was well enough by Sunday to rehearse. The band wanted her to conduct them to make sure they did not get the numbers out of order, and she reluctantly agreed. Emma had hoped Dora might take her place with Damon, but he would have none of that now. "No mo' swopin'," he said. "Besides Miss Dora needs to get her strength back before she gets hot on the dance floor." Knowing he was right, Emma did not try to make any more changes.

The night of the show Emma and Dora were tripping around the stage as light and as bright as peacock tail feathers in match-ing blue-green pants suits shimmering with gold rhinestones. As a tribute to Jarret, the senior band leader, the student who allegedly had fallen asleep drunk in Jarret's room and stayed all night, introduced the first song, "Tomorrowland," as Jarret's theme song. The whole choir and all the performers in the show came out on stage and sang. From there the pace went from fast to faster as the band played the numbers from the 50s and then the 60s. Only a couple of individual numbers were less than transforming. The first two of the six dance numbers that Emma and Damon performed with the other fifteen dancers did not come off as electrifying as she felt they had in rehearsal. And then she realized that it might be because she had not smiled. She had not let herself go as she had in rehearsal before Jarret's death. She remembered Jarret's words: "Don't be so self-centered. You take yourself too seriously. I mean, who will be watching you?" Before the next dance performance, Emma walked over to Dora and said, "Something's not right. The students are tense because you and I are. Let's let go and they'll follow."

Emma knew she must close her mind to the fact that Mr. Franklin and most of the school board sat right in front of the stage. She would think only of dancing, uninhibited as she had done with her sister on her grandmother's porch when she was fourteen and Martha twelve. It worked. She sensed Damon relaxing. Everyone on the stage moved together with one beat as if they shared the same pulsing blood in their veins. The last two songs were Marvin Gaye's. During "I heard It by the Grape Vine," Emma noticed Dora's mother in the audience standing and swaying her hips, raising her arms first one and then the other, keeping time to the music. Several students joined her and started singing and dancing at their seats. The auditorium resounded with applause. The students shouted, "More! Ya'll can't quit! We want more! We want more!"

The last dance performance was to "I Ain't Got Time." The band and dancers had voted to end with it, and it turned out to be the clincher they had predicted. As Emma faced the audience she could see all the students, white and black, standing and dancing at their seats. Some moved into the aisles. Then the parents and teachers stood swaying and moving their feet with the beat. Only Mr. Franklin and the board members were not standing. They looked as if they did not know whether to join in or walk out, so they just stood trying to look sophisticated among the throbbing unity of soul. The band started over at the end of the number, mesmerized by the audience. Emma danced Joseph over to Dora and said, "Let's quit before they call the cops on us!" Dora smiled and nodded. At the end of the number, the curtain dropped and the audience yelled, "No! Ya'll Can't Quit!" Ya'll Can't Quit!" But they did and stood together to bow while the band played "Tomorrowland" as the curtain fell again. The curtain rose once more, and Damon took a bow, Emma hiding behind the curtain until the audience cried her name, and Damon pointed to her. "Come out here, right now, Miss Applewhite. They're calling your name!" She did come out and bowed and then turned her hand toward Dora and the band, still playing Jarret's song. The audience went wild, and the curtain dropped for the last time.

It was midnight before Dora and Emma sat in Emma's room and cried, remembering the night they had sat with Jarret and drunk champagne and sung "Tomorrowland." There were only two weeks left in the school year. They had almost made four years.

The list of graduates was circulated among all teachers, and Emma looked at her senior homeroom. They had all made it. The student she was most proud of, Sharon, the one who had been her right hand for four years, bright and stable, announced that she was not going to college. "Why?" Emma asked. Sharon wasn't getting married. Why in the world? Her prize student whom she had nurtured. The girl just didn't think she would like college. What kind of answer was that? And then Emma knew the answer. The girl was too mature. She was ready for the world of work. She was smarter and wiser than any of the other students she would encounter in college. Still, Emma was disappointed.

Tommy, a slow student whom she had sheltered and pro-tected for four years, came by after school once he found out he would graduate. He had spoken very few words in the four years she had had him in homeroom and the junior year he was in her class. "I wanted to thank you, Miss Applewhite, for all you've done for me." And he handed her a rather limp one dollar bill. Anger shot through her. How dare he belittle her now that he was free to do so. After all she had put up with, his coming in late, not doing his work, her having to ask over and over for his work, talking every week to his mother. Tommy looked at her. "Please take it. I know it's not much, but I just wanted you to know I appreciate all you done for me." And Emma took the bill, knowing this action might be illegal but realized Tommy was completely sincere. What did it matter from a retarded student who was just wanted to thank her?

"I haven't done anything for you that I haven't done for other students," she lied. "Thank you and good luck."

Mr. Franklin asked to see Emma the day after all final grades were in. Graduation over, there were only three teacher work days left. She really could not think of what he might want.

"Come in, Miss Applewhite," he said. "Sit down. I have been

assessing our year, which for the most part was very successful. I think you've done a good job teaching this year. I must say my son learned a lot and had to really think for himself, something he had not been challenged to do in previous years. You know, teachers tend to tell the students what the theme is, for example, instead of pulling ideas out of them. That sort of thing you did a good job of in your discussions from what he said."

"Well, I didn't realize I had a spy in my room," Emma laughed. However, she had known very well she had a spy.

"About the extracurricular projects for next year—I'd like for you and Dora and whoever takes Jarret's place to do the talent show again. Only ... we don't want to offend people next time."

"Offend people?" Emma did not get it.

"Well, I would have warned you that the board, even the black member, Mr. Spellman, did not approve of the jungle bunny atmosphere with you a white teacher dancing so provocatively with a black student, not once, but six times, and getting the audience riled up—dancing in the aisles." Emma's blood began to boil. She said nothing. "This is not Los Angeles or New York City, Emma. This is good old country people. I mean, for example, Damon whirling you around in the air and sliding you between his legs on the floor. I was surprised. I really didn't know you were that kind of person. Of course, I can monitor things and better prepare you for next year." He spoke, not really looking at her and she was reminded of the day her Uncle Milton had asked her if she had any colored students and when she said yes, he had said, "Some people will do anything for money," and never realized she was "some people."

Emma stood up. "Well, Mr. Franklin, I don't think I will be around for the next talent show. You see, I am that kind of person, and it took you to make me realize it." She turned and walked out of his office, tears burning her eyes, that boiled egg stuck in her throat again. She got in her car and drove to the college, parallel parked on the street, and walked to the English Department. The chair happened to be in and was available to talk with her. He confirmed what Professor Di Yanni had told her. He believed she could get into the master's program linked to the opportunities to work with drama and dance. He gave her an application packet and told her to get it back to him as soon as she possibly could. Some of the professors she had as an under-graduate would gladly recommend her, and her 4.0 average would not hurt.

Professor Di Yanni would be a good reference, and Emma decided to look him up. The offices of the music professors and art professors were in an old building at the edge of the campus on the side opposite the building where the English courses were taught. She had never been in the building. The concerts were held in the new classroom building or the auditorium. She looked at the directory on the wall. She didn't see his name, so she walked around the first floor looking at the names on the doors. A young woman came out of an office, and Emma asked her where Professor Di Yanni's office was. She said she didn't know the name.

Finally Emma saw the music department office and walked in. An elderly woman sat at a side table eating some kind of greens and fried corn bread and drinking tea. "I'm looking for Professor Di Yanni, ma'am. Can you help me?"

"Professor Di Yanni," the woman repeated. "What do you need to see him about?"

"I want to ask him if he will provide a reference for my application to graduate school. I thought his office was in this building. He is a visiting music professor."

"There was a Professor Di Yanni here years ago, a brilliant black musician, but he was killed in an accident. I remember so well because it happened the night before my birthday, and he had told me he had a surprise for me. The professor, his wife, and daughter had been to visit his sick mother over in Wynn County. His mother had been sick a long time and had taken a turn for the worse. On their way home that night a drunk driver hit them head on. Only the drunk driver survived. Let's see. That has been fourteen years ago."

"My professor must have been a relative of your professor," said Emma, in disbelief."

"Professor Di Yanni was a kind and gentle man, so down to earth, but so eloquent at the same time. He always made every-one feel important just by looking them in the eye and asking genuinely how he or she was feeling and what was going on. His daughter was only thirteen when she died. He had brought her into the office a few times. She wanted to be a writer, especially a playwright. He had taught her to treat everyone with respect as he did. I know God made him an angel. I would not be surprised if he is not amongst us as we speak." The old woman looked at Emma, who stood seemingly in shock. "I will go get some pictures of him and his daughter taken at an office party one Christmas. Wait here."

"Never mind," Emma said. "I'll find him." But she didn't. His name was not on any of the doors. She did not see him listed in the phone book in the phone booth outside. Well, he would hear when she returned to graduate school and pop up some-where, most likely literally bumping into her. She blocked out what she could not comprehend. The old woman was senile.

Emma wanted to visit her mother and sister to tell them she would be a poor student again soon for a couple more years. She would work in a restaurant at night to supplement the teaching assistantship if she needed to. There had to be a way to get her master's degree and start over.

When Emma went to her classroom to clean out her desk, she found a note taped to the door. It was from Mr. Franklin. He wanted to see her. She packed everything personal in her book bag, leaving pens, paper, paper clips, and scissors—a lot of materials she had purchased—in the desk. She decided to leave the posters she had bought also as well as the custom made lectern, wooden with a Formica top, made for her by a student as his project for shop. She had tried to pay him but he wouldn't take any money. On her way out, she did knock on Mr. Franklin's door.

"Come in, Emma. I have reconsidered after talking with the board chair and would like to talk with you if you will step in and sit down."

"I ain't got time." The words rolled out of her mouth in the tone of Marvin Gaye before her brain knew what she said as if Marvin Gaye had possessed her brain, and seeing the shock on Mr. Franklin's face, she closed the door and walked on.

In the fall, graduate courses started the last week in August. Emma took just two courses to begin with and taught two freshman courses. The stipend she received would not be enough to live on. She sold her car and got a cheaper room within walking distance of the campus. She would have to get a part-time job.

The eight o'clock class, The Age of Samuel Johnson, was a tough one. The first day after class, Janet, one of the students in the class who had taken a previous course with Dr. Mellon, warned Emma that he asked questions about the reading homework. He didn't mind putting you on the spot. Janet had gone into the master's program straight from undergraduate school, working in a record shop during the summer.

"Thank you for the tip," said Emma. Looking at Janet, she

thought her extremely tiny. "How do you keep so thin?" asked Emma in a complimentary tone.

"I don't eat," Janet answered, looking at Emma as if she had a lot to learn about the life of a graduate student.

Despite Janet's warnings, Emma was thrilled to have the opportunity to work on her master's. She seemed to float across the campus to class that first morning. Arriving at seven-thirty at the seminar classroom for the eight o'clock class with Dr. Mellon, Emma gave significant thought to which seat to choose at the long, rectangular table. Janet arrived second, balancing her books, her half-eaten doughnut and coffee.

"Good morning!" said Emma as cheerful as a new robin. "I'm so glad to see you in this class. I've already taken the best seat, besides the head of the table, reserved for Dr. Mellon! But here, sit next to me!"

Janet flopped down, putting her coffee on the table and biting her doughnut. She swallowed, took a sip of coffee, and looked at Emma as if she were a Big Sister sophomore. "How can you be so damned happy so early in the morning!" said Janet.

And Emma's grin widened.

ABOUT THE AUTHOR

Mi Mi Roberts has written poems, short stories, and a novella, founded a writer's group; and co-founded the *Neuse River Anthology*. Many of her poems and stories, as well as her novella were lost; however, several of her poems were published in NC literary magazines, including *A Carolina Literary Companion*, *The Wayah Review*, and *The Arts Journal*. Her chapbook of poetry, *Down the Dirt Road*, was published in 1985 by St. Andrews Press. She co-authored *The Write Stuff*, a college textbook, published by Prentice-Hall, and wrote the biography of an entrepreneur in eastern North Carolina, *What Goes Around, Comes Around: C. Felix Harvey III*, published in 1998 by B. Williams in Chapel Hill, North Carolina.

Roberts lives with her husband on a farm in eastern North Carolina.

www.ingramcontent.com/pod-product-compliance
Lightning Source LLC
Chambersburg PA
CBHW061552170626
46811CB00001B/170